ONCE BURNED

FIREHOUSE FOURTEEN
BOOK 1

LISA B. KAMPS

Lisa B. Kamps

Once Burned
Firehouse Fourteen Book 1

Lisa B. Kamps

ONCE BURNED

ONCE BURNED
Copyright © 2016 by Elizabeth Belbot Kamps

All rights reserved. Except for use in any review, the reproduction or utilization of this work in whole or in part in any form by any electronic, mechanical or other means, now known or hereafter invented, including xerography, photocopying and recording, or in any information storage or retrieval system, is forbidden without the express written permission of the author.

All characters in this book have no existence outside the imagination of the author and have no relation to anyone bearing the same name or names, living or dead. This book is a work of fiction and any resemblance to any individual, place, business, or event is purely coincidental.

Cover and logo design by Jay Aheer of Simply Defined Art
http://www.jayscoversbydesign.com/

Lisa B. Kamps

All rights reserved.
ISBN: 153028032X
ISBN-13: 978-1530280322

ONCE BURNED

Lisa B. Kamps

DEDICATION

In Memory of Randy P. Meyer
May 27, 1959-April 11, 2009
You were taken too soon.
I miss you, my friend.

ONCE BURNED

Contents

Title Page iii
Copyright v
Dedicatiom ix
Other titles by this author xv

Chapter One 17
Chapter Two 24
Chapter Three 30
Chapter Four 35
Chapter Five 42
Chapter Six 47
Chapter Seven 55
Chapter Eight 66
Chapter Nine 74
Chapter Ten 81
Chapter Eleven 92
Chapter Twelve 99
Chapter Thirteen 111
Chapter Fourteen 116
Chapter Fifteen 124
Chapter Sixteen 134
Chapter Seventeen 143
Chapter Eighteen 152
Chapter Nineteen 157
Chapter Twenty 166
Chapter Twenty-One 174
Chapter Twenty-Two 185
Chapter Twenty-Three 191
Chapter Twenty-Four 204

Chapter Twenty-Five	211
Chapter Twenty-Six	218
Chapter Twenty-Seven	226
Chapter Twenty-Eight	236
Chapter Twenty-Nine	243
Chapter Thirty	251
Chapter Thirty-One	259
Chapter Thirty-Two	267
Chapter Thirty-Three	274
Chapter Thirty-Four	282
ABOUT THE AUTHOR	291

ONCE BURNED

Lisa B. Kamps

Other titles by this author

THE BALTIMORE BANNERS

Crossing The Line, Book 1
Game Over, Book 2
Blue Ribbon Summer, Book 3
Body Check, Book 4
Break Away, Book 5
Playmaker (A Baltimore Banners Intermission novella)
Delay of Game, Book 6
Shoot Out, Book 7

FIREHOUSE FOURTEEN

Once Burned, Book 1
Playing With Fire, Book 2
Breaking Protocol, Book 3

STAND-ALONE TITLES

Emeralds and Gold: A Treasury of Irish Short Stories
(anthology)
Finding Dr. Right, Silhouette Special Edition
Time To Heal

Lisa B. Kamps

Chapter One

Mike Donaldson stood frozen just inside the doorway, her hand clenched around the axe handle, squeezing until she imagined she could feel the impression of the raised grains along the poorly varnished wood through her thick gloves. The urge to hurl the axe across the room, to tear into walls and smash everything around her, grew. Overwhelming. Suffocating.

She didn't need this shit. Not now, not today. Not any day.

She swallowed the destructive urge with a mouthful of smoke and bit back a cough. Dammit to hell anyway.

What the hell was wrong with her? She shouldn't be hesitating, shouldn't be questioning. She had a job to do, why the hell wasn't she doing it?

Because her conscience, something she thought long dead and buried, had picked today, this minute, to come roaring back to life. And what the hell was up with that? Since when did she let anything get between her and her job? Why was she standing here, breathing in smoke, practically frozen in place while her long-lost conscience pricked the nerves behind her eyes and soured her stomach?

Dammit. She didn't need this shit. Not now.

The only thing Mike wanted to do was tear the room apart. Pull the ceiling down, rip holes in the wall. Break the windows and enjoy that split-second sound of shattering glass.

She wanted to grab that guitar in the corner and splinter it into a million pieces. That damned fucking guitar. It couldn't be. No. No way in hell. That would be a twist of fate too cruel for even her to tolerate.

"Yo Mikey, what are you waiting for already?" Somebody knocked into her from behind and she took another step into the room, moving out of the doorway. "You got this room or what?"

"Yeah, I got it," she answered, her mind on autopilot as she looked around once more. A haze of smoke hung over the room, already staining the ceiling and top fourth of the walls a sooty gray. She breathed through her mouth, not worrying about the mask that hung limply around her neck: the fire downstairs was out and they were on the clean-up phase.

Salvage and overhaul. Seek and destroy. The best part of the clean-up phase was the chance to take your aggressions out on the house around you. But not today. Not here, not now. No, for some reason, her damned conscience wasn't going to let her play fast and loose, wasn't going to let her stretch the rules this time.

Shit. She pinched the bridge of her nose with her free hand and squeezed her eyes shut, trying to stop the nervous twitch building in the left one. An ominous rolling in her stomach quickly followed and she groaned, cursing herself for drinking too much the night before. Maybe it wasn't her conscience that was souring her stomach. Maybe it was all that freaking tequila from the night before. Whatever was causing it, it needed to go away. She wasn't in the mood to deal with any of it.

Mike squeezed her eyes closed once more, took another shallow breath through her mouth, then opened them and looked around. Nope, everything was still the same. First she had to deal with a colossal hangover, and now this.

Great.

Her gaze drifted back to the set-up on the far side of the room, clearly visible through the haze. Several amps of different sizes were stacked neatly alongside narrow hard plastic cases that no doubt held microphones. A wooden bookshelf held a variety of binders and folders, probably sheet music. Several guitars, both in and out of their cases, were grouped together. There was no doubt in her mind that this room was being used as a music room. Yeah, it didn't take a genius to figure that one out.

But whose room was it?

Mike stepped closer, not caring that her turnout boots tracked wet and sooty marks along the beige carpet. She wanted, *needed*, to get a closer look at that damn guitar in the corner, to make sure she wasn't seeing things.

"What are you doing?" The voice snapped her out of her daze. She looked over shoulder and shot an impatient glare at her partner, Jay Moore. He was leaning against the doorframe, the shoulder of his turnout coat smudging the painted wood. His flint gray eyes were rimmed in red, though whether from the smoke or from his own hangover was anyone's guess. It was the expression in them that she didn't care for: studying, worrying, maybe a little cautious, like he wasn't sure what she was doing. Yeah, right. Jay, of all people, knew better.

"Just checking something out. I said I have this room, so go already."

"Are you okay?"

"I'm fine, now go." She pivoted on her heel and took another step then lowered herself to one knee, leaning closer to study the guitar.

As far as instruments went, it was a beautiful piece of craftsmanship. Book matched flamed maple top and a cherry burst finish that glowed on its own. Abalone inlays in an ebony fretboard and gold-plated hardware. She knew without touching it, without studying it too closely, that the body and neck of the guitar were crafted from Hawaiian Koa wood.

It was a Carvin DC400 Limited Series, and cost its buyer a tidy sum of money when it was purchased more than twelve years ago. She knew because *she* was the one who bought it all those years ago, *she* was the one who had ordered the custom hardware installed. It had taken her what seemed like forever to save enough money to buy that damn guitar.

And she had given it away. A gift.

God, had she really been that fucking stupid? That utterly and hopelessly naive?

Yeah, she had been. Dammit.

Mike cursed under her breath and pressed the heel of her hand against her twitching left eye. It was possible, likely even, that the guitar had been sold to someone else at some point in time in the last twelve years. It was possible that she was *not* kneeling in the music room of a man she had not seen in a decade, a man she hoped to never see again.

Yes, it was possible. Please, God, let that be the case. Just thinking of the alternative was enough to send the tequila sloshing in her empty stomach and threaten to make a reappearance. And wouldn't the captain just love that? Nothing like giving him even more ammunition to use against her. The bastard.

She muttered a quick prayer that she was right, that this was some complete stranger's house, and slowly stood. The sudden and intense desire to smash everything in sight was an overwhelming urge that had nothing to do with completing overhaul at the scene of a fire. Mike took a deep breath and squeezed the axe in both fists to stop it.

An image of Nicky Lansing popped into her mind, unbidden and completely unwelcome. Laughing brown eyes, black hair that cascaded past broad shoulders, an incongruous dimple in his right cheek that had ultimately led to her downfall. Nineteen-year-old Nicky Lansing, a modern-day, leather-clad rebel who had gone for a ride and taken her down with him.

In more ways than one.

The axe came up and started swinging, almost on its own accord, almost as if it was possessed. The blade stuck into the top of the wall near the soot mark; Mikey pulled it out with a grunt before swinging again and again, not stopping until a one-square-foot hole marred the plaster. She lowered the axe and stared at the damage in front of her, then back at the equipment in the corner.

At the damn guitar.

Shit. She wasn't in the mood for this. Not today.

"Dammit," she muttered. There was so much more damage she could do, *wanted* to do, but some inner voice stopped her. She tossed the axe to the floor, where it landed with a heavy thud, then turned to leave the room. Jay collided with her as she turned the corner.

"Hey, look out." He pushed her back with a steadying hand, his gray eyes narrowed in his lean face. "Are you sure you're okay? Your eye's twitching again."

"Yeah, whatever. I'm fine."

"If you say so. Where are you going? Did you check for any extension up here?"

Mike looked at Jay then back at the room she had nearly run out of to escape. She shook her head. "None that I can see, just some smoke damage. I'm going to get some tarps, though, and cover that equipment so it doesn't get ruined."

"You, getting tarps? Since when do you worry about that shit?"

"Can it, Jay. That's expensive gear in there." She hooked her thumb in the direction of the room then pushed past him, shaking her head at her own actions. Jay was right, she rarely worried about that kind of thing. In fact, none of them really worried about it, not very often. Usually, on the fires they had, there wasn't much left to worry about protecting.

But this was a simple room and contents fire downstairs with limited smoke and water damage. To tear down ceilings and open walls when it wasn't necessary would be a waste. To needlessly destroy the equipment in that room would be a sin, even if it did, by some impossible long shot, belong to *him*.

Mike took a deep breath and blew it out in a rush as she descended the stairs and made her way to the fire engine outside. There was a chance, a very good chance, that the guitar had been sold sometime in the past decade. She couldn't destroy such a beautiful piece of work out of spite.

Even she hadn't fallen that far.

She stopped on the sidewalk and turned to look at the house, noticing the trimmed lawn and careful landscaping. The probability of Nicky Lansing living in this immaculate split-level in this upscale neighborhood was nil. Slim, at the very least.

After pulling several blue plastic tarps from a side compartment of the engine, she paused again to study the expensive landscaping that framed the front of the house. Her mood lightened at the sight of a multitude of colorful late summer flowers and well-maintained greenery that gave the impression of June instead of early-September.

No, there was no way Nicky Lansing could be living here. He would have had to change too much, would have had to grow up. And the Nicky she knew was incapable of that.

Chapter Two

"Mr. Lansing, I had a question about this assignment."

Nick paused in the middle of tossing files in the briefcase and closed his eyes at the sound of the soft voice, searching for patience. He mentally counted to ten, took another deep breath, then opened his eyes and faced the girl leaning in the doorway.

"Yes, Sheila. What is it?"

The girl straightened, a slight smile turning up the corners of a mouth overdone with lipstick, and took a few steps into the room. She perched one hand on her jean-clad hip and stared at him with a look entirely too old for her sixteen years. "For this report, do we have to actually read the book or can we just download the movie?"

"I'm going to pretend I didn't even hear that." Nick turned back and added another file to the briefcase then closed it with a soft click, noticing from the corner of his eye that the girl made no move to leave. He sighed again, preparing to usher her from the room if necessary, but was stopped by a deeper voice that boomed with authority.

"Move along, Ms. Curtis, or you'll miss the bus." The girl darted her eyes at the newcomer then turned and left the room with a stomp of one foot, mumbling under her breath. Nick was too far away to catch the words, but apparently Chris wasn't. He rolled his eyes in the direction of the retreating student then quirked an eyebrow at Nick. "How do you do it?"

"Do what?"

"Catch the attention of every female between six and sixty. Is there no one immune to your charms?"

Nick stared at his friend and colleague Chris Dalton, opened his mouth for a comeback then thought better of it. He lowered himself into the worn desk chair with a weary sigh. The metal creaked under his weight, sounding nearly as decrepit as he felt. He reached up and tugged at the noose around his neck, sighing again as the knot of the tie loosened.

"Despite your faith in me, I do not attract as much attention as you think. And certainly not as much as you do."

Chris laughed, a deep booming noise that rumbled from his broad chest. Even though he was dressed in khakis, polo shirt, and tennis shoes, he looked exactly like what he was: a football player. Or rather, coach of Buckley High's football team, as well as head of the school's physical education department.

"Yes, well, you can't deny you get your fair share." Chris's laughter subsided and he leaned his massive frame against the desk edge, studying Nick with a shrewd amber gaze. "So, how's the house coming along? Need more help with anything?"

"No, it's just minor stuff now. The drywall guys finished yesterday, and the professional cleaners have been through the place from floor to ceiling. I swear I can still smell smoke on everything, though." Nick suppressed the urge to sniff his shirt in demonstration, knowing that the smell was only his imagination. "Hopefully the painters will have finished today, and I can get back to some sense of normalcy."

"Well, you're lucky. It could have been worse than it was, you know."

Nick muttered a noncommittal grunt, his focus on the pen that he was rolling back and forth between his palms. Chris was right, it could have been worse. The fire itself had been extinguished quickly, according to what he had been told. A few pieces of furniture downstairs had been destroyed and the walls of the room where the fire had been needed to replaced. There were a few walls upstairs that needed to be patched but that was it, other than the smoke damage throughout the rest of the house. Everything was covered by insurance, nothing sentimental had been destroyed, and his music equipment had been untouched and undamaged.

Yes, it could have been worse.

His stomach still clenched at last week's memory of arriving home only to discover that his house had caught fire. A small fire contained to a single downstairs room, he had been assured by the single uniformed man who had met him in the driveway. Nick briefly wondered if more people would have been on hand to greet him if the fire had been more catastrophic in nature, then shook the bitter thought away. It didn't take an army to deliver bad news, after all.

And even Nick had to admit that it seemed as if whoever had put out the fire did a professional job of it. At least, as far as he could tell. He remembered the tarps someone had tossed over the assorted music equipment and again said a brief prayer of thanks to whichever fireman had thought to add the protection.

"I know it could have been worse. They said the firemen that responded did a nice job of stopping it from spreading."

"Isn't that what they're supposed to do?"

Nick shrugged and glanced at his watch, then hoisted himself to his feet. "I guess. Regardless, though, I thought I'd swing by the fire station and drop off something for them, as a little thank you."

Chris raised his eyebrows in question, the corner of his mouth tugging upward in a smile. "A thank you? Isn't paying their salary enough? They do get paid using tax dollars, you know."

"I'm sure they do," Nick replied, pulling the briefcase from its perch on the desk. "Probably just like we teachers get paid."

"Too true, my friend, too true." The laughter echoed off the walls of the empty classroom, sounding loud to Nick's ears. Of course, with Chris, the laughter always was loud.

The two men left the room, walking in silence down the deserted corridors. The soles of Chris's athletic shoes squeaked on the polished tile floor, muffling the dull sound of Nick's own loafers. He breathed in the mingled odors that were as much a part of the school as the students and faculty, and wondered briefly if it had smelled the same when he was a student. If it had, he hadn't noticed. Then again, what teenager ever did?

"I heard you got roped into heading up the drunk-driving awareness program this year. How's that going?" Chris's voice seemed out of place in the surrounding silence and Nick inwardly flinched at the sound. Chris was a great friend, but he had no inclination of how *loud* he could be sometimes.

Nick sighed and shifted the briefcase from one hand to the other, digging in his pocket for the car keys as the two of them exited the building. He squinted against the afternoon light, flipping through the metal ring until he caught the ignition key between his fingers. "It's not yet. I tried calling the police department, and they transferred me to their public relations department. And then *they* transferred me to the fire department, who transferred me to *their* public relations department. I'm still waiting. Apparently, there's supposed to be some kind of pilot program that they're implementing to help with this kind of thing."

"Hmm. Typical bureaucracy." Chris pursed his lips in concentration. "Sounds different, anyway. Think it'll work?"

"Well, how often did you pay attention to your teachers when you were in high school? At least it can't hurt."

"True." They reached the faculty parking lot and Chris paused. "You guys playing Saturday night? I might break down and finally take Melissa to hear you play."

"Yeah, but I'd hold off on bringing Melissa. We're at a place called Duffy's, and I don't think it's her kind of place."

"That bad?"

Nick shrugged, not really knowing how to answer. "I don't think it's 'bad', but it's not like the places we usually play. I've never been there, but I heard that it's more of a local hangout than anything else. That usually means it's a dive."

"How'd you get roped into playing a place like that?"

"Who knows? I think Brian's doing a favor for a friend."

"Hmph. I'm surprised you even had an open night to play someplace different. Aren't you guys pretty much booked solid?"

"For the most part, but there's always room for flexibility." Nick glanced at his watch and sighed. If he left now, he might have time to swing by the house and change before visiting the fire station. Chris must have noticed the small motion because he said his goodbyes and headed back to the school, no doubt to get ready for the upcoming football practice. And Nick thought he had a full schedule; thinking about the extra hours Chris devoted to sports made him cringe.

He walked over to his car, a nondescript Volvo wagon that fairly shrieked respectability, unlocked the door and tossed the briefcase on the front seat before climbing in. Nick still wondered what had possessed him to buy the car a few years ago. Probably some psychological need to prove his maturity to the woman he had been seeing at the time. He mentally shook his head at the memory. The purchase didn't accomplish anything more than adding to his monthly bills, and the relationship had fizzled out. But hey, he still had the car, and it was finally paid for. And it did give an illusion of respectability, something that came in handy once in a while.

Sometimes image was everything, even if it was nothing more than illusion.

Chapter Three

Nick pulled into the entrance of the fire station two hours later, doing his best to swallow his impatience as he followed the drive around the square brick building and pulled into an empty parking slot. He was surprised that he had so much trouble finding the place. He was even more surprised that he hadn't noticed it before tonight, considering it was only a few miles from the neighborhood where he had been living for the last five years.

So much for his keen powers of observation.

In his defense, though, he had to admit that the building was designed to be unobtrusive. A large but simple single-story structure constructed of pale brick and glass, it sat well back off the road, hidden by an expanse of trees and overgrown shrubbery. The design and location was obviously a concession to the nearby residents who probably wanted protection close-by but didn't want to deal with the potential eyesore.

Nick stepped out of the car then reached into the

back seat for the bushel of steamed crabs, cursing under his breath when he saw the small stain on the floor. Perfect. Now his car would reek like crabs and Old Bay seasoning for the next month. It wasn't bad now, but give it a few days and the aroma would turn into the thick smell of rotten seafood. Just what he needed.

He slammed the door shut with his foot and tried to remind himself that the crabs were still a good idea, that there was nothing wrong with saying thank you. Unfortunately, the minor disaster that had greeted him at home took some of the zing out his gratitude.

How could something as simple as repainting turn into such a fiasco? Remembering the off-white puddle in the middle of the floor, Nick was thankful that at least the carpeting hadn't been replaced yet. As he walked around to the front of the building, he grimly wondered what else might possibly go wrong, then forcibly pushed the pessimistic thought away, not wanting to encourage another disaster by thinking about it.

The cracked sidewalk stopped at a metal and glass framed door. Manipulating the heavy bushel to free a hand, Nick reached out to pull the door open only to mutter under his breath when it wouldn't budge. He peered through the glass but could see only an empty hallway, so he knocked. A long minute passed with no answer. Sighing, he sat the bushel on the sidewalk then walked over to the two huge garage doors and looked through the thick clear plastic panes set inside them.

Two large fire engines sat side-by-side in the cavernous room. At least it looked like somebody *should* be there, Nick thought. Unless there was other equipment there he didn't know about. He squinted through the streaked glass, looking for signs of life, and was ready to knock on the oversized garage door when the glass door he had first stopped at was finally pushed open.

An average-looking man in his late thirties with a drooping mustache peered at Nick, his square face expressionless.

"Can I help you?" The question was obviously mere courtesy, spoken in a tone laced with barely-restrained boredom.

"Um, yeah. I was told that this station responded to a fire at my house last week." The statement was greeted by a blank stare and Nick suddenly felt foolish. He cleared his throat and closed the distance between himself and the fireman. "The house is on Benson Road."

A spark of recognition flashed in the dark eyes that stared at Nick. The man nodded but didn't say anything else. Nick shifted his weight, waiting for the man to say or do something, and again wondered why he thought this would be a good idea. He ran a hand through his thick hair then gestured at the bushel on the sidewalk in front of him.

"I brought these as a thank you. For putting out the fire," he added unnecessarily. The man finally looked down and noticed the crabs on the sidewalk; this time when he met Nick's gaze, there was a wide smile on the rugged face.

"Hey man, thanks. Come on in. The guys'll get a kick out of this." The fireman opened the door wider, motioning for Nick to come inside. He retrieved the bushel then followed the man, not even surprised that he was the one who had to carry the crabs.

After walking through a maze of connected hallways that led through a cavernous room, they finally went through a set of swinging doors that opened into a large kitchen. Spacious and utilitarian, it was obviously designed on a local government budget: worn but polished off-white asbestos floor tiles, cinder block walls painted a pale gray, and more metal-framed glass windows that took up the entire outside wall.

The far wall was converted into counter space with the necessary kitchen fixtures of sink, stove, and three refrigerators, while another wall was covered with a large combination chalk board/bulletin board. Four large wooden tables, their varnished surfaces scarred and yellowed with age, were placed haphazardly in the open space. Around them sat a hodge-podge collection of chairs, all facing the focal point of the third wall: a large flat screen television set. Several of the room's occupants looked up from the local news and stared at Nick in silence as the fireman who had greeted him stopped in front of a man wearing a white shirt.

"Hey Cap, look what we got. Crabs!" The man motioned at Nick, who was standing stupidly just inside the door. Warm crab juice leaked from the bushel down the front of his khaki trousers. Nick barely noticed, sparing the leak the briefest glance before returning his open-mouthed stare to the woman standing in front of the kitchen sink, who was staring back at him in undisguised horror.

The bottom of Nick's stomach dropped open with a sickening thud that matched the hollow sound of the bushel when he dropped it on the closest table.

Everything in the room disappeared except for the young face eight feet away: oval shaped, framed by long curling wisps of chestnut hair that brought out the deep green of the wide eyes staring back at him. No, that wasn't right. Nick squeezed his eyes closed, reopened them.

The face morphed, no longer as young as he remembered, no longer as soft or full. Her hair was a little lighter than he remembered, pulled back in a functional ponytail instead of flowing past her shoulders. But the eyes. Her eyes were still the same shade of mossy green, the color rich and vibrant. And they were still focused on him in horror. Nick clamped his mouth shut with a click and swallowed back the guilt that rose like sour bile up the back of his throat. He swallowed again, his voice croaking like an adolescent's when he spoke.

"Michaela?"
"Oh shit."

Chapter Four

"Oh shit," Mike repeated under her breath, too horrified to do anything more than force herself to breathe. Not an easy task, considering she was literally frozen to the spot. She willed herself to move, to do something, anything, except stand there like an idiot. Her fist tightened around the sponge she had been using to wash the dishes left over from the day shift, her nails digging into the flesh of her palm.

Unsure what else to say or do, wondering if there was anything she *should* do, she forced herself to draw another deep breath into her burning lungs then tossed the sponge in the sink behind her. The air was thick with heated tension. The buzzing in her ears made it impossible for her to hear anything.

Shit, it's Nicky. Shit, it's Nicky. The phrase kept spinning through her mind until she thought she'd be sick with the dizziness of it. Her chest heaved with the effort to breathe and her pulse beat in a crazy tap dancer's rhythm.

Did anyone else notice the sudden change in the

room? Mike forced herself to look away from that face from her past and quickly glanced around. Five sets of eyes fixed on her with varying degrees of bewilderment. She could still feel *his* eyes on her, too, filled with stunned disbelief.

Feeling like she was trapped in a nightmare where everything moved with the speed of molasses, Mike pushed away from the counter and walked across the room, straight past the frozen figure of Nicky Lansing and through the swinging door. She turned a corner and rushed through a second door that opened into the engine room, not stopping until she reached the engine on the far side, where she promptly collapsed on the back step.

Heedless of the dirt and grime, she let her head drop against the back compartment door, ignoring the length of hose line in her way. Her breathing came in shallow gasps that did nothing to help the lightheadedness causing black dots to dance across her closed lids.

Hyperventilating. She was hyperventilating. The calm, rational part of her—she was surprised she still had one—told her to lean forward, to get a grip on herself and her breathing. Now bent over, sitting with her head between her knees, Mikey grabbed the running board with both hands and concentrated on the feel of the diamond plate cutting into her palms.

The spots faded away and her breathing slowed to something closer to normal. One last deep breath and she straightened, only to choke on a scream when she came face-to-face with Jay, his brows lowered in a frown as he studied her with concern.

"Jesus! Don't scare me like that!" She pushed him away then stood, only to sit back down when she realized how bad her knees were shaking.

"Scare *you*? What is wrong with you? Are you okay?"

"I'm fine. I couldn't be better! Don't I look fine?"

"You look like you're ready to pass out. What the hell is going on? Do you know that guy? He looks like he's seen a ghost!"

"He probably thinks he has." Mike moved over and motioned for Jay to sit down, ignoring his scrutiny as he twisted sideways and continued staring at her.

"Are you going to explain that?"

"No." She ran her hands through her hair, muttering when she pulled a thick hank of it loose from the ponytail. Sighing, she reached back and pulled the elastic band loose, then quickly rearranged her hair into a more secure hold. Jay watched her intently then nudged her leg with his when she continued to ignore him.

"Well?"

"Well nothing. He's just somebody I used to know, that's all."

Jay snorted. "Bull."

"Okay, fine," she conceded. "He's also somebody I never wanted to see again." Mike reached down and gingerly touched her right side, trying not to remember but unable to forget. If Jay noticed the motion, he didn't say anything.

They sat in silence, the familiar background noises of the station virtually unnoticed. A few minutes went by before Jay spoke again. "You sure you don't want to talk about it?"

Mike shook her head, ready to make a sarcastic reply when the sound of footsteps echoed through the engine room. The steps paused then changed directions before walking around the side of the engine, coming closer. Mike knew without looking who it was: the steps were those of a stranger, someone who didn't know his way around.

Nicky stopped at the back of the engine, not saying anything as Jay slowly stood and positioned himself slightly in front of Mike, shielding her. She touched his arm briefly, in a gesture both of thanks and of reassurance that she was alright. Jay looked back at her, one brow cocked in question, then reluctantly walked away at her nod. Mike didn't see where he went but she knew he would be close by in case he was needed.

She stood slightly, changing her position on the running board so she was leaning on it instead of sitting, then crossed her arms in front of her, covering the jagged scar that ran along her left forearm. The stance was as close to aloof and detached as she could manage considering her insides were making a milkshake of her early dinner. Too late, she remembered the sunglasses hanging around her neck, and wished she would have thought to put them on to hide any emotion in her eyes.

With an effort that took more strength than she wanted to admit, she let her eyes slowly, coolly rake the man in front of her from top to bottom.

Dammit. The Nicky Lansing from her past had been ruggedly handsome with dark looks and boyish charm; this Nick Lansing was dangerously gorgeous. A little taller than she remembered, he stood just over six feet, and was definitely broader through the shoulders and chest. The boy she remembered had finally filled out, to all the best advantages.

The long hair of his past was gone, cut to a length that brushed just past the collar of the light blue shirt he wore. Still too long to be squeaky clean, but short enough by today's standards to be rated as professional. His eyes were the same, though. A dark chocolate brown framed in sinfully long lashes, they invited a person to swim in their depths and lose their soul without a second thought.

She would know, since she had done just that.

Those eyes were watching her now and she briefly met his direct gaze without meaning to. They had changed, she realized. There was an inner depth now, a maturity that had been missing those many years ago. And in that brief second when their eyes had met, she thought she glimpsed something else. Guilt? Regret? Somehow she doubted it.

Nicky shifted his weight from one foot to the other and jammed both hands into the pockets of his trousers. Mike watched his nervousness with a sense of satisfaction and refused to do anything to ease it. He cleared his throat, looked around, then finally returned his gaze to her. The corner of his mouth twitched in a forced smile, showing a glimpse of that damned dimple, then abruptly died.

"I, uh, I wasn't expecting to see you here," he finally said. His voice was deeper than she remembered, smooth and mellow. Probably soothing to the listener, too, if it had been anyone but her.

She didn't move, didn't respond, just stood there watching him as she fought the twitch she could feel building in her eye. He shifted again, removed one hand from his pocket and ran it through his thick hair. His eyes met hers then darted away.

"You look good, Michaela."

"Compared to the last time you saw me?" The words, full of bitter resentment, tumbled from her mouth before she could stop them. She watched him cringe at the accusation but refused to do anything to lessen his discomfort. His suffering now was nothing compared to what she had gone through.

"Kayla—"

"Don't call me that!" Mike uncrossed her arms and pushed herself off the running board, standing so there was less than a foot between them. She narrowed her eyes at Nick, clamping her mouth shut against all the words she wanted to pummel him with. Anger, red-hot and bone-deep, coursed through her, scaring her. Her emotions hadn't been this close to the surface for a long time and she hated him for the sudden lack of control that swamped her.

"I'm sor—"

Mike stepped forward, cutting him off, and jabbed a finger in his direction, not quite touching him. "No! Don't you even dare say it. You—"

A shrill alarm cut her off, startling Nick. She ignored him and cocked her head, thankful for the interruption as she listened to the radio that suddenly blared through the engine room. Hurried footsteps echoed around them, coming from different directions as the station came to life. Mike shot one last glance at Nick, who was obviously surprised at the sudden commotion, then walked away without saying anything.

She felt his eyes on her as she threw on her turnout gear, felt them following her as she ran to the engine and climbed into the jump seat. The smell of diesel exhaust filled the room as the engine roared to life and pulled out of the station, the siren beginning its mournful wail. Mike risked one last look out the window and saw Nick walking around the side of the building, his back to her as he walked away.

It was the view of Nick she was most accustomed to.

Chapter Five

Mike slammed on the brakes, causing the old CJ7 to fishtail in the loose gravel of the parking lot. She reached over and turned down the stereo's volume, stared at the lot full of cars, then faced Jay.

"Are they giving something away tonight?"

Jay shook his head, looking around the lot with open-mouthed astonishment. "I have no idea."

Mike glanced at her watch. Half-past ten. She shrugged, then maneuvered the Jeep around the edge of the parking lot, finally finding an empty space around back. Well, not exactly a space. It was a patch of gravel and overgrown weeds between the dumpster and the encroaching woods, but it suited her purpose just fine. She drained the can of beer she had been drinking, reached above the roll bar and tossed it into the dumpster, then climbed out of the Jeep.

A deep booming bass shook the walls of the bar as they walked around the side of the clapboard building. Jay paused, listening to the beat before shooting her a crooked smile.

"Sounds like they have a band tonight. That's a first."

"Yeah, and so is this crowd," Mike added, shaking her head in disbelief. Their shift had been coming to Duffy's for a little more than two years now and never before had there been this many people here, not even on a Saturday night. That was the charm of Duffy's. It was out of the way, a run-down local dive that served cold beer and frozen pizza to the few loyal patrons who preferred its rural flavor over the influx of high-priced clubs and sports bars a few miles down the road.

Mike tugged on the wooden door and braced herself against the loud music that washed over her when they entered. The press of bodies forced them to elbow their way to the back, away from the crowd formed around the area where the band was set up. Mike pushed up on her toes to make sure the rest of the shift was at their normal table, then continued through the crowd.

"This place is too small for this," she complained in a near-shout as she and Jay finally took two seats that had been saved for them. The crowd that had temporarily parted to let them through closed again, effectively shutting out the view of the rest of the bar.

"Yeah, well. At least they're good." Their lieutenant, Pete Cook, filled two plastic cups from one of the pitchers of beer on the table. He passed them to Mike and Jay, then leaned back in the wooden chair and crossed his arms, a frown tugging at his already drooping mustache. Mike took a sip, only half-listening to the music surrounding them.

"Not bad," she agreed. "So why the lack of enthusiasm?"

Dave Warren, the paramedic from their shift, leaned over and jabbed a brooding Pete in the ribs. "Ignore him. He's just upset because they took the pool tables out for tonight."

The comment was greeted with a small spattering of laughter which was immediately drowned out by the combined noise from the band and crowd. Mike refrained from reminding Pete that he wasn't that great of a player anyway and pushed her chair closer to the wall. She took another sip of the beer then tilted the chair backwards so she could rest her head against the cheap paneling.

The headache that had been plaguing her since early evening was threatening to worsen, no doubt aided by the commotion going on around her. She noticed Dave muttering something in Jay's ear, watched as both of them turned carefully blank looks in her direction. Mike raised an eyebrow in silent question only to have both of them look away and direct their gazes into the crowd.

Which was probably for the best, she thought, draining the cup in two long swallows. Knowing those two, they were no doubt gearing up to give her a lecture on drinking too much. Again. The guys at work were closer to her than her own sparse family, but sometimes they took the role of surrogate brotherhood entirely too far.

Folding her hands around the now-empty cup, Mike closed her eyes and let the bass line of the music seep through her. The last strands of the current song faded away, only to be immediately followed by the raucous introduction of an old rock hit. The crowd applauded its approval, nearly drowning out the voice of the lead singer. Mike frowned and opened her eyes, staring at nothing. For a minute she thought the voice had been Nick's.

Ridiculous. She just had a bad case of Nicky-on-the-brain, something that had been plaguing her since Thursday night when he had shown up at the station. It was a temporary illness, that was all, nothing that another beer couldn't cure. She let her chair topple forward and motioned to Pete for a refill, raising her cup in silent thanks before taking a sip.

Her gaze wandered to the crowd pushing in on their private space, faceless bodies writhing to the steady beat, and part of her suddenly wanted to join them. Giving into the impulse, she stood and grabbed Jay's arm, tugging, trying to urge him into the dancing crowd.

"What are you doing? Are you nuts?" He protested, pulling against her and exchanging a glance with David. She let out a weary sigh and slumped into the chair, shaking her head at both of them.

"No, I'm not drunk, so you two can knock it off. In fact, I'm not even planning on drinking that much tonight."

Jay shot her a disbelieving look. "Uh-huh. In that case, maybe we should go someplace else."

"What?" Mike glanced at the two of them, then at Pete, who was engrossed in a conversation with someone else. "You guys want to leave already? Why?"

Dave and Jay stood up at the same time, pulling Mike with them. She stumbled to her feet and nearly fell in her attempt to stop them from dragging her across the floor. At the same time, the music stopped, the sudden silence punctuated by an amplified announcement that the band was taking a break. Mike froze, her eyes searching the far corner where the band had set up.

Nick stood less than fifty feet away, his eyes fixed on hers as he absently propped a too-familiar guitar against the wall. She ripped her gaze from his and shot a panicked look first at Jay then at Dave, who shrugged helplessly.

"Nobody knew who it was at first. We figured you might want to leave."

Leave. God, yes, she wanted to leave. But she wouldn't. This was her bar, her hangout, and damned if she'd run.

Straightening her shoulders, Mike took a deep breath and reached into her pocket, digging out the keys to the Jeep. She turned her head and met Nick's gaze straight on as she blindly tossed the keys to Jay.

"We're staying. And I changed my mind. I've decided to do some serious drinking tonight."

Chapter Six

Nick paused on the make-shift stage, his hand loosely wrapped around the neck of the guitar as common sense and intelligence warred with emotion. Kayla's gaze met his and even from this distance he could see a spark of defiance in the green eyes. He was a fool ten times over for even thinking about going over and talking to her, especially since it was obvious she had no desire to see him. He got that message loud and clear from the frosty glare, the tilt of the chin, the crisp turn of her body when she walked back to the opposite corner.

Going within twenty feet of her would rank right up there in the top ten list of stupid moves.

But nowhere near as stupid as his move ten years ago.

Nick tightened his hold on the guitar, closing his eyes against the memory and the flare of pain. The moment was brief and unwelcome, but decisive. Kayla had obviously put everything behind her and didn't want to see him for old times' sake. The least he could do was respect that. He busied himself with straightening the equipment around him, a mindless task that wasn't even necessary.

"I'm getting a beer. Do you want anything?"

"Yeah, I could handle a soda." Nick turned toward Brian and stifled a groan when he saw the small group of women gathered in a knot by the stage behind him. They were dividing their hungry gazes evenly between Brian and him. Nick's groan grew louder when he recognized the faces from some of the other places where the band had played. "On second thought, I'll go with you."

Brian rolled his eyes, careful not to let the cluster of groupies see him do it. The two of them smiled cordially as they pushed their way through the crowd and headed to the bar, angling for an empty space so they could get the barmaid's attention. A few minutes passed before someone shoved against Nick, clearing the space next to him. He shot the newcomer an irritated glance and realized it was the man who had come in with Kayla, the same one who had hovered around her the other day at the fire station. The same one she had tossed her keys to just a few minutes ago.

Nick clenched his jaw against the sudden irrational emotion that spiraled through his gut, an emotion he had no business feeling. The man studied Nick through flint gray eyes, an eerily vacant stare that sized him up while radiating some kind of feral warning. Nick met the stare head-on, refusing to look away, and was gratified when the man nodded slightly then called the barmaid over. Nick's irritation grew at the immediate service the man received. He didn't miss the look of interest on the barmaid's face as she smiled at the man.

"Hey Angie. We need two more pitchers and Mikey wants some tequila. Might as well just give me the bottle." Resignation laced the man's voice as he leaned against the bar, his eyes still on Nick as he waited for his order to be filled. A charged silence hovered between them and Nick shifted uncomfortably, waiting for something, wondering if the man was going to say anything—or just stare at him the entire time. A minute crawled by as the man grabbed a stirrer from the container on the bar and chewed on it, openly studying Nick.

Nick ignored him while he gave his order to a second bartender then stood back to wait.

"Soda, hm?"

The question startled Nick. After the intense sizing up he had been given, he hadn't expected the man's first words to question his choice of beverage. "Yeah, soda. I don't drink." Anymore, he added to himself.

"Hm. Wish you could give Mike some pointers on that." The man chewed on the stirrer some more, considering, then held out his hand. "Jay Moore."

Nick stared at the outstretched hand then grudgingly shook it, introducing himself. "So, everyone calls her Mike?" It wasn't the question Nick wanted to ask. Not even in the top ten. But he had no business asking questions, no business prying into Kayla's personal life. Not anymore. He'd never had that right, not even ten years ago. He sure as hell didn't have it now, not after everything that had happened.

"What else would we call her?"

"When I knew her, she went by Kayla."

Jay studied him some more then shrugged,

leaning over the bar to pull the tray the barmaid sat in front of him closer. He rearranged the pitchers, bottle, and shot glasses then picked it up, instructing the woman to put everything on their tab. He turned back to Nick with another penetrating stare. "I get the feeling that was during another life for her. See you around."

Nick turned and watched him walk away, dodging through the crowd with the cumbersome tray, making it to the table without dropping anything. Laughing faces greeted him as the small group reached hungrily for the fresh drinks, Kayla the first in line. Nick was astonished when she grabbed the bottle of tequila and drank heavily, not even bothering with a glass. None of the men she was with reacted to it at all, not even a single raised eyebrow or a funny joke. Maybe it was normal for her, normal to them—but not to him. Not from Kayla, at least. The Kayla he remembered would never take long swallows from a bottle. The Kayla he remembered would give him hell if he'd done the same thing.

He closed his eyes, imagining the bitter liquid draining down his own throat. His stomach clenched painfully, even as his mouth watered with a distant craving. Nick grabbed the soda from the bartender and took a sip, washing away the phantom taste of alcohol.

What had Jay said? That he wished Nick could give some pointers on drinking soda to Kayla? Apparently her name wasn't the only thing that had changed in the long years since he had seen her last.

He continued watching the table in the corner, not worrying about getting caught staring since nobody was paying any attention to him.

Kayla was obviously the center of attention, her laughter heard even from this distance. She wore her hair down tonight, a thick mass of loose chestnut waves that curled past her shoulders. As he watched, she shoved a strand of long hair out of her face and leaned over the table to say something to the man across from her. Nick's eyes automatically dropped lower, resting on the shapely bottom that was being shown off. He swallowed, his mouth suddenly dry at the sight of her tight, denim-clad curves. Kayla had always had a nice body, soft and curvy, comforting. There was no doubt that time had only enhanced it as she matured. She still had curves but she was leaner now, her body toned and tight. It was the body of someone who worked out, who stayed in shape—maybe a little too much.

She straightened and motioned wildly with one hand, drawing more laughter from the guys surrounding her. He recognized a few of the faces from his brief visit the other night and he wondered if everyone at the table worked with her. Not that it was any of his business, he told himself.

The gap he had been watching her through filled with people when the jukebox kicked on. The first strands of music were lost in the noise of the crowd before the volume was turned up. Nick's stomach tilted when he recognized the old slow song and he craned his neck to catch a glimpse of Kayla to see her reaction.

She was sitting now, the chair tilted back against the wall, her arms wrapped around her middle and a frown on her pale face. Someone leaned over and said something to her; she seemed to shake herself and forced a smile before downing the shot she had been given.

Nick tossed back the remainder of his soda and hesitated. He wanted to go over to her, to talk to her. The saner part of him told him that to do so would be the same as ramming a serrated knife into his gut and twisting. Repeatedly.

Without realizing he had made the decision, Nick pushed through the crowd, not stopping until he reached the table. A second went by before one or two of the men noticed him, another second before Kayla seemed to sense the change around her and slowly looked up. Glassy green eyes finally met his, unfocused at first, then full of emotion that was quickly hidden behind a cool glare.

Pain ripped through him. And regret. He knew she hadn't meant for him to see, that she'd be horrified if she realized it. But in that split-second when she first looked up at him, before she had a chance to put on that cool detached mask, Nick had glimpsed sorrow and longing in the dark green depths of her eyes. He swallowed against the silent accusation that was now being thrown his way. *You did this to me*, the look seemed to say. And he had. Ten years ago when one reckless night changed their lives forever.

"What do you want, Lansing?" Her voice was cold, unwelcoming, and Nick inwardly flinched. Had he really expected a warm reception? Could he really blame her for how she obviously felt?

Several pairs of eyes were focused on him and he squirmed under the scrutiny, wondering if any of them knew. Probably not, or the looks would be more hostile. He cleared his throat and turned back to Kayla, who was busy downing another shot. She shook her head and exhaled a breathy sigh, slamming the glass on the table and motioning for a refill. The bottle was barely half-full. Hadn't it been a new bottle when the barmaid gave it to Jay? He couldn't remember, didn't want to think it had been, not when he was wondering how many shots she had downed in such a short amount of time.

"I was wondering if you wanted to dance," he finally asked, motioning to the floor behind him. He wasn't surprised when she forced a laugh and promptly told him to go to hell.

"Go on, Mike, go dance."

"Yeah, go have some fun."

The phrases of encouragement coming from her friends startled Nick, but apparently not as much as they startled Kayla. She looked around the table in horror, her eyes narrowing on the nearest victim, who happened to be Jay.

"I. Do not. Want. To dance." The words were short and clipped, uttered through clenched teeth. She let out a quick breath, looked up at Nick, then back at Jay. "Especially with *him*."

"Mike, go dance," Jay ordered, pushing the shot glass out of her reach. "Maybe it'll sober you up some."

"I am not dancing with him. And I don't want to be sober!" Kayla leaned across Jay and tried to rescue the glass from his grip, only to tilt forward and nearly fall into his lap. Nick instinctively reached past Jay to catch her, grabbing her by the shoulders in a gentle grip.

It was the wrong thing to do.

Kayla stiffened at his touch, freezing for a split-second before throwing his hands off her and suddenly swinging out at him. Nick stumbled back as Jay caught her flailing arm with both hands. She shook her hair out of her face but made no other move, allowing Jay to push her back into the seat as she glared at Nick.

Surprised glances were shared around the table as the men with her looked first at Nick then at Kayla. The accompanying silence was strained, made more so because of the music and noise that continued around them. Jay rested a hand on Kayla's shoulder and nudged her until she looked at him.

"Mike, what is with you? All he asked was for you to dance."

Kayla hung her head, her arms wrapped protectively around her middle once more. "Just tell him to get lost."

Nick remained rooted to the spot, pity and guilt filling him as he watched the sudden change in her. No longer fiery or defiant, she was looked lost, defeated. He couldn't shake the feeling that he was responsible—no, he *knew* he was responsible. There was no question or doubt about that. He should leave, should just walk away and pretend she wasn't here, pretend he didn't know her. But he couldn't. He didn't know why, knew it was irrational, but he couldn't leave, not yet. Not without saying something. "Kayla—"

"Go away!"

"Mike, calm down. Jesus. What is wrong with you?" Jay asked, watching her in astonishment. She uttered a short laugh that sounded forced and faced Nick, pinning him with a look of hatred so clear it sliced him, deep and quick.

"Wrong with me? Why don't you ask him? He's

the son of a bitch who almost killed me!"

Chapter Seven

"So are you going to talk about it?"

Mike took a gulp from the plastic bottle in her hand and swished warm water through her mouth before leaning over and spitting it out. The sudden motion made the ground under her feet tilt at an odd angle and she reeled sideways, catching herself against the dumpster. She closed her eyes and took a deep breath, trying to focus on Jay's question.

"Talk 'bout what?"

"About tonight."

"Nothin' to talk about," she muttered, resting her forehead against the side of the dumpster. The metal was rough on her skin but cool. Cooler than her skin, anyway. Her stomach rolled and she swallowed several times in an effort to calm it, taking a deep breath when it cooperated. For now.

"How can you say that? Christ, Mikey, you're close to tossing cookies with your head in a dumpster!"

"My head…is not…in the dumpster." Mike took

another deep breath and straightened, carefully easing her eyes open. She turned her head and squinted at the unfocused blur leaning against her Jeep. "Let it go."

The blur moved, motioning in her direction and making her head spin again. "I'm not going to let it go. What was that all about earlier? I've never seen you like that before."

"Jay, please. Just, take me home. Please." She hated the begging whine in her voice but didn't really care at this point. Tomorrow she'd kick herself for it, but tonight she just wanted to go home.

"What are you going to do about that guy Nick?"

"Huh? Nothing." Mike pushed away from the dumpster and lurched toward the Jeep, stumbling blindly until Jay placed a steadying hand under her elbow.

"You're going to have to do something, Mike, because I don't think he's going to go away."

"Sure he will. Always does. It's his specialty." She climbed over the front seat, muttering under her breath when her knee banged the stick shift before she rolled into the passenger seat. Her stomach tilted again and she closed her eyes, resting her head against the roll bar.

"Yeah, well, it doesn't look like he's going away to me."

"Huh?" Mike pried one eye open and squinted at Jay, who pointed at something over her shoulder. With careful effort she slowly turned her head and tried to focus. No good. The outside security light was too bright, making her vision swim. A darker blur wavered in the light and she squinted again, trying to make it out. Still no good. Letting out a deep breath, she closed her eyes and let her head fall back against the seat.

"Mike? Mike! C'mon, wake up."

"Uh-uh."

"Mike, you have company."

"Hm. Uh-uh."

"Is she alright?" The question came from somewhere to her right and the voice didn't belong to Jay. She tried to open her eyes, wanted to see if she was imagining the voice, but the effort to move hurt too much and she gave up.

"Yeah, she'll be fine."

"She doesn't look fine to me. Does she do this a lot?"

"Enough." There was a pause as the Jeep dipped slightly on the driver's side. Mike swallowed, trying to control her stomach's roll at the motion.

"Are you sure she's okay? She's not going to fall out?" The question was accompanied by another motion to her right, a touch against her shoulder and waist as someone buckled the seat belt around her. She pushed at the strap across her stomach, trying to ease the pressure, then finally cracked one eye open and glared at the figure next to her. Him. Again.

His eyes met hers, full of sorrow and, God help her, pity. She didn't need Nicky Lansing's pity. Or anything else he might try to give her. She cleared her throat and let her eye drift close, searching blindly for the water bottle. "Go away, Nick. You've done enough already."

"Kayla."

She waved a hand in his direction, trying to ignore him, to brush him away as she continued her search for the water. She leaned forward and grimaced as the lap strap pulled tight against her stomach, tried to swallow, to stop the rolling in her stomach as more of the tequila sloshed around, but it was no good. Her will was no match for the alcohol, and neither was her empty stomach. She reached out, groping, unhooking the seatbelt in time to lean over the passenger side so the feeble contents of her stomach would hit the ground instead of the inside of her Jeep.

A deep chuckle from her left told her she would have made it, if Nick Lansing hadn't been in the way.

***

Laughter and music. Loud music. The roar of wind blowing, a scream. Burning rubber as tires squealed and metal twisted. A disembodied face, staring. His face.

Nicky.

Mike woke with a strangled sob and pitched upright, then grabbed her head with both hands before it could topple off. Maybe she'd be better if it did topple off; it would save her from the pain of what promised to be her worse hangover yet.

Head still held firmly between two hands, she rolled sideways on the bed, groaning, and swallowed against the rotten taste in her mouth as memories of the previous night assaulted her memory. Tequila. Yuck. Why had she insisted on drinking the stuff, knowing what it did to her?

The memory of why was too clear, and she groaned again.

"I see you're finally alive. Barely."

Mike peeled open one heavy lid and tried to glare

at Jay as he leaned against the railing at the top step of her loft bedroom. The glare wasn't very successful, if his grin was an indication. He strolled into the room, looking relaxed and disgustingly sober and clear-headed. He leaned over and placed a cup of coffee on the nightstand, along with a bottle of ibuprofen. She stared at it for a second then closed her eyes, the effort to move too much.

"What time is it?"

"Oh, almost one o'clock. I was beginning to think you had died when I wasn't looking."

"I'd be better off if I had." Silence settled over the room, broken by the squeak of the bed as Jay sat down next to her. She moved her foot to give him more room, groaning as the bed dipped, thankful it was her head spinning and not her stomach. That had been emptied the night before.

"Mikey, you've got to stop doing this to yourself. I've never seen you as bad as you were last night. It's like you're deliberately trying to self-destruct."

"Not now, Jay."

More silence, then a long sigh. Mike held her breath, waiting for the lecture to start, waiting for the words she damn near knew by heart. But there was nothing but silence, heavy and more damning than any words could be. She opened her eyes and looked up. Jay was staring at her, his gray eyes dark with concern as he sat there in silence.

"So who is this guy Nick?"

It was Mike's turn to sigh. If she could have managed it, she would have hit him, but her whole body felt as if it had been battered and she couldn't make the effort. Instead, she closed her eyes again and pretended to ignore him.

"C'mon, Mike, fess up. Who is he?"

"Nobody." God, she sounded so freaking pitiful, even to herself. No wonder Jay looked so worried.

He grunted his disbelief but said nothing else. The bed dipped again as he shifted and before Mike realized what he was doing, he had pulled the bottom of her shirt up, revealing her stomach and the jagged scar that ran across her right side. "Does he have anything to do with this?"

Mike glared at him then pulled the shirt from his hand and tugged it back down. "You know, people are going to start thinking there's something going on between us if you keep doing shit like that."

"Yeah, right. How long have we known each other? Eight years? It would be like sleeping with my sister."

"Gee, thanks for the compliment. And I really didn't need the visual, either."

"I aim to please. Stop trying to change the subject."

"I'm not changing the subject, because there is no subject. Let it go." Mike slowly pushed herself to a sitting position, wincing at the sharp pain behind her eyes when she moved. She reached out a shaking hand for the coffee, took a long swallow, then fought with the cap on the bottle before dumping out four of them and tossing them back with another gulp of coffee. It was sheer fantasy thinking they'd do anything to help, but at least they wouldn't hurt. Unless you counted the ache of moving.

"So who is he?" Jay's tone of voice said he wasn't going to be put off easily. Mike eased herself back down on the bed and ignored him. "Well?"

"Jay, I love you dearly, but if you don't let it go, I

will kill you. Got it?"

More silence. Several minutes ticked by and Mike felt herself drifting off into oblivion, only to be pulled back when Jay roughly lifted her off the bed, causing everything to swim. She bit back a scream and grabbed for him, searching for an anchor in the suddenly spinning world but coming away empty-handed. The bathroom loomed before her and this time she did scream, but not before Jay managed to toss her in the large tub, clothes and all.

Her mouth filled with freezing water when Jay turned on the shower but she could do nothing more than just sit there, letting the cold water rush over her, pasting her clothes to her shivering body. She was too stunned to move, too shocked to do anything but stare up at him. He was leaning over her, careful to stay out of the water spray, pointing a finger at her with a look of steely determination on his face.

"You're going to sit there until you come to your senses. Then you're going to get dressed and come out and tell me what the hell's going on. Got it?" He didn't wait for an answer, just stared at her for another second then turned on his heel and stormed out of the room, slamming the door behind him. Mike winced as the loud noise pierced her skull. She muttered to herself, choosing a few of the more colorful words in her vocabulary, then turned on the warm water and pulled herself to a standing position while she yanked the shower curtain closed.

She continued her half-hearted swearing as she peeled off the wet clothes and stood under the spray, letting it wash over her, wishing it would wash away the memories as well. How could she even begin to explain Nick? She couldn't. Not to Jay, not to anyone.

Hell, she couldn't even explain to herself. Not twelve years ago, not ten years ago. Certainly not now. It hurt too much, dredging up the old memories. Not that she'd ever really forget. Her hand strayed over the roughness of the scar, a jagged tear on otherwise smooth skin. No, she would never be able to completely forget. But she thought she had at least moved on.

Forcing herself to push everything out of her mind, Mike finished her shower and dried off, then pulled on the sweat pants and t-shirt Jay had left in the bathroom for her. The hangover still held her firmly in its grip, but at least she looked a little better. Maybe. She grimaced at the reflection in the mirror, at the pale skin and the shadows under red-rimmed eyes. A walking corpse. That's what the reflection reminded her of.

The comparison was too close, too disturbing. She shook he head, forcing the memories from her mind as she walked out of the bathroom, ready to face Jay.

He was waiting for her downstairs in the living room, sprawled out on the sofa, playing channel roulette with the remote control. She walked by him and pulled it out of his hand, then flopped back on the love seat, groaning at the throbbing in her head. A basketball game blared on the television and Mike snapped it off with the remote, welcoming the silence with a grateful sigh.

The silence was short-lived, as she knew it would be. Jay sat up and stared at her, sighed, then went straight for the kill. "So fess up, Mike. Who is Nick Lansing?"

"Ex-boyfriend. See? Nothing deep, dark, or

mysterious."

"You want to tell me something I haven't already figured out? What I want to know is why you react so…I don't even know what to call it. I've never seen you act like that before. So why? Why were so volatile around him?"

Mike sighed and rested her head against the cushions, wishing she could disappear in the comforting softness. She couldn't, though, so she tried to decide how much to tell Jay. He was her best friend. What did it mean that he didn't know the full history? That she'd never told him. Never told anyone. And she couldn't tell him now; she wasn't ready, didn't think she'd ever be ready.

She took a deep breath, let it out slowly, and stumbled over the words. "Not just ex, then. I guess you could call him my 'first love'. We didn't part on good terms."

"And?"

"And nothing. Christ Jay, what more do you want?" Mike shifted on the love seat and pushed up on one elbow, watching him. "How would you act if you suddenly saw your first love again after ten years?"

He appeared to consider it for a full minute then smiled a slow, insinuating smile. Mike threw the remote at him in frustration, sparing a brief second of sympathy for whatever woman thought she could reel Jay out of the bachelor pond.

"Yeah, well, I know a lot more now than I did back then." His expression grew serious as he slid to the end of the sofa, leaning closer to her. "Mike, I know there's more to it than that. I've never seen you as bad as you were last night. Are you going to tell me it had nothing to do with him?"

"No, I'm going to tell you it was one big coincidence. Don't read so much into it." Her voice was carefully flat, expressionless. If Jay heard just one nuance of emotion, he would pounce on it, and she didn't want to travel down memory lane. Not today, and certainly not about Nick. She didn't want to think about how he had abandoned her, broke her heart.

Left her for dead.

Minutes crept by, quiet minutes where Mike knew, just *knew* that Jay was wondering how much more he could push her. He must have realized he was nearing the edge because he let out a heavy sigh and sat back. "Fine, you don't want to talk about it, suit yourself. Think you could at least manage to talk about this fun-filled program I got suckered into?"

Mike managed a laugh, at Jay's desperate tone as well as the image of him teaching a drunk-driving awareness program for high school students. "What do you want me to say? You're the one who was stupid enough to volunteer. Sucker."

"Ha ha. And I didn't exactly volunteer, I was just in the wrong place at the wrong time. You're going to help me, right?"

"What?" Mike struggled to a sitting position and stared at Jay in open-mouthed shock. He was watching her in wide-eyed innocence, his gray eyes sparkling with humor as he brushed a lock of blonde hair off his forehead. "Now I know you're cracked in the head."

"C'mon Mikey, I need help. I don't know what the hell I'm doing with this."

"And I do? Go talk to somebody in Public Affairs. This whole fiasco was their idea, wasn't it?"

"Yeah, but that doesn't mean they know what's going on. Throw together a new program for good PR, forget about how to make it work. You know how it goes. So you're going to help. Right?"

"Help how? What makes you think I can do anything that you can't?"

"Because you're better at that whole instructing thing."

"This isn't instructing."

"So? Just come with me tomorrow afternoon when I meet the teacher liaison. I'll owe you one."

"You already owe me about a thousand as it is."

"So add it to my tab." Jay stood and stretched, his muscles flexing under the faded denim that hugged his legs. He reached down and grabbed his keys from the coffee table then walked to the door, pausing to study Mike with a look she didn't like. "So I'll pick you up tomorrow afternoon?"

Mike closed her eyes against Jay's concern and nodded, wondering why she was agreeing to get herself involved in something that would probably prove to be nothing more than just another huge headache.

Chapter Eight

Nick leaned back in the chair and stared at the clock on the wall. *Tick, squeak, tock, squeak.* The seconds ticked away in time to the rocking motion of the chair, the only sounds in the deserted classroom. A stack of essays was piled neatly on the scarred desk, demanding his attention, but his mind was somewhere else.

So much for making use of the last period of the day, his only free one on Mondays.

He let out a deep breath and ran his hands through his hair in another unsuccessful attempt to rid himself of the one image that had haunted him all weekend: Kayla, drunk and sick in a bar parking lot. Christ, why couldn't he stop seeing her like that?

Because as bad as that was, it was better than his memory of the last time he had seen her, his conscience piped up. He closed his eyes and swallowed, tasting the bitterness of guilt deep in his throat. Ten years was a lifetime ago, and he still couldn't get rid of it. The guilt, the regret, all of it was still imbedded deep inside him, eating away at him even when he thought he had buried it with his past. Seeing Kayla had made him realize that the past wasn't quite as buried as he thought it was.

"I don't need this," Nick mumbled to himself. His voice bounced back at him, too loud in the empty room. He ran his hands through his hair again then leaned forward and propped his elbows on the desk, thinking. He'd prefer not thinking, but he had tried that already and it hadn't worked.

Part of him wondered if it would just be better to seek Kayla out, to talk to her and try to resolve their past once and for all. He had a feeling that the idea was easier said than done. First, he had no idea where to even find Kayla except at work, and this was the kind of conversation that needed to be done in private. Second, he was pretty sure that Kayla wouldn't want to speak to him even if he did track her down.

So why was he sitting here agonizing over the whole thing? There was very little chance that he'd run into her. Running into her twice last week was a quirky fluke that wouldn't happen again. Did he really want to dredge up the past, to pick at old injuries, just to ease his conscience now?

No, he didn't. The time for that was long past. He'd lived with the consequences for ten years; he couldn't dredge it all up now just to ease his own guilt.

A picture immediately came to mind, an image of the older Kayla superimposed over the younger, more innocent girl he remembered. And clearer than the picture in his mind was the certainty that he was largely responsible for the lack of innocence he sensed in her now.

Just forget it. Nick rubbed his eyes with the heels of both hands. Forget the guilt, pretend it didn't exist. And forget the pity, both for himself and for Kayla. Both of their lives had changed, they were different people now, and their paths would never cross again. He had to let it go, get back to who and what he was now. He let out a deep breath and pulled the first essay from the pile, determined to grade at least a handful before his three-thirty appointment.

An hour later he was still staring bleary-eyed at the first essay, the typed letters blurring illegibly in front of him. He murmured a silent thanks when the room intercom buzzed and the school secretary announced that his visitors were on their way down. Nick tossed the essay back in the pile and stood, stretching until his back popped. He ran one hand through his hair in an attempt to smooth it, straightened his tie and jacket, then opened the classroom door at the knock and immediately froze when he saw who the visitors were.

"You have got to be fucking kidding me." The cool smile on Kayla's face disappeared with her blunt statement. She spared a glance at Nick then turned to face Jay Moore with an accusing glare. "Did you know it was going to be him?"

Jay looked as stunned as Nick felt, and was barely able to shake his head in response to Kayla's question. Silence stretched tight around the trio then finally snapped when Kayla spoke again. "All yours, Jay. I'm out of here."

"Wait, hold on!" Jay reached out and grabbed Kayla by the arm then ushered her past Nick and into the classroom, closing the door behind him. He kept hold of her arm as he led her to Nick's desk and pushed her into the chair. She held herself stiffly upright, her arms crossed defiantly as she stared straight ahead, her jaw clenched. Jay leaned down and said something to her, but Nick was too far away to hear it clearly. Whatever it was apparently didn't please Kayla because she shot Jay a withering look before turning it on him.

"Okay, now, time to get to the bottom of this and find out what's going on. You," Jay pointed at finger at Nick, "get over here. If I can't get an answer from her, maybe I'll get one from you."

Nick raised an eyebrow at the demand but wisely said nothing as he closed the distance between the door and his desk. He risked another glance at Kayla and felt the guilt and regret wash over him again. Had she really become that cold and hard, or was it just a show for his benefit? He was almost afraid of the answer.

"Now that we're all together here, someone help me out. First—are you the teacher we're supposed to meet to set this program up?"

"The awareness program? Yes," Nick confirmed. Jay muttered under his breath, obviously not happy with the answer. He rubbed the back of one hand across his mouth and sighed, staring at Kayla. She stared back at him, sending him some silent message that Nick couldn't interpret. A flash of jealousy, unexpected and unwelcome, seared his veins, and he wondered if the couple in front of him had a history. They must have, to be able to communicate so swiftly and silently. And it was none of his damned business, so why was he even worrying about it?

"Perfect. Just great." Jay released another sigh

then looked at Nick, those odd gray eyes filled a hardness he didn't understand. "Okay then. Is there anyone else besides you that we can work with?"

"Excuse me?" Irritation exploded deep inside. Not just irritation; something else, something darker from his past, a feeling of inadequacy, of once again wondering what else he needed to do to atone for the sins of his past. Nick forced his jaw to relax, forced himself to meet the other man's gaze with his own unflinching one. "No, I'm afraid there isn't."

"Kind of hypocritical, don't you think? You, heading a program against drunk driving?" Kayla's words were icy, bitter. Nick faced her then immediately recoiled from the look she leveled at him. Accusation, anger. And why shouldn't he see those things in her eyes? He opened his mouth to say something then promptly shut it against the defensive comeback he had been about to utter. More than anyone else, Kayla had every right to throw the accusation at him.

"I don't drink anymore." Nick's quiet response seemed empty and hollow to his own ears. From the expression on Kayla's face, it was obvious she didn't believe him. She pushed herself out of the chair and walked several paces away, putting more distance between them. Her back and shoulders were rigid, her jaw clenched even tighter than before. He watched her carefully as she started pacing, the pony tail of her slicked-back hair swinging against the shoulders of the shapeless blue uniform shirt with each angry step.

Nick sighed and ran a hand through his own hair in frustration. And despair. The air around Kayla crackled with emotion so tense, so thick he could feel it. He braced himself for the explosion he was sure would come. But there was no explosion, only a damning silence that was a hundred times worse—because it made Nick realize that this woman in front of him was nothing like the Kayla he remembered from all those years ago. Laughing, innocent, quick to show what she was feeling, no matter if it was good or bad. This Kayla, the woman in front of him now, looked as if she never smiled, as if she kept things too deep inside, buried and hidden. Almost as if she didn't feel—or as if she was afraid to let the world know she felt.

They were the same, yet completely different. He didn't know this woman in front of him, no matter how closely she resembled the girl from his past. He closed his eyes tight and immediately saw an image of the younger Kayla, vibrant and laughing, full of life and hopes and dreams.

Over that came another image, an image of twisted metal and broken bones and torn flesh. And blood.

Oh God, the blood.

Nick shuddered and opened his eyes, trying to banish the memory that he had worked so hard to forget. His breath caught in his throat as his eyes met Kayla's, at the bitterness etched on her face. And something else, a deeper emotion he couldn't read but that made him uncomfortable regardless. He looked away, unable to meet her direct gaze any longer, and cleared his throat, swallowing against the thickness that clogged it, making it hard to breathe.

"For what it's worth, I am sorry. I never meant..." He trailed off, immediately recognizing the mistake of saying anything. Fire flashed in the depths of her green eyes as she closed the distance between them, jabbing a long finger in his direction. She didn't touch him, made sure there was still space separating them, but the physical threat was there nonetheless. It took more willpower than Nick thought it would not to step away from her.

"Don't you even say it! Do you hear me? You had your chance for sorry ten years ago and you weren't man enough to do it then, so don't try to do it now!" Kayla's voice was soft, tightly controlled despite the tense emotion of her words. He swallowed and stepped back, remembering they weren't alone in the room only when Jay's quiet words shattered the tension surrounding them, suffocating them.

"What the hell is going on between you two?" His gray eyes, full of concern, rested on Kayla for a few long seconds. Then he shifted his gaze to Nick, his eyes cold and filled with suspicion. The silence was broken by Kayla's laugh, brittle and sharp.

"Going on? Nothing. It's just funny that he should be warning anyone about the dangers of drunk driving. I mean, you do it so well, Nicky, don't you?"

"Kayla—"

"No, let's get it all out." Her voice betrayed none of the emotion that flashed in her eyes, cold with fury as she stared at him. Quiet seconds went by before she looked away, turning her attention to Jay. "I wasn't joking when I told you the other night that he almost killed me. One night, just over ten years ago, Nicky decided he was okay to drive and I was stupid enough to believe him. He walked away from the accident. I didn't. And that was the last time I saw him."

Kayla turned back to face him, those green eyes

that used to be so full of life and laughter now cold and flat, completely devoid of all emotion. "So you see, Jay, there really was nothing mysterious about it like you thought. Just an ex who means as much to me as I do to him. Does that sound about right, Nicky?" She turned back to Jay and offered him a brittle smile. "Sorry pal, but you're on your own with this one. I'll wait outside for you."

Nick watched her open the door and walk out, felt the familiar guilt sweep over him once more, harsher and more painful than ever before. And this time, the guilt, all the other emotion he had been trying to deny, scared the shit out of him, twisting his gut and knotting his throat. And he was scared. Scared because his worse fear from that long ago night had actually come true, no matter how hard he tried to convince himself otherwise.

He had been kidding himself all these years, telling himself that Kayla was alive and well, blindly believing that of all the things he had done, he could at least be thankful that he hadn't killed her.

With the image of the woman who had just walked out of the room still burning clearly in his mind, Nick realized he had been wrong all these years. The Kayla he remembered *was* dead and gone, had been for ten years.

And he was the one who had killed her.

Chapter Nine

Unbelievable. Utterly unbelievable.

Mike didn't know whether to laugh or cry, a decision made harder because neither reaction would help. So instead, she took a deep breath and lashed out again with her fists, her pent-up anger finding some release in the repeated blows against the stuffed bag. It remained still for the first set then swung wildly under her last assault.

"Hey, would you take it easy?" Jay stepped away from the bag and rubbed at a spot on his chest, apparently the same spot where the bag caught him when he lost his grip. Mike gave him a dirty look and threw two more heavy punches, followed by a hard kick, just to make sure Jay understood what kind of mood she was in. She wiped the sweat from her forehead then stepped away from the bag and shot him another murderous glare.

"Okay, so it was stupid. *I* was stupid. I wasn't thinking."

"There's an understatement." Mike sat down on

the bench and wiped more sweat from her face, then draped the towel around her neck and reached for the water bottle. She took a long swallow, wiped her mouth with the back of her hand and then glared at Jay. The workout had helped nothing. Her frustration and anger were still there, simmering just below the surface, aching for release. She took a deep breath, let it out, took another and held it, counting to a slow ten before releasing it.

"Mikey, c'mon, please. I'm sorry. How long are you going to stay mad at me?"

"For as long as it takes."

"Mikey..." Jay's voice trailed off and he stepped away, slowly pacing back and forth before coming to a stop in front of her. He ran a hand through his hair, causing the short blonde strands to stick up at crazy angles. He dragged the hand down his face and sighed. "I'm sorry. I screwed up, okay?"

"That's putting it mildly."

"I didn't know! Okay? I didn't know. I had the damned paperwork filled out before we even went to that school. How was I supposed to know they'd send the stuff in before our shift even started?"

Mike took another deep breath and leaned her head against the wall, closing her eyes to block out the sight of Jay's misery. There was probably some comfort to be found in that, knowing that she wasn't the only miserable one, but it didn't help. Not now. And all because Jay had, for once, actually done his paperwork. Any other time, forms were misplaced or waylaid or sent in late. Or Jay just forgot to do them at all. But not this time. Of course not. And why in the hell couldn't that have happened this time?

Because fate was a bitch with a twisted sense of

irony.

She and Jay had been called into the captain's office right before lunch so he could read them the letter he had received from the Public Affairs Office. Out loud, like they were a couple of school kids who weren't able to read for themselves. The letter commended them—no, it commended the captain, who was hell-bent on making Chief—for doing such an outstanding job in launching the pilot awareness program.

Mike leaned against the doorjamb in stunned silence, listening to the captain's voice, smug with satisfaction, drone on and on as he read the letter. But Mike didn't care what it said, didn't care how smug the captain was. She could only stand there, her jaw clenched, and stare at Jay. He stared back at her, his face twisted in horror, his mouth opening and closing silently as red flamed across his face and neck.

Captain Nelson had stopped talking and was watching both of them with that keen sight that let him see too much, then abruptly asked them what the hell was going on. The question—and the captain's impatient glare—was directed solely at Mike. She opened her mouth to speak but was cut off by Jay, who promptly explained that he sent the wrong paperwork in, that Mike couldn't help because of another obligation, that this would be Jay's solo project.

Only it wouldn't be. Not anymore.

Because Jay had outlined such a great program that he wouldn't be allowed to do it solo.

Because Jay needed someone with a higher certification than his to oversee it, and the captain had already put her name on it.

The unspoken threat was there, loud and clear. Mike would be in charge, and she better not screw it up.

And absolutely not, no, they could not find someone to take Mike's place, because that would mean going to another shift. Captain Nelson strongly advised against even thinking about it. Of course he would, because that wouldn't reflect positively on him.

Which meant that was pretty much that.

So now Mike was stuck helping with a program she didn't care about. Stuck working with a man she wished she had never met, a man she really, really wished was dead.

Oh yeah, fate definitely had a twisted sense of irony.

"Mikey, I swear, I'll figure something out. I mean, there's nothing saying you actually have to go to the meetings. You can just sign-off on them. And then, during the actual program, you can just sit in the back and—"

"Jay, stop." Mike took another deep breath and opened her eyes, almost wanting to laugh at the pitiful expression on Jay's face. Almost. She wasn't in much of a laughing mood right now. "I'm not mad at you. Well, nothing I won't get over, anyway. And I can't just sign-off on the paperwork. You know as well as I do that Cap is going to be looking at this too closely. I can't give him any excuse to come down harder on me than he has been. You know that."

Jay sighed and nodded, then dropped down next to her on the bench and leaned against the wall, his position a mirror of hers. "I just wish they'd promote his ass and get him out of here. He's only been here for six months and he's damn near destroyed the shift."

Mike snorted. "Yeah well. At least he doesn't have a hard-on for you. I just wish to hell I knew what I did for him to be watching every move I make."

"It's not just you, Mikey. It's all of us. I think you just notice it more. Or let it get to you more."

She wanted to argue, to tell Jay that it was more than that. She didn't bother. Yes, the captain came down hard on all of them, for all the wrong reasons. But with her, it was a little more personal and had been since his first trick at the station. Mike was so used to the rhythm they'd established over the years, of getting to a scene, sizing it up, and just doing what needed to be done. How was she supposed to know the new captain didn't want anyone so much as twitching an eye before he barked orders? Like the crew was nothing more than a bunch of imbeciles who didn't understand their jobs. One call, that was all it took. One strike for doing nothing more than her job. If the captain had his way, she would already be out. Written up, disciplined, transferred. It didn't matter, the threat was there.

And she couldn't do a damn thing about it.

She uncapped the bottle and took another long swallow, then nudged Jay's leg with her knee. "Don't worry, I'll figure something out. I'll just clench my jaw and deal with it if I have to."

They sat side-by-side for several quiet minutes before he spoke, his voice quiet, almost sympathetic. "So I guess you really loved the bastard, huh?"

Mike froze at the question. She should have expected it, should have had an answer ready. No, Jay hadn't pushed for more information, but she still should have expected it—especially from Jay. He, of all people, would come right out and ask. Especially since he had been dancing around it, subtly asking for more information, for the last several weeks.

Yeah, she should have expected it, should have had an answer ready. But she didn't. And she had no idea how to answer, didn't think she ever would. That part of her past—it was still too painful, too bitter. She tried to put it behind her, tried not to think about it. Ever.

Mike swallowed against the tangle of emotions, trying to figure out how to answer. She decided to be as honest as she could be, for now.

"I was too young and stupid to know what love was."

"Hmph. If you say so." Jay reached out and gently grabbed her hand, squeezing it once before letting it go. "So how long did you wait for him? After the accident, I mean."

"Jay—"

"Sorry. Forget I asked." There was a long pause, the silence unhurried, companionable. Down here, in the basement of the station, they were away from the noise and jokes and bickering and carrying on that accompanied work. They didn't have to worry about being interrupted. Mike knew that was the only reason Jay had felt comfortable enough to bring up the subject. He shifted beside her and cleared his throat. "I am sorry, Mike. I had no idea and now, because of me, you're going to have see him again. Of all the times I pick to do something ahead of time, it had to be this time."

Mike sighed and stood up, absently straightening

the weights and mats as her thoughts echoed Jay's exactly. She didn't think he'd appreciate hearing that, though.

"Hey Jay, Mikey! You guys are relieved!" The announcement was bellowed from the door upstairs, echoing off the block walls around them. She glanced at her watch, surprised at the time, then grabbed her uniform shirt from a hook and pulled it on over the dark blue t-shirt, feeling Jay's eyes on her the whole time.

She finished buttoning the shirt then finally looked over at him. "What?"

"I am sorry, Mike, I really am."

"Jay, if you apologize one more time, I'm going to hit you. I know you're sorry, enough already." She paused, watching Jay gather up his things, then headed for the stairs. "And who knows? Maybe it won't be so bad."

"You are such a liar."

"Yeah, well, you can't blame me for trying. Besides, when has there ever been anything I can't handle?" She reached the top of the stairs and leaned back to flip the light switch off, hoping the words wouldn't come back to haunt her.

Chapter Ten

Mike sat in the front seat of the Jeep, trying her best to ignore the knot twisting in her stomach, trying to convince herself that she was *not* nervous. Not her, the queen of cool. She was *not* anxious. And she most certainly was *not* panicky.

Yeah, right, sure she wasn't.

She clenched her fists tightly around the steering wheel and took several deep breaths, wishing she could be anywhere but where she was, wondering again how this had even happened. Talk about cruel twists.

Giving herself a mental shake, she climbed out of the Jeep, wanting only to get the whole thing over with as soon as possible. Not that this afternoon would be the end of it. No. This afternoon was just the beginning, God help her.

The outside door of the school opened with a muted creak and Mike stepped through, pausing to let her eyes adjust to the dimness of the hallway. It looked like any other school hallway and smelled of wax and chalk; the combination threatened to send her back in time, to her own high school days, and she shuddered. That was too long ago and she had no desire to travel down memory lane. Not when Nick would have the starring role in most of those memories.

Mike finally reached the partially opened door of Nick's classroom and paused outside, taking a deep breath to rally her nerves, then stepped across the threshold. She opened her mouth to say something but stopped, her heart stuck in her throat at the sight of Nick. He sat at the desk, bent over with his head resting in his hands. His fingers, long and strong, splayed through his thick hair, giving it a gently-mussed look. He looked...lost. Lonely. Dejected.

No. She couldn't think of him that way. Not now, not ever. Not if she wanted to survive this. Nick wasn't lost or lonely. Impossible. No, the boy she remembered—the man she watched—was too strong, too independent to be lost or lonely. She needed to stop seeing things that weren't there, need to see him for what he was: someone from her past, someone she was being forced to work with for right now. A teacher, nothing more, nothing less.

Except he looked nothing at all like a teacher, sitting there with his elbows carelessly propped on a pile of papers.

Of course, he probably wasn't a real teacher, Mike realized. He probably helped with teaching music or band or something like that, because there was no way her Nicky could be responsible for anything more than that.

Her Nicky? Where had that awful thought come from? Biting back the sudden anger that accompanied the mental slip, she pushed the door until it hit the wall with a muffled bang, her steps loud as she moved into the room. Nick jumped at the noise, his elbow sliding off a stack of papers and hitting the edge of the desk with a thump she could hear a few feet away. He raised his head, his dark eyes shadowed, almost haunted. No, she must have been seeing things, because the expression was gone as soon as he blinked. His lips tightened into a straight line and he looked away, suddenly focused on gathering the scattered papers and putting them in a neat pile, completely ignoring her.

Two could play that game, she thought, knowing even as she did that it wasn't true. No matter how much she wished otherwise, she'd never been able to ignore Nick. That had always been the problem, was going to be the problem now. But she could at least pretend. Her gaze wandered around the room, slowly taking everything in without really seeing anything. And then one detail in particular jumped out at her.

"Where's Jay?"

Nick glanced at her then down at his watch. He tossed some papers into the open briefcase that sat on the desk then shrugged. "He's obviously running late."

Oh, that was just great. Mike swallowed her groan and took a seat at one of the desks, trying to look casual and collected, trying to distance herself from any emotion. And trying not to watch Nick as he moved, trying not to study him.

He continued gathering items from his desk, tossing some into the briefcase, putting others into a drawer. Each movement was precise, controlled. Mike stared at his hands, at the strength in each of them.

They were broad and well-sculpted, the fingers long and tapered. She remembered how well those fingers could dance along the strings of a guitar—still could, apparently. And she remembered what else those hands, those fingers, were capable of doing.

Mike swallowed another groan and closed her eyes, mentally kicking herself. How could she be sitting here, remembering those things? She had no business remembering at all, she should be concentrating instead on what had happened after— No. What she needed to concentrate on was getting this program finished so she would never have to see Nick Lansing again. Maybe then she could put this all behind her and move on.

Again.

"I have aspirin if you need some."

"Excuse me?" Mike opened her eyes and looked at Nick. He was leaning against the edge of the desk, his arms folded across his chest, his long, jean-clad legs stretched out in front of him. She pretended not to notice the way the worn fabric clung to his muscular thighs, or the way the material of his gray polo stretched across his chest and shoulders.

"Aspirin. For your hangover." Nick's deep brown gaze pierced her, studying her with a coolness she didn't quite understand. Watching. Assessing. She narrowed her own eyes in response and sat a little straighter, wishing now that she was standing because sitting put her at a definite disadvantage.

"I am *not* hungover."

"Oh." Nick continued studying her with that cool gaze and it took all of her control not to squirm beneath it. Just what, exactly, did he think he was doing, anyway? "For your headache, then."

"What? I don't have a headache!" Mike ground the words out between clenched teeth, knowing that she *would* have a headache if this kept up. Was this Nick's lame attempt at casual conversation to kill time? They'd both be better off if he just kept quiet. At least, she would be; she didn't care about him.

Nick watched her for a few more quiet seconds then shrugged and straightened, moving to take his seat behind the desk. The chair squeaked under his weight as he shifted, propping the heels of his booted feet on the corner of the desk and resting his elbows on the arm chairs. He glanced at his watch again, the move slow and calculated, then turned back to her. "So, is your friend always late?"

Mike glanced at her own watch and sighed. "Not usually, no." And the fact that Jay was running late was beginning to worry her. If something had happened, he would have called her, but the cell phone in her back pocket was silent. For his sake, she hoped he had a really good excuse.

"So tell me, why are you here? You made it pretty clear the last time that you weren't interested in helping out." Nick steepled his fingers and stared at her, his dark gaze unwavering in its scrutiny. If she didn't know better, she'd think he was baiting her, trying to get some kind of reaction from her. Part of her wanted to give in and give him all the reaction he could handle but she didn't. Instead, she took a deep breath and counted to ten, telling herself not to lose control.

"I didn't have much choice in the matter," she finally admitted. Nick's eyebrows shot up in surprise but he didn't say anything. Mike took another deep breath and rubbed the palms of her hands along her legs, hoping the desk hid the action. "Listen, Nick, unless something changes, we're going to be stuck working together for a while. Maybe we should just, you know, call a truce or something."

"A truce? I didn't realize we were at war." Nick's words were short and clipped, matching Mike's mood exactly. She clenched her jaw tighter and stared at him with the coolest look she could manage, hoping the gaze let him know in no uncertain terms exactly what she felt. He returned her look with an intensity that added to the discomfort racing through her. Time stretched around them, tense and silent until Mike could no longer stand it. She pushed herself out of the chair then slammed it against the desk, muttering an obscenity.

"This is ridiculous. What right do you have to sit there and act like you're the injured party? Tell me that! After all these years—" Mike choked back the rest of what she wanted to say, appalled at the emotion in her voice. Too much time had gone by; none of this should matter anymore. But it did, and she hated herself for it.

She ran a shaking hand across her eyes, pushing her thumb against the left one to stop the tell-tale twitching she could feel building in it. Her gaze traveled to the closed door and she had to stop herself from bolting toward it and running. Yes, she could do it. Run out the door, out of the building, just keep on running. But no matter how far she ran, she wouldn't be able to escape. Escape was only an illusion.

"Kayla." Nick's voice was thick with emotion and entirely too close, making her jump. She whirled around and nearly fell into him, he was so close to her. He reached out and placed a hand on her shoulder to steady her, which only made her stumble more. Heat seared her where his hands rested, one on her shoulder and the other now on her waist. Her pulse kicked up, her heart pounding in her chest, too tight, too heavy. Mike froze, unable to breathe, unable to think, aware only of Nick's touch and the intensity of his gaze as he stared down at her.

No. She had to be imagining it. There was no way he could still have this effect on her, not after all these years. Not after everything that had happened, after everything he'd done.

His hands tightened on her then slowly drew her in, his arms wrapping around her in a hesitant embrace. She closed her eyes as he tightened his hold, refusing to lean into him but unable to pull away. She could feel his heart hammering in his chest, felt the warmth of his breath against her cheek as he held her. God help her, part of her wanted to lean against him, to hide in the strength of his hold. To just let the years fall away as he held her, safe and secure.

"Kayla." His voice was soft, rough with emotion. His arms tightened even more and she felt herself leaning against him, giving in, forgetting. "I'm sorry. So sorry. I never meant to hurt you, not like that."

Mike heard the anguish in his voice and focused on that, instead of the words. She leaned closer, shutting everything out except the feel of his arms around her. Time slowed, meaning little while he held her. And with the slowing came an awareness of the electric tension surrounding them, a thick heaviness in the air that made it difficult to pull air into her lungs. She recognized it immediately as the same heaviness, the same tension that had always surrounded them in the past. It was a living thing, combustible, threatening to explode and consume her.

Even now, after all these years, after all that had passed between them. How? How could she still be so weak, so needy, when it came to this one man?

Her breathing hitched in her chest, echoing Nick's harsh gasp. Slowly she opened her eyes, the lids heavy as she raised her head, already knowing what was to come, her body welcoming it even as her mind screamed out in warning. His mouth descended, slowly, his dark eyes locked with hers. And in that split-second Mike saw something that chilled her.

Pity.

She took a deep breath and pushed Nick away, cursing herself for forgetting, cursing him for making her forget.

Not the heat or the passion. There had always been that between them, a heavy awareness that had consumed them both and threatened to destroy common sense. She had never found anything close to it since then and she had never been able to forget it. Just like she had never forgotten what Nick had done to her.

Until just now.

To see his pity on top of everything else was more than she needed, more than even she could handle. She didn't want—didn't *need*—his pity and she didn't need his words of apology. In fact, she didn't need anything from him.

Mike turned her back on Nick and paced around the small room, frustration adding an edginess to each step. She paused to rub one hand across her eyes, annoyed at the slight shaking in her fingers. She took a deep breath and held it, let it out slowly, searching for some kind of inner calm. What a joke. How could she be calm when every single nerve was dancing with anger and, worse, awareness?

"Kayla." From somewhere behind her came Nick's uncertain voice and she resumed her pacing, wanting nothing more than to put more distance between them. When she went as far as she could, she turned and faced him, hoping her expression betrayed no sign of the emotional battle being waged inside her. She forced herself to stand straight and meet his gaze head on, refused to waver in the face of his obvious confusion.

"What exactly is it you do here, anyway? Teach band or something?"

"Excuse me?"

Mike ran a shaking hand through her hair and forced a slight smile as she repeated her question. Nick stared at her for a long second then shook his head, as if he had trouble understanding her. He sighed then walked over to the desk, leaning against it with his arms folded across his chest while he fixed her with a steady gaze as blank as her own. She had the uncomfortable and very distinct impression that he was seeing too deeply inside her.

"No, I do not teach band." The words were clipped, maybe a little defensive even. "I teach English literature."

"I'm sorry, excuse me?" Mike made no attempt to hide her surprise, wasn't sure she could have hidden it even if she tried. Her eyes widened as she stared at him in disbelief. Nick taught English? She must have heard him wrong.

"Why does that surprise you so much?"

"I...it just does, that's all," she finally admitted. She tried to picture him standing where he was now, teaching high school kids the finer points of Shakespeare and Tennyson. The image refused to materialize, no doubt hindered by the way he looked, dressed in snug jeans and a polo shirt that pulled tight across his broad chest, with thick wavy hair that hung just below his collar. English teachers didn't look like him. She cleared her throat and made her final admission. "It sounds too responsible for someone like you."

"Someone like me?" The sudden cool edge in his voice was unmistakable. Mike ignored it and continued to watch him. He straightened and fixed her with a stern look as something flickered in his eyes, there and gone before she could really see what it was. Irritation? Anger? She didn't know. Then he sighed and finally shook his head, a brittle smile twisting one corner of his mouth. "People change. But then, I guess you know that firsthand, don't you?"

"Yeah, I do," Mike agreed. She recognized the verbal bait for what it was but didn't care. She charged ahead and met it with her own dig. "Just like I know that not everybody has a choice. Sometimes people are forced to change because of things that happen. Because of things that are done to them."

Nick paled at her accusation and for a minute she thought he would say something, but he didn't. He just shook his head again and sat down in the creaking chair, his shoulders slumped in something that closely resembled defeat. "You were right. If we need to work together, maybe we should call a truce. Pretend there's nothing..." He stopped and cleared his throat. "Pretend that we never met."

Mike listened to his halting words and heard an undercurrent of emotion she didn't understand. She opened her mouth to say something, preferably something sarcastic, but was stopped when the classroom door opened. She turned around to see Jay standing there, a look of caution etched on his face. His gaze rested briefly on Nick before he turned to face her, hesitant and obviously worried. Mike glanced at her watch, noting how late he was. He offered her a look of apology then closed the door behind him with a soft click.

"So, did I miss anything important?"

Chapter Eleven

Nick shifted in the chair, trying to focus on the outline in front of him as Jay droned on about his idea. None of it mattered, because he wasn't hearing it. His attention was centered instead on Kayla, who had been sitting in the back of the classroom, silent for the last hour.

He had expected her to be the one to go over the details with him, to explain how the program would work. It had been difficult for him to hide his surprise when he learned that Jay would be the one orchestrating everything and that Kayla was only there to oversee it. To supervise Jay.

It was just one more surprising thing he was learning about this new Kayla.

He shifted so he could watch her without seeming to. She was sitting sideways in the hard wooden chair, her head propped up on one hand, the careless posture closely resembling that of some of his bored students. Her long hair fell to the side, partially hiding her face, and he couldn't tell how much she was paying attention to what was going on, or if she was paying any attention at all. Part of him wanted her to look at him, to silently acknowledge his presence.

To admit that she was as aware of him as he was of her.

Nick shifted again and silently cursed himself for being such a fool. She had every reason to avoid him, to stay as far away from him as she could. He knew that, but he still wanted her to notice him.

Fool.

He had been surprised when she walked into the classroom because he hadn't expected to see her, not after she had made it so clear that she wanted nothing to do with him or the program. But for all his surprise, part of him had been pleased, too. And for that brief moment when he held her, when her body eased against his, he had forgotten all about their history and remembered only the sweet fire that had burned between them.

That obviously still burned between them, whether he wanted to admit it or not. He wondered if Kayla had felt it, too, that swirling flame of need and want that had instantly wrapped around them.

Which didn't say much for any respectability he thought he had. Christ, he had almost killed her and now, the first time he touched her since he ran away all those years ago, all he could think of was how they had been when they were together. Yeah, he could try to convince himself he had changed all he wanted, but the truth was obvious. When it came to Kayla, he hadn't changed at all. And what the hell did that say about him?

His eyes drifted back to where she was sitting,

still looking carelessly bored. She shifted position, slouching in the seat with her legs stretched out in front of her, her feet crossed at the ankles and her arms crossed in front of her. Her appearance was a complete contradiction. She should have looked cool and reserved, detached and maybe a little masculine, in the shapeless dark blue uniform pants and t-shirt, but she didn't. To him, she looked innocent and lost. Like she was only playing at this other tough persona he didn't really understand.

Or maybe it was just his own guilt that made him see what he wanted to see, because he didn't want to admit he was responsible for her loss of innocence.

"That sounds good to me." Kayla's voice broke into his thoughts and he looked up in surprise, thinking he had spoken out loud by mistake. But no, she was standing next to Jay, leaning over his shoulder as she hastily signed some form. She glanced at her watch then gave Jay's shoulder a friendly pat before walking to the door. Nick stared after her in surprise, watching in silent bewilderment as she left without saying a word.

He finally noticed the silence that followed her departure and turned to find Jay watching him.

"So tell me, Lansing, did you even hear anything that I said? At all?" Jay asked the question as he scooped papers and forms into a haphazard pile and tossed them into a battered folder.

"Of course I did. Why wouldn't I?"

"Because your attention was focused somewhere else the entire time."

Nick started to deny it then thought better of it. He didn't think he had been obvious, but maybe he was wrong. And did it really matter if the man across from him had noticed? Not really. Not unless—the thought trailed off as Nick studied Jay more closely. Then another thought, unwelcome and irritating, popped into his mind. He straightened in the chair and pushed at the papers in front of him, striving for a nonchalance he didn't feel. "My apologies. I didn't realize you two were involved."

Silence greeted his statement for a whole second before it was shattered by a loud laugh. Nick looked up in surprise at Jay's reaction, not knowing what to make of it.

"Sorry," Jay muttered, still chuckling. "I'm not laughing at you, just at the image of me and Mike involved."

"So you two aren't...you know?"

"No, we're just friends. Very good friends." The amused expression left Jay's face as he studied Nick with a cool seriousness. "I'm closer to Mike than I am to a lot of people, and I care about her. I don't want to see her hurt."

"I'm not planning on hurting her."

Jay continued to study him, his light eyes stern and assessing. "Good. Because you've already hurt her enough. More than enough, I think."

"I know that." Nick's admission obviously startled Jay. It startled him to a point, as well. He *had* known, all these years, how much he had hurt her physically. He could imagine only too well how his cowardice and shame had hurt her emotionally. It had been easier to convince himself that she was better off. That the years between then and now would have made it easier for her. But he'd only been lying to himself. And he had never admitted it before, not out loud and certainly not to anyone else, let alone a complete stranger.

"At least you admit it. That says something, I think." Jay shifted in the chair and continued studying Nick. After a long minute, he spoke again, his voice low and quiet. "I haven't made up my mind about you yet, Lansing, but I'm going to tell you something anyway. Mike isn't as tough as she looks, and she's one hell of a lot more vulnerable than she'll ever admit. Probably more than she even knows. Just remember that."

"How long have you known her?"

"About eight years, ever since I got into the department. We came through the Academy together. Are you asking if I knew about you? No, she never mentioned you until the night you showed up at the station. Did I know about the accident? Yes, for the most part."

"So you knew about the accident, but not me?"

Jay gave him one long look then stood, gathering his stuff into a pile and tossing it into a soft-sided case. "That's right. But I knew Mike well enough to be able to figure out that the accident involved someone she was close to. I didn't need all the details. Hell, after seeing that scar, I didn't want the details. I've seen enough in the field to figure out how bad it was and what she went through."

Nick's throat closed, threatening to choke him. He swallowed, forcing the sensation away, and looked up at Jay. His words were hoarse, forced through a too-tight throat. "Scar? How bad? I mean—"

Jay looked at Nick with an expression of disbelief, mingled with astonishment and something else Nick didn't want to define, something that increased his guilt a hundredfold. "You never saw?

No, I guess you didn't. Mike said she never saw you after the accident, but I thought—"

"I did see her. Once."

"But she said—"

"She didn't see me. It wasn't long after the accident, and she was still in Shock Trauma. I only got to see her through the glass of the room cubicle for a minute. She wasn't even awake. Or conscious, I guess. Then her father showed up and—well, he never liked me to start with, you know? Besides, they only allowed me a few minutes. I had to leave anyway."

Silence greeted his quiet admission but he refused to look at Jay and focused instead on the scarred surface of the desk. He forced himself to remember again that long ago day that he had pushed to the back of his memory, and the sight of the battered figure huddled on a hospital bed, parts of her body hidden by thick bandages, surrounded by foreign equipment and tubing.

He remembered the noise that had escaped him, a deep rumble of anguish that clawed its way out of his throat. And the coldness. Not from outside. No, this coldness was a thousand times worse. Sharp, biting, almost burning as it broke free inside him, from somewhere deep that he had never known existed. It spread its way across his body, wrapping around him until he couldn't breathe.

And he remembered raising his hand, resting it on the glass window that separated him from Kayla. Remembered thinking that if only he could touch her, if he could hold her in his arms, then everything would be fine, nothing else would matter. But another hand had reached out and grabbed him, shaking him violently and throwing him against the wall, yelling, threatening.

Nick shook his head, trying to clear the images from his mind.

God, how he had tried to forget, knowing even as he did that he never would. A noise pulled him from his thoughts and he mentally shook himself again, not surprised to see that Jay was looking at him expectantly. Nick shrugged in apology and Jay repeated his question.

"You said you had to leave. Where did you go?"

Nick laughed, a bitter sound to his own ears that accompanied the bitterness of his confession.

"To a drug and alcohol rehab to dry out."

Chapter Twelve

Nick stared down at his watch, surprised that so much time had passed, surprised that nobody had noticed his car parked so conspicuously on the small street. It wasn't a regular neighborhood, this quiet community of Victorian houses that formed something close to an old village, nestled in the rolling hills of the north county. Any strange vehicle should stick out.

But then, he was driving a Volvo and wearing a tie. Who else would think to even look twice at him?

Nick bit back a muttered oath and shook his head, still not sure why he was here. He looked down at the packet of pictures sitting next to him. He could have waited until next week to return them. For that matter, he could have just given them to Jay.

His gaze darted back to the small renovated two-story barn, taking in the red paint and white trim, the inartistic landscaping that dotted the front here and there, the trees that gave an illusion of privacy. It was a contrast to the lusher landscape of the old Victorian farmhouse a hundred yards away.

A Jeep sat in the small graveled lot off the driveway that circled the barn before leading up to the house. Nick shook his head again in surprise. Not at the fact that Kayla was home—he had been pretty sure she would be on a Thursday night—but at the changes in the barn. The last time he had seen it, it had been a ramshackle building that gave an impression of dilapidation despite the sturdiness and cleanliness inside.

He looked at his watch again and sighed. He was turning into a stalker.

Almost three weeks had passed since the meeting where he had made his quiet admission to Jay. There had been two more meetings since then, each quiet and subdued. Kayla had been at the last one for a total of five minutes, long enough to toss a packet of pictures on Nick's desk. Graphic images of accidents, all the result of drunk drivers, she had explained before walking out. Nick had thumbed through the pictures, curious.

Graphic.

Yeah, that was one way to describe them. He had come close to being sick when he looked at them.

Jay had given the pictures no more than a cursory glance then continued going over notes for the program. At the end of the meeting he had suggested, not too subtly, that Nick go over the pictures some more then return them to Kayla. At home. Nick wasn't sure what Jay was up to, but here he was, taking the man's advice and not really knowing why.

Nick sighed and started the car, calling himself all kinds of names as he drove the short distance from the street to the barn. He turned the ignition off and sat for another minute before finally getting out of the car, the pack of pictures held tightly in one hand. He didn't want to think of Kayla's reaction when she saw him. She was bound to be surprised. And angry.

He took a deep breath and quickly knocked on the door, afraid to hesitate in case he lost what little nerve he had. Muted music drifted through the closed door, blocking out any other sound there might have been. He knocked again, harder this time, and waited. A minute went by. The music suddenly quieted a second before Kayla opened the door, a smile on her face.

"I thought you said—" The smile died as her voice trailed off and Nick realized she had been expecting somebody else. "What are you doing here?"

Nick shifted uncomfortably, taking in the baggy sweat shorts and paint-stained tank shirt she was wearing. The smell of fresh latex paint drifted out of the open doorway and he realized she had been painting. He congratulated himself for being so observant and offered Kayla an apologetic shrug. "I just wanted to drop these off."

She looked down at the packet in his hand then back up at him, her eyes narrowed in suspicion. Several long seconds went by while she studied him, then she blew out a long breath between pursed lips. She stepped back and opened the door further, motioning for him to come in. Nick muttered a thanks and closed the door behind him, looking around. The inside had changed as much as the outside, he realized.

The downstairs had been converted into a large living room with a high ceiling, airy and spacious, decorated in a neutral sand color with muted blues and greens. A decent-sized combination kitchen and dining room was off to the left, decorated with the same color schemes. A closed door was to his right and at first he thought it must be the bedroom. Then he looked up and noticed the open loft above him. From what he could see, the entire barn had been redone instead of just a portion of it, which meant Kayla had plenty of room for herself. Nick was surprised, but he wasn't sure why.

"It looks really different. Nice," he commented. Kayla narrowed her eyes at him again but didn't say anything. She turned and walked into the kitchen area and Nick followed her, part of him still waiting for her to throw him out. She went to the refrigerator and opened it. Nick's gaze drifted downward, noticing her slender, well-muscled legs. He looked away when she straightened, a can of beer in her hand. She watched him, still silent, as she popped the pull tab with a little hiss and took a long swallow.

She leaned against the counter, her arms loosely crossed, and took another sip. She studied him for a few long seconds, her green eyes carefully blank. "Did you want a beer or anything?"

"Uh, no. No thanks. I told you, I don't drink anymore."

"Hm. So you came to drop the pictures off?"

"Yeah."

"Hmmm." She took another long swallow of the beer, watching him over the rim of the can. "Fine. You can leave them on the table on your way out."

"Kayla, I..." Nick let his voice trail off, not sure what to say. She raised one eyebrow in his direction, obviously waiting for him to finish. He shifted under her stare and searched for something, anything, to say. A thought popped into his head and he grabbed it in desperation. "I don't think we can use these. Some of them are too graphic. I'm afraid of the impression they might leave."

"Too graphic? Fine, it's your program. I didn't realize you wanted to gloss over the effects of drunk driving." She drained the beer and tossed it into the trash can, then walked by him and out of the kitchen. Nick stared after her, biting back the brief flare of anger he felt at her words, then abruptly followed her.

"Kayla—"

"I'm busy. I'm painting. I don't have time." She tossed the clipped words over her shoulder as she climbed the steps to the loft. Not stopping to think, Nick followed her, only half-surprised when she didn't turn around and kick him down the stairs.

He paused at the top, not hiding his surprise. The loft was huge, used mostly as a bedroom. A king size bed was pushed to the middle of the floor, covered with tarps. Other furniture, a dresser and nightstands from their shape, were pushed close to the bed and also covered by tarps. The smell of paint was stronger up here. It looked like Kayla was painting in sections as time allowed. The back half of the room was finished. If the color and decorations already there were any indication, the room was going to be the ultimate definition of romantic intimacy.

Nick closed his eyes, shutting them against several sudden and very vivid images, pictures he had no right imagining. He swallowed and opened his eyes, glad that Kayla didn't seem to notice. She was busy dipping a roller into a paint tray, then applying the paint with vicious strokes that made it look like she was attacking the wall instead of painting it. She reached up with a grunt, stretching to get the top of the vaulted ceiling. Her shirt pulled up with the motion, revealing an expanse of flat belly and tanned skin.

And torn flesh.

Nick's breath left him in a rush, as if someone had sucker-punched him in the gut. A jagged scar ran across Kayla's stomach at an angle, marring the otherwise perfect flesh. It started somewhere above the shirt's hem and ran down along her right side, disappearing into the waistband of her shorts. He must have made some kind of noise because Kayla halted what she was doing and turned to him, her face expressionless. She studied him for a minute then tossed the roller down, splattering paint on the tarp.

"What's the matter, Nick? Oh, that's right. You never saw your handiwork before, did you?" Her voice was flat and emotionless. Nick looked up at her, at the coldness in her eyes, and silently shook his head, unable to speak. Before he realized what she was doing, she grabbed the hem of the shirt and lifted it, pulling it off in one angry movement so she was standing there in only a black sports bra and those loose, low-hanging gym shorts.

Nick's knees wobbled and he sagged against the wall, looking for some kind of support. She closed the distance between them, not stopping until she was a foot away from him, standing in front of him in the sports bra and sweat shorts, her hands placed defiantly on her hips.

"Go on, Nick, take a hard look. Then tell me again that those pictures are too graphic."

Nick watched her face for a long second, at the

defiance etched so clearly on her features, and at the fear hidden so carefully in the depths of her eyes. Then he lowered his head and looked, because he was helpless not to.

The scar started at the base of her breastbone, thin at first, then turning into a thick mottling of puckered flesh as it ran down her stomach and angled to the side. The scar thinned again, smoother and faint until it disappeared into the waistband of her shorts. Nick swallowed hard. The scar was hideous, causing his stomach to sour and roll.

But not for the reason Kayla so obviously thought. The scar was hideous because *he* had put it there. *He* was the one responsible for marring an otherwise perfect and beautiful body. For destroying a life so full of promise. His breath left him on a groan and he closed his eyes, unable to bear the evidence of his irresponsibility any longer.

"Yeah, pretty disgusting, isn't it?" Kayla's voice was hoarse, the words harsh. Nick opened his eyes and saw the vulnerability in her gaze before she had a chance to hide it. He reached out, grabbing her hand to stop her from turning away.

"No. No, it's not." His grip tightened on her when she tried to pull away. He stared into her eyes, not breathing, his mind racing to find the words to explain what he was thinking and failing. He closed his eyes again and dropped to his knees, resting his forehead against her stomach. Her breath hitched in her chest and she tried to pull away again, but he wouldn't let her. With one hand still wrapped firmly around her wrist, he reached out with his free hand and gently traced the ragged scar with a trembling finger, surprised at its smoothness.

"Nick." Kayla's voice wavered, his name an uncertain whisper that pierced the tension surrounding them.

"Shhh." He whispered the reassurance and lowered his head. Nick placed one gentle kiss on the scar, then another and another, dragging his lips across the marred flesh, trying to heal what couldn't be healed. Her body shivered under his touch until she finally pushed him away and dropped to her knees.

"Nick, don't."

He looked into her eyes, saw the fear and uncertainty in their depths, saw the tears clumped at the edges of her lashes as she studied him. He shook his head to silence her, then reached up and gently traced her lower lip with his thumb before lowering his mouth to hers. She stilled under his touch, not giving in but not pulling away, letting him set the pace.

He cupped her face with both hands and rubbed his lips lightly across hers. Gently at first, then more firmly as she responded to his touch. He deepened the kiss until her mouth opened under his and his tongue immediately, instinctively swept inside, meeting hers in a wild frenzy. Kayla moaned, a small sound that was lost between them. She leaned into him, meeting each thrust of his tongue with her own. Her hands wrapped around his neck, her fingers playing in the hair at the edge of his collar.

With a harsh gasp Nick broke the kiss, his breathing heavy as he dragged his lips along her jaw and down across her neck. His hands drifted across her shoulders then lower, to the heated flesh of her bare back. He hooked two fingers into the waistband of her shorts then dipped his hands inside, cupping her firm bottom and pulling her hips against his. Her body arched against him and she moaned again, a small sound of desperation as she hungrily kissed his throat.

"Kayla, oh God." Nick shuddered as her hands ripped at his shirt, freeing it from his pants until her fingers raked the bare skin of his back. She pressed more fully against him, her hips fitting themselves tightly against his erection, searching. Her breathing was raspy and harsh, an echo of his own. She was demanding too much too fast, her hands already fumbling with the zipper of his pants, reaching in and grabbing him in a desperate grip that made time stop. He clenched his jaw, his head falling backward at the intense sensation of her touch. Her frenzy was contagious, sweeping him along in an insane whirlpool of need and desperation.

Biting back a curse, he reached between them and grabbed her hand, stilling it but not moving it away, not yet. He lowered his lips to hers again in a hungry kiss, taking as much as she was before he pulled away with a frustrated growl.

"Not so fast, Kayla."

"Nicky, please," she pleaded, her hand again moving between them, stroking him. He gave up trying to stop her, gave into the mindless pleasure her touch brought. His own hands slipped further down her hips, pushing the shorts lower, uncovering her until his fingers found her opening, moist and slick. She moaned and rocked against him, her teeth nipping at his lips. She fell against him, leaning and pushing until he toppled backward, her warm body sprawled on top of him.

There was something wrong, something that niggled at the back of Nick's conscience. Kayla was too frantic, too fast. Too desperate. Nick tried to pull back, to slow her down. "Kayla, easy, not so fast."

She ignored him, her touches becoming harder, frantic. He gritted his teeth and reached between them, pulling her hands away, holding them firmly in his grip. He wrapped one leg around hers, forcing her body to still as he kissed her, long and slow. Her body molded against his, her hips still searching, rocking. With a groan he rolled over, trapping her beneath him as he trailed slow kisses along her jaw and up to her ear.

"Not so fast, Kayla," he repeated, his voice sounding strangled to his own ears. "I'm sorry, so sorry. I want to make love to you. Let me show you how sorry I am. Please."

Her body shuddered under his as he moved his lips down her throat and across her collarbone. Mindless seconds disappeared around them before she suddenly stiffened and pushed against him. Another few seconds went by before the change in her registered with Nick and he pulled away, looking down at her. Her icy stare met his, cold and emotionless.

"Get off of me. Now." Her voice matched the look in her eyes. Nick continued to watch her, confusion dulling his senses as he tried to figure out what happened, what changed. She pushed against him again, hard, and he rolled to the side, still watching her as she struggled to sit. "Get out of my house."

"Kayla—"

"I said get out!" The words were angry and

harsh, more so because they were whispered instead of shouted. Kayla pushed to her feet and rearranged her clothes, the movements jerky and uncoordinated. She bent down and grabbed her tank shirt from the floor and pulled it back on, her back to him. He frowned and slowly stood as well, tucking in his shirt and zipping his pants as he stared at her stiff back.

"Kayla, what happened? Did I—"

She whirled to face him, effectively cutting him off as she pointed a shaking finger in his direction. "I don't need your pity or your guilt, so just get out!"

"What are you talking about?"

"Just what I said. Are you going to deny this just happened because you felt sorry for me?"

"No! I mean yes. I mean, Christ!" Nick took a deep breath and ran his hands through his hair in frustration, trying to understand what had happened. "What just happened has nothing to do with pity or guilt."

"Doesn't it? 'Oh Kayla, let me show you how sorry I am!'" She threw his words back at him, mocking and sarcastic. A coldness settled over Nick at the look in her eyes as she stared at him.

"That's not what I meant," he said quietly.

"No? Are you going to tell me you don't feel sorry for me? That you don't feel guilty?"

She was twisting his words. Nick hadn't meant for them to be taken the way she was taking them and he tried hard to understand how she felt. But his own anger simmered close to the surface, threatening to erupt. He took a deep breath and let it out slowly, pacing back and forth with short steps as he tried to think of something, anything to say.

"Do I feel guilty? Yes, dammit, I do. How could

I not and still be human?" He pointed at her, at her stomach. "Look what I did to you! *I* did that, nobody else. *I* was the one driving. It was my goddamn fault!"

Nick's voice broke and he swallowed, his breathing harsh in the silence around them. "I almost killed you, Kayla. There hasn't been a single damn day that's gone by that I haven't thought about it. I've had to live with what I did for more than ten years, to live with the knowledge that someone I loved came very close to dying because of something *I* did. Guilt? Yeah, you better believe there's guilt."

He paused again, staring at Kayla, watching her as she made a point of not looking at him. Was she even listening? Nick didn't know. He sighed and shook his head. "I've dealt with the guilt for ten years, Kayla. Am I sorry? Yeah, and if I could, I'd tell you that every damn day. But this? What almost happened here? No, this had nothing to do with guilt. Or pity. Or being sorry. This was something else entirely, and I don't mean just sex."

Kayla didn't move, gave no indication that she was listening. Nick bit back a curse of frustration, knowing that nothing he did would do any good right now—nothing except him leaving. He straightened his tie and turned to leave, then paused. Without thinking too much about what he was doing, he closed the distance between them and leaned down, placing a quick kiss on Kayla's cheek. He wasn't surprised when she turned away. He gently squeezed her shoulder then left without saying anything else.

Chapter Thirteen

The last day and a half had drifted by in a fog, flowing from hour to hour with no meaning or purpose. Mike wasn't sure what she thought about that, if she should get used to it or if she should fight it. The only thing she could say with any certainty was that the fog beat the current alternative.

Mike let out a deep breath and finished the whiskey and soda in her hand. The alcohol had definitely helped bring the fog on, but that wasn't the main reason for it. The main reason for the fog was Nick. Or rather, to forget Nick. To forget his words and the instant inferno that had erupted between them.

She leaned back on the overstuffed sofa and closed her eyes, trying to erase the memory, trying to erase the sensations. She had intended to throw her deformity in his face, thinking the scar would revolt him like it had so many others. But the plan had backfired on her. Instead of being revolted, Nick had dropped to his knees at her feet and caressed the scar, tenderly traced it with the tip of his shaking finger, with his mouth. The emotion in his eyes as he looked at her had been her undoing.

Mike shuddered at the memory and sat up, squeezing her eyes against the slight spinning her quick movement caused. If he hadn't muttered the word 'sorry', if he had remained silent, they would have had sex right there on her bedroom floor. She hadn't cared. All he had to do was touch her, and feelings that had been held back for far too long broke free. She had been frantic to touch him, to taste him, to feel him.

To have him inside her.

What the hell was wrong with her? She had wished Nick dead so many times, had wished to never see him again because of what he had done to her. Because of the way he had just left her, never seeing her again, never even bothering to find out what had happened to her. That was what hurt her the most, though she would never admit it to anyone. Hell, she had a hard time admitting it to herself.

And she still felt that way, the past so hard to bear sometimes, even though she knew she should be over it by now. It was far past time to forget, to move on. So how could she feel that way, wishing him dead, wishing she had never met him, and still want him like she did? Why did the memory of his touch send heat spiraling out of control through her?

She sighed and put the empty glass on the table then, because part of her felt like continuing her self-torture, she leaned over and grabbed her phone and listened to her voicemails one more time.

The first message was from Thursday night, several hours after Nick left. His voice immediately filled the room, hesitant but clear. He apologized again, but said he didn't regret what had happened. If she felt like talking, she could call him.

The next message was from yesterday—Friday. Nick's voice again, not quite so hesitant this time, telling her he had been thinking about her, that he wanted to see her, to talk to her.

The final message was from this afternoon, from Nick again. Not hesitant, but not entirely sure of himself, either. He had just called to talk, to see how she was doing. And to let her know he was playing tonight, in case she felt like seeing him, that he hoped to see her.

The voicemails ended, plunging the dim room into a deep silence. Mike swung her legs over the side of the sofa then leaned forward and rested her head in her hands. With a muttered curse she picked up the glass, stood and walked to the kitchen, playing her voicemails one more time.

She opened the freezer and grabbed two ice cubes, dropping them into the glass with a *clink*, then grabbed the whiskey bottle off the counter and poured amber liquid into the glass until it was half-full. Mike tossed the empty bottle into the recycle bin then leaned against the counter and sipped the drink, listening to Nick's voice in the background.

"Dammit," she muttered. She took another sip and shook her head in disgust. If she was smart, if she had any common sense at all, she would lean over and just delete every single one of Nick's messages. Then she would go take a shower and get to bed early. Tomorrow was the first day in of her normal two-day, two-night trick. There was no reason for her to go out tonight, no reason to even think about going to the club where Nick was playing.

But she *was* thinking about it, and she didn't know why.

Scratch that. She did know why. It had nothing to do with wanting to see Nick again because she *didn't* want to see him, absolutely not. What she wanted was to let him know that he had no effect on her, that she had her own life and it had nothing to do with him. Nothing. She had moved on, moved away from her past—a past that included Nicky Lansing.

So the smart thing to do would be to erase the messages and not show up. That should give Nick the message, loud and clear.

Mike took another sip, thinking. Yeah, ignoring him would be the smartest thing to do. Except she had never been smart when it came to Nick. Never. From the first time she had met him when she was fifteen, to almost a year after the accident when she was barely nineteen. Even then, throughout that entire horrible year, after everything she had been through, she had kept waiting for him to come back. *Hoping* for him to come back. No, she had never been smart when it came to Nick, not even as recently as Thursday afternoon, when he had knocked on her door and she had let him in.

Yeah, she was normally an intelligent human being, except when it came to Nick.

"Dammit," she repeated, because she knew she was going to be stupid again. She drained the rest of the drink, put the glass in the sink, and walked back into the living room. Mike tapped the screen of her phone, her thumb hitting her favorites list without even needing to look. From the other end came the sound of ringing. Once, twice, three times. She almost hung up when a breathless voice answered, "Hello?"

"Hey, it's Mikey. What are you doing tonight?"

"Tonight? I have a date. Why?"

Mike paused in surprise. It wasn't the answer she had expected. Jay never had 'dates', he had 'encounters'. To Jay, dating was too big of a commitment, not quite on the scale of marriage but close.

"Are you still there?"

"Huh? Yeah, I'm here. You caught me off-guard, that's all. I don't think I remember you ever having an official date before."

"Yeah, well, I'm still not sure how it happened. So, what's up? What did you need?"

"Uh, nothing. It wasn't important. Never mind."

"You sure? I can cancel if it's important."

Mike knew that, which was why she said nothing. She had no business interrupting Jay's personal life because she was planning on being stupid. She just wouldn't go, that was all. It was for the better, anyway.

"No, it was nothing, don't worry about it," she assured him. They exchanged more small talk before Mike finally hung up. Jay had a date, which meant she would, for once, be smart when it came to Nick Lansing. She would have gone tonight in a heartbeat if someone—if Jay—had gone with her. But there was no way she would go by herself.

Absolutely no way.

Chapter Fourteen

The club was crowded. Huge and crowded.

Of course it would be, though. It was just after eleven on a Saturday night, the perfect time for a large crowd at a nightclub. And wasn't that the whole purpose of going to a club? To blend in with the crowd, to meet new people, to mingle?

Mike wasn't too sure about that last part, since she wasn't accustomed to going to clubs by herself. She had never been into the crazy club scene, which was the main reason why she frequented smaller bars like Duffy's in the northern portion of the county. No noisy crowds, no unwelcome attention. No need to dress up.

She pushed her way further into the throng, grateful that she didn't look out of place wearing black jeans and a black-and-white print sleeveless turtleneck. Or maybe she did stand out, if some of the glances thrown her way were any indication. Careful to keep a neutral expression on her face and not make any eye contact, she continued through the crowd, following the sound of the music.

A large bar conveniently sat in the middle of the club and Mike made a beeline for it, edging her way to the front of the crowd surrounding it. Minutes went by before a bartender came over to take her order for a soda. A plain soda. She could probably use something stronger, no doubt would wish she had opted for something stronger, but she was driving. She might not have been smart enough to stay home, but she wasn't completely stupid, either.

Drink in hand, she stepped away from the bar and edged closer to the dance floor. Singles, couples, groups—they were all out there, moving to the music, some with rhythm and some definitely without. Mike sipped her soda and looked around, trying to see over the heads of the crowd, to get a closer look at the band. She hadn't paid much attention that night at Duffy's, but the band sounded different tonight. Rock had been the primary choice in Duffy's but the music here was more Top 40. Maybe they changed their routine with the crowd.

Someone tapped her on the shoulder and she whirled around in surprise. A young guy in his early twenties was standing behind her, a slight smile on his lean face. He leaned in closer, raising his arm and propping it on the wall behind her. She stared at him expectantly, waiting but not encouraging. His smile faltered for a split-second then resumed.

"Hi, I'm Kyle," he introduced himself with the arrogance of youth and alcohol. Mike barely refrained from rolling her eyes at him and said nothing. "And you are?"

"Not interested."

"Oooo-kay." Kyle straightened and walked away,

much to Mike's amusement. She shook her head and turned back, her eyes roaming the faces around her. Young. Fun-loving. Eager for the company of the opposite sex. What the hell was she doing here? She didn't fit in with this crowd, she never had. And she had absolutely nothing in common with anyone here.

She was accomplishing absolutely nothing by being here. What did she think she was going to prove? That she could be in the same place as Nick and what—pretend he wasn't there? Act like she didn't care? If she really didn't care—and she didn't—she would have stayed home. Coming here was ridiculous and proved nothing, except that once again she had allowed Nick to goad her into do something she didn't want to do.

Proving once again that she had never been smart when it came to Nick.

No harm, no foul. Nick hadn't seen her, couldn't have seen her from his place on the stage. Mike could leave, go back home, and not have to admit to anyone how stupid she was. She drained her soda and turned to go, only to slam straight into a solid body. She stepped back and mumbled an apology then tried to walk around. A warm hand rested on her shoulder and she bit back an insult, her hand already curling into a fist. She looked up then stumbled back in surprise when she saw Nick standing in front of her. His grip on her shoulder tightened and his eyes narrowed momentarily. Mike knew without a doubt that he thought she was drunk and if she hadn't been so surprised, she would have said something to correct his misconception. As it was, she could barely talk without stammering.

"Nick! What? But aren't you...? I thought..." She

finally closed her mouth and pointed behind her at the band that was still playing on the stage.

"We played earlier," he said, as if that explained it all, and Mike guessed it did. She swallowed and nodded. How could she have known that more than one band played a night? If she had, she certainly wouldn't have shown up.

God, she was an idiot.

"I didn't think you'd show up," Nick continued, easing her out of the flow of bodies to a deserted section next to the wall. Mike looked around, hoping for a stampede or other distraction. Seeing none, she sighed and looked back at Nick.

He looked different from the other night. Gone was the shirt and tie, what she had come to think of as his 'teacher outfit'. Tonight he was wearing worn faded jeans and a short-sleeve Henley that showed off his broad shoulders and broad chest, his sculpted arms and—Mike squeezed her eyes closed and reminded herself that she felt nothing for Nick. Nothing at all.

She opened her eyes to find him studying her, his dark gaze fixed on her with an intensity that made her knees weak and her stomach flutter.

"Actually, I was just getting ready to leave. It's late and I have to work tomorrow and—"

"Then why did you show up?"

"Excuse me?"

"I said, why did you show up? Why come here if you weren't planning on staying?"

"I, um—" Was it her imagination, or was Nick moving closer to her? He was. She swallowed nervously and stepped back, bumping into the wall. "I was meeting someone."

Nick's expression told her he didn't believe her. He watched her for a long second then made a show of looking around, searching. "So where are they?"

Mike gritted her teeth so hard she was surprised they didn't break. Why was she even bothering? She didn't have to explain anything to him, and she certainly shouldn't be backing away from him like she was intimidated. Taking a deep breath, she squared her shoulders and straightened to her full height. Thanks to the boots she was wearing, that almost put her at eye level with Nick. All the better to give him her coolest glare and tell him exactly where he could go.

Nick laughed, a smooth warm sound that did nothing to calm or amuse her. He reached out and grabbed her hand, folding it in his large one and squeezing gently before tugging her into the crowd. "C'mon, I'll buy you a soda."

"I said I was leaving." Mike pulled against him, but not as hard as she could have. She told herself that it would be easier to duck out when they got closer to the door. A tiny voice called her a liar.

Nick continued leading her through the crowd—away from the door. Mike tossed a single glance over her shoulder, wondering if she really should just leave. She didn't. Instead, she followed Nick to a small high table with, surprisingly, two empty stools. Or maybe not surprisingly. When she finally looked up, she realized the table was one of a group being held by a number of people, apparently friends of Nick from the way they greeted his return.

Mike nodded briefly as Nick made introductions which she quickly forgot. If she was smart, she would turn around and leave. There was nothing to be gained by staying here, not when staying here could only lead to trouble and worse, possible hurt. Sighing in defeat, she sat on one of the stools, hooking her boot heel around the rung as Nick motioned for the waitress at the next table.

"A seven and seven, please," Mike corrected when Nick ordered two sodas. The waitress took their order and disappeared, leaving them as alone as two people could be in a crowded nightclub. An uncomfortable silence stretched around them, made more awkward by the look that Nick leveled at her. Intent, curious. Heated. She shifted and finally looked straight at him with a questioning stare. "Is something wrong?"

Nick continued watching her, the expression in his dark eyes suddenly hooded. A long minute went by before he shook his head and looked away, leaving Mike suddenly more uncomfortable than before. His expression had been strange, one she had been unable to read but left her feeling like she should understand. She shrugged the sensation away and glanced around, looking for a distraction. In a place this size, with so many different people, it should have been easy. It wasn't.

The waitress finally reappeared, saving Mike from her squirming. She reached out and grabbed the drink with something close to desperation and sipped it, thankful for something to do at last. She would finish this then go home.

Mike was getting ready to take another sip when Nick abruptly stood and grabbed her arm, coming close to knocking the glass from her hand. She opened her mouth to say something but never got the chance because he was suddenly dragging her across the floor.

"What the hell are you doing?" Mike finally asked, forcing the words out through her clenched teeth. Nick just looked at her, not stopping until they reached the dance floor. He turned and wrapped her in his arms, pulling her entirely too close.

"Dancing," he answered. Mike stared at him in shock, her body rigid as he began swaying to the slow music. She tried to pull away, only to have him tighten his hold on her.

"I don't want to dance."

"Well, I do."

"Oh for crying out loud." Mike tried to pull away once more than gave up. His arms were wrapped too tightly around her; if she kept pulling away, he would end up squeezing the last breath out of her. It would be easier to just finish the dance then leave.

"Relax. You look like a stiff board. I'm not going to attack you," Nick reassured her. It wasn't much of a reassurance, not with his mouth was so close to her ear, not with his hand gently rubbing small circles on her back. Mike swallowed, trying to keep her body stiff when all she wanted to do was melt into a puddle at his feet.

She closed her eyes, trying to think of something, anything, besides the feel of Nick's body pressed so close against her. It didn't work so she opened her eyes, only to find him staring at her with that intense gaze again. Her heart jumped into her throat and she tried to look away. Nick dipped his head closer, leaning in, and she tried to pull away before his lips brushed against hers in a soft kiss.

"Kayla, don't." His voice was hoarse and soft, his breath warm against her mouth. She felt her resolve disappearing, felt herself leaning toward him no matter how hard she fought the pull. His mouth claimed hers, softly at first, then more firmly, demanding.

Owning.

Mike stepped back abruptly, breaking the kiss and the embrace, causing them both to stumble. She stared at Nick, saw the confusion in his eyes as he watched her. She shook her head and took another step back.

"Nick, I can't do this. I can't."

"Kayla—"

"I'm sorry, but I can't. I have to leave." She looked at him for another second then turned and left, weaving her way through the crowd, imagining that she heard his voice behind her.

Chapter Fifteen

Mike sat in the watch room, her eyes focused on the blank screen of the television as thoughts tumbled one after another through her mind. Saturday night had been a disaster but she had nobody to blame but herself. She was the one who had been stupid enough to show up at the nightclub, even knowing what could happen. The worst of it was that she hadn't been able to think of anything else for the last three days. How could she still find herself drawn to Nick, after everything that had happened between them? After so many years had gone by? After what he had done?

She sighed and rubbed her eyes, mentally cursing herself. Paperwork was scattered on the desk in front of her, the pages filled with her small handwriting. The top pages were nothing more than an update on the damn program that had been thrown in her lap. Right along with Nick. It should have been easy. All she had to do was let Jay run the show, like they had discussed. All she had to do was sit quietly in the back and do nothing. She didn't need to be involved. Except now she was—because of Nick. And now, for the first time in a long time, she doubted her ability to do something, because she really didn't think she could do this anymore.

Because of Nick.

The other pages were nothing more than heartfelt venting, a way to work through her anger and frustration. The rambling words were addressed to nobody, meant only for her eyes as she laid out all the reasons she could no longer take part in the project. It was just a draft, allowing her to vent her frustrations, to get everything out of her system. She wouldn't turn it in. As much as she wanted to, she couldn't, even if she had thought about putting in a formal request, to make it real.

No, that was the one thing she couldn't do, no matter how much she wanted to. There would be too much backlash, too much retaliation from Captain Nelson. Against her. Against Jay.

But that didn't make taking part in the program any easier. Part of her really thought she couldn't do it anymore. Being around Nick was taking too much out of her. And helping Jay out wasn't worth her sanity. But she'd stick with it. Because Jay had always stuck by her, no matter what. And because part of didn't want Nick to win.

Mike stood and stretched the kinks out of her back then grabbed the paperwork and stacked it in a neat pile, the report on top. Maybe if she talked to the captain, explained why—without going into too much detail. If she could explain why, give him a sound, reasonable explanation, then maybe he'd be willing to work something out.

Mike chewed on her lower lip, her mind running through all the possible scenarios and outcomes. Her mind made up, she left the watch room and headed back to the officers' room. She had to tell Captain Nelson she couldn't do it. Her nerves would never last the next few months—not if the last month was any indication. Her sanity was more important.

Her steps faltered, doubt filling her. Who was she kidding? She couldn't tell Captain Nelson she wanted off the project, no matter what reason she gave him. He'd be livid. But maybe she could work something else out, offer a compromise.

Yeah, as long as she could come up with something brilliant in the next thirty seconds.

She paused at the closed door, took a deep breath, and knocked, waiting for the muffled invitation before opening the door. "Cap, can I—"

Her words were interrupted by the shrill noise of the alarm. Time froze for a few heart-pounding seconds as the disembodied voice of a faceless dispatcher announced a vehicle rescue. Time snapped back and life erupted around the station. Mike threw the paperwork on the captain's desk then ran into the engine room, gathering her gear before jumping in the back of the engine with Jay. He wiggled his eyebrows and gave her a thumbs-up, but the traditional lucky sign failed to bring even a hint of smile to her face. Jay studied her as she pulled on her gear, finally shouting over the roar of the engine as it pulled out of the station.

"You okay?"

Mike waved his question away and settled back in the jump seat, trying to clear her mind as the engine sped through the late evening traffic on its way to the interstate. She turned in the seat, craning her neck to peer out the front window at the stopped traffic clogging the road in front of them. Rush hour should have been over an hour ago, which meant something else was causing the standstill. Mike turned back around and slammed on the engine cover to get Jay's attention, then motioned out the window. She reached over and pried a Halligan bar from its bracket, then pulled a handful of latex gloves from the box wedged beside her.

The engine slowed, the tires rumbling over the rough shoulder before coming to a stop. Mike threw open the door and climbed out, following the captain around the front as the spot lights on the side of the engine lit the scene.

One car rested against the guardrail at an awkward angle, the back and driver's side caved in. A second car was on its roof in the culvert off the shoulder, apparently having flipped over the guardrail. Jay made his way to the first car while Mike climbed over the damaged guardrail and slid down the small incline, taking in the scene immediately surrounding the vehicle. A quick glance showed one person inside the car, still strapped in the passenger seat and hanging at an awkward angle.

Mike signaled to the captain, holding up one finger to indicate the number of people, then dropped to her knees and climbed in through the broken driver's door window. The middle-aged woman grabbed for her, sobbing and muttering words that made no sense. Mike tried to comfort her with soothing words, doing a quick visual assessment of the patient then looking around for the driver. There was no one else in the car.

"Ma'am, I need you to calm down. Can you tell me what happened?"

Mike listened as the woman muttered something about being late for a party, something else about her boyfriend, but Mike couldn't make much sense of it. She backed out of the car and waved to the captain, motioning that she needed him.

"Cap, we have a missing driver. Anyone up there see anything?"

"Let me check." He turned and headed back up, his feet sliding under him as he struggled up the incline before finally reaching the road and disappearing into the gathering crowd. Mike muttered an obscenity to herself then crawled back into the car, doing a physical assessment of the woman while listening for the tell-tale sound of the ambulance's siren. Minutes went by before the medic unit finally arrived and Mike mumbled a quick thanks when Dave joined her by the car.

"What do you have?" He sat the large trauma box and collection of collars on the ground next to the car then tapped her on the leg, guiding her as she crawled out.

"Possible neck and back and she's complaining about her right ankle. I can't get in close enough to see. Possible ETOH. Not to mention a missing driver." She lowered her voice for the last part, not wanting the woman to overhear Mike telling him she had been drinking and that her boyfriend was nowhere to be found.

"Great." He climbed into the car, only to reappear two minutes later. "Get the backboard for me and have them call for the helicopter. I'm going to send her downtown."

"Will do," Mike assured him, grateful to be doing something besides patient care. She keyed the mike hanging from her turnout coat and relayed Dave's request as she made her way back up the hill. Several minutes later, she had the long board from the medic unit and was making her way back down to the overturned car, her eyes searching for any sign of the driver. There was a slight chance the body could be under the car; if that was the case, there would be little hope for him.

Dave was quiet as he treated the woman, calmly answering her hysterical questions while Mike helped out in silence. They finally maneuvered the woman out of the seat belt and were positioning her on the backboard when a raging bellow exploded around them. Dave and Mike both stopped what they were doing, startled, and looked up as a ragged man came hurtling toward them from the sparse wooded area on the other side of the culvert.

The man screamed obscenities, running at them like a raging bull. Mike figured he was over six feet tall and weighed a solid two hundred-forty pounds. From the blood streaming down his battered face, there was a good chance he was their missing driver.

The thought whirled through her mind with lightning speed, followed immediately by the realization that the man was charging them, his meaty fists already swinging through the air as he moved closer. Mike's instincts took over. She turned, facing the threat head-on while positioning herself in front of Dave, who had lowered his end of the backboard to the ground and hovered over the patient in an attempt to shield the injured woman.

From the corner of her eye, Mike saw a flurry of

action on the road above them as police officers jumped over the guardrail. The raging bull was much closer, bellowing at them to leave the woman alone as he lunged toward them. Mike knew it was coming, saw the large arms swinging before he even reached them. She braced herself and lowered her shoulder, hoping to at least stop the man before he ran right into the patient. Her reflexes were fast but the man was faster. A fist the size of a bear's paw caught her in the face and she toppled backwards, managing to fall to the side and avoid Dave and the patient.

The crazed man fell on top of her, knocking the wind from her as he continued swinging. Both of them struggled, Mike trying desperately to draw breath through what she was sure had to be a collapsed lung. The man's struggle suddenly ceased, turning him into nothing more than dead weight on top of her. A second went by before the weight was moved by the late-arriving police. She rolled to her side, her arm wrapping around her middle, her chest heaving.

"Shit! Mikey, are you okay?"

She blinked and turned her head, watching as Dave hovered over her, his hands already pressing in on her arms and side, assessing. She shoved his hands away and pushed herself to her hands and knees, still trying to drag air into her lungs as blessed numbness spread along her face.

The disjointed noise around her was suddenly magnified, echoing with the buzzing between her ears. Mike closed her eyes and rested her head against the cold ground while she concentrated on breathing, finally able to pick out individual words with her first lungful of air.

"Second helicopter—"

"No, he's combative...by land..."

"Bruised ribs at least—"

"...one helluva shiner." Mike finally opened her eyes and looked up to see Jay peering down at her, a cold pack in his hand. He reached out to help her stand then held the cold pack to her face as he led her away from the commotion by the car. She took a few steps then stumbled, forced to lean against Jay so she wouldn't fall down as he led her up the incline.

"Oh, man, everything's swimming," she muttered, reaching up for the cold pack. Jay steadied her as they walked the remaining distance to the road, then she gingerly sat down on the guardrail. The earlier bustle that had erupted with the stranger's startling presence had slowed into organized chaos. Mike took a deep breath and immediately wished she hadn't when a sharp pain pierced her side. She wrapped one arm around her chest and leaned forward, taking baby breaths through her mouth.

"Mikey, you're not looking so good. Maybe you better get in the ambulance."

"No, I'll be fine."

"Yeah, right. I'm getting someone."

"Jay." Too late, he was gone. Mike didn't bother calling him back because he was right. The charging bull had caught her by surprise and she was starting to feel the damage. Part of her wanted to do nothing more than just go home and sleep it off, but that was wishful thinking. There was no doubt she'd be making a trip to the hospital, whether she wanted to or not.

She closed her eyes again, shutting out the turmoil taking place around her. The dizziness wasn't so bad with her eyes closed but the darkness magnified the sounds of the scene, which made her head hurt. Biting back a wince she opened her eyes again, in time to see Dave approaching her with the trauma bag in hand. A paramedic from the second medic unit was behind him, directing the transport of both patients up to the road.

"How are you feeling?" Dave asked, kneeling in front of her and opening the bag.

"Like I've been run over, how do you think?" Mike watched as the two patients, both on backboards, were lifted over the guardrail and taken to the nearest medic unit. "How's the guy?"

David glanced at the medic unit then turned back to her, shrugging. "I'm pretty sure he's got a closed head injury. Both pupils are shot. Raccoon eyes. Not to mention the combativeness. Not good signs."

Mike grunted, not really having anything to say, then closed her eyes as Dave poked and prodded and examined. His hand pressed against her side and she winced.

"Hmm. You're definitely going to need X-rays. Other than that and the side of your face, you look okay. C'mon, let's get you to the hospital and get you checked out."

"Gee, I'm so lucky. And here I was looking forward to going on another call." Mike stood then swayed as a wave of dizziness washed over her, making her stomach roll. She closed her eyes and reached out, feeling Dave's arm go around her to support her. A second passed before the world righted itself and she could open her eyes.

"Alright, sit back down." Dave lowered her back to the guardrail, still supporting her as he called for

Jay to bring a stretcher.

"I don't need—"

"I'm in charge here so don't even bother. You're going on the stretcher whether you want it or not."

"David—"

"Forget it. Just remember that nothing good ever comes from being a smartass. Next time, try not to use yourself as a barrier wall. You'll be better off."

Mike opened her mouth to say something then decided against it. She didn't have the energy to put up a fight, not right now, not when she knew she'd lose anyway. Her head hurt too much to argue, and her chest hurt too much breathe. Let Dave have his way on this. He was the paramedic, after all.

She finally nodded her agreement, wincing at the pain the movement caused, then closed her eyes and let her head fall against his shoulder.

Chapter Sixteen

Nick let a minute go by before he knocked on the door for the third time. He knew Kayla was home: her Jeep was parked next to the barn and he could hear noise coming from inside, muffled and faint. He bounced from one foot to the other and blew on his closed hands, trying to get some warmth circulating in his limbs. The day was gray and damp, typical for early November.

He muttered to himself and raised a hand to knock again, then jumped back in surprise when the door opened. Nick's mouth opened in shock when he saw Kayla. "Holy mother of—What the hell happened to you?"

She stood in the doorway, her body limp as she leaned against it and peered at him through one good eye. The other one was partially closed with swelling, the flesh distorted and discolored. The left side of her face was swollen and bruised, a mottled coloring of blues and purples edged in a grotesque green.

"Just what I needed. What do you want?" Her

words were quiet and strained, like she had been forced awake after a long nap. Or been resurrected from the dead.

"What happened to you? Are you alright?" The damp air still seeped into him but that's not what caused Nick's sudden chill. He stepped forward, reaching out for her but touching only air when she turned and walked into the living room. Nick paused in the doorway, hesitating. Screw it, he thought, then boldly stepped inside, closing the door behind him.

Kayla lowered herself to the sofa, grabbing her side and wincing when she lay back on the pillows and stretched out. She shifted, slowly rolling to her side, then closed her good eye and sighed. A minute went by before she reopened it and focused a glare on him when he sat down on the loveseat. "What are you doing here, Nick?"

"Nobody showed up at the meeting yesterday and I just wanted to see if everything was okay. I guess not."

"Jay probably forgot to call. Guess you didn't think about using a phone, either."

"No, I did. I just didn't think you'd talk to me if I called."

"Hmm." Kayla closed her eye again and sunk deeper into the cushions, taking a deep breath. A brief expression of pain creased her face then disappeared when she shifted positions again.

Nick watched her for a long minute, feeling more like an intruder than he could have imagined. She looked lost and vulnerable. Fragile. But the image of fragility didn't fit her. Not now, not even all those years ago when she had been young and innocent. He shifted on the loveseat and cleared his throat. "Do you need anything?"

A shallow sigh, followed by, "No."

"So. What happened?"

Kayla mumbled something he couldn't hear then slowly rolled over and pushed herself to a sitting position, wincing again. She opened her eyes and fixed him with a cold glare that rivaled the chill outside. The silence stretched so long that Nick didn't think she was going to answer. Her words were short and clipped, tired. "I got into a fight with a patient at the scene of an accident."

"You did what?" Nick didn't bother keeping the surprise from his voice. A second went by before he realized she must be joking with him. He offered her a quick smile. "Yeah, right. If you look this bad, how's the other guy?"

"Dead," she answered, her voice flat.

More time went by, the room around them so quiet that Nick could hear her raspy breathing when she lowered herself back onto the cushions. She didn't say anything else, didn't even look at him, and he suddenly realized that she didn't look like she was joking. He leaned forward, his hand stretched out, reaching for her. He realized what he was doing and let his arm drop. "Are you serious?"

"Yes, Nick, I'm serious. Is there anything else you want? Because I've got to tell you, I really don't know why you're here, and I'd really love to be alone right now."

"My God, Kayla. What happened? Are you okay? I mean, you didn't—that is, he's not dead because—"

"I didn't kill him, if that's what you're asking."

"No. I mean, oh. Then what happened?"

"For crying out loud." She leaned up on one

elbow and stared at him. "There was an accident. The guy was thrown out of the car. Major head injuries. He was combative and came after us. I was closest. He died at Shock Trauma. There, are you satisfied? May I please get some rest now?"

Her voice was worn and tired, too tight and laced with stress. And pain. Nick looked closer and realized her face was pale and sweaty, her features drawn. He stood up and moved toward her, no longer caring if she snapped at him, if she argued with him or pushed him away. She was in pain and trying so hard to hide it. From him? Or just because that's who she was now? It didn't matter, not really. He leaned over and fluffed the pillows for her, arranging them so she'd be more comfortable. The look she shot him made him feel foolish and inadequate. At least she didn't say anything, just lowered herself and watched him with a wary expression.

He reached out and smoothed a strand of hair from her face before he could think about what he was doing, before he could stop himself. Surprisingly, she didn't push his hand away. "You look like hell, you know."

"I feel worse."

Nick pulled away, a slight smile playing on his mouth as he stared down at her. "What? No sarcastic comeback? You better watch it or I might think you're getting soft."

"It's not me, it's the drugs. Being mellow is a side-effect. Luckily for my image, they're starting to wear off."

"Did you need me to get you anything? Water or something?"

"No." Kayla paused and glanced at the oak

coffee table, then up at Nick. "Maybe some fresh water. I think that's probably warm by now."

Nick picked up the glass. "Anything else? Something to eat maybe?"

"Water's fine."

Nick walked into the kitchen and opened the refrigerator, searching for a pitcher of water. All he found was a sparse scattering of left-overs, soda, and beer. Shaking his head, he grabbed some ice from the freezer and filled the glass from the tap, then returned to the living room. Kayla roused from a half-sleep and took the glass from him, taking a sip before reaching for the medicine bottle on the coffee table. Nick grabbed it for her so she wouldn't have to stretch, then fought with the top.

"How many?"

"Two."

Nick shook out two of the large pills and dropped them in her hand. Kayla popped them in her mouth and followed them with another sip of water. She handed the glass back to Nick then lowered herself again with a sigh and a muttered thanks. Not knowing what else to do, he put the glass on the table within her reach then sat back down on the loveseat, taking his coat off as he did.

A few quiet minutes went by, filled only with the soft music coming from the stereo in the corner and Kayla's soft breathing. Nick took advantage of the lull and studied her. She looked so different from when he knew her last; different, but the same. There were times when he looked at her that he saw the young girl from another lifetime.

But not the other night.

The other night he had seen the woman that girl

had become. He remembered when she had walked into the nightclub, her steps sure and direct as she headed first for the bar then edged closer to the dance floor, studying the band through the crowd. He had been surprised to see her, surprised at the burst of pleasure that warmed him when he realized she had shown up. And when he got a good look at her, at the tight firm body and long legs, showcased by skin-hugging black denim and heeled boots—to deny that he had felt a surge of masculine desire and possessiveness would be a lie.

Nick didn't think that Kayla would appreciate knowing the extent of heated desire he still felt for her. If anything, it was stronger than the rampant teenage hormonal passion they had shared so many years ago. And he was pretty sure that the attraction, the desire, was mutual.

He closed his eyes and sighed. If there hadn't been so much history between them—bad history that eclipsed everything else—he wouldn't hesitate to start another relationship. Or at least try. But Nick didn't think Kayla would be open to the idea, no matter how big the attraction was between them.

So where did that leave him?

Absolutely nowhere. Because Kayla was partly right when she accused him the other week of acting out of guilt and pity. He did still feel guilty, he probably always would. And yes, a small part of him did pity her—not because of what happened, but because of what she could have been. She had such a promising future in front of her. Her music, her talent. College scholarships. A full life, just waiting. She had been bright, witty, full of life. And he had never appreciated it, not really. Even after all these years, part of him still wondered why she had chosen him to be with him, wondered what she ever saw in him. He'd been a rebel, focused on music and cars and partying. He'd been her first, and he still didn't understand why she had given him so much of herself in the years they had been together. Her innocence. Her love.

Did he pity her? Yes, maybe a small part of him did. But what Kayla didn't know was that he felt more pity for himself. It was an absolutely useless emotion and didn't say much for his character, but there it was.

And damned if he knew what to do about it.

A whimper from the sofa caught his attention and he turned in time to see Kayla try to shift position. He went over to her and leaned down until she opened her good eye, the green glazed with medication and pain.

"Wouldn't you be more comfortable in bed?"

"Hm, probably."

"Then why don't you go upstairs?"

"Too stiff, hurts to walk."

"Then let me help," Nick said. Before she could object, he leaned down and gently moved her to a sitting position so he could maneuver her into his arms. Her head rolled sideways and rested against his shoulder as he lifted her. She hissed in pain when he wrapped his arm around her and he drew back, afraid he had hurt her.

"Bruised ribs, be careful," she whispered sleepily. Nick grimaced, knowing he must have hit the sore spot dead center. He repositioned his arm and lifted her the rest of the way, moving slow as he straightened with her weight in his arms. He shifted and carefully walked to the stairs, climbing slowly so he wouldn't jostle her.

A small bedside lamp was turned on, the only light in the room. He walked over to the king size bed and gently lowered her to the mattress. She shifted with a small whimper and helped her ease under the fluffy comforter, noticing that there was a feather mattress on top of the regular one. He bit back a groan and tucked her in, trying to ignore her happy sigh. "Better?"

"Hmm-hmm," she mumbled, curling on her side so she faced him. She looked up and offered him a small smile then snuggled deeper, sighing again.

Nick straightened and tore his gaze from her resting figure, looking around the room. She had obviously finished her painting and decorating. Gauzy lace and soft muted colors, bold abstract prints in bright colors, silk flowers and piles of overstuffed pillows. The loft had been turned into a cozy romantic getaway, which only made him stifle another groan. He should probably leave, for both of their sakes, but he wasn't sure if she should be left alone. What if she needed something? Would she be able to get back downstairs if she did?

"Are you going to be okay?" Nick asked, looking back down at her. Her eyes were closed, her breathing shallow and even. A minute went by before he realized she was asleep. Nick sighed and ran a hand through his hair, wondering what he should do.

She would probably be fine if he left. After all, she had been by herself when he got here and she certainly wasn't helpless. And if she really needed something, her father was home, still living in the old Victorian a hundred yards away. There was nothing he could do for her that her father couldn't.

And he doubted if she'd really want his help even if she did need it. Sure, she had let him help just now. But Nick was pretty sure that had more to do with her medication than anything else. Unless she really was in enough pain not to care who helped.

He hesitated for only another minute then made up his mind. He would stay here a little longer, in case she woke up and needed something. If she wanted him to leave then, he would.

Nick looked around for somewhere to sit and noticed the two upholstered chairs arranged in the far corner in what was obviously a reading nook. A smile lifted one corner of his mouth as he recalled her voracious love of reading. It looked like that, at least, hadn't changed.

But then he frowned, studying the chairs, thinking they didn't look very comfortable if you planned on sitting in them for a long time. Of course, he could go downstairs and stretch out, but then he might not hear her if she needed something. His gaze moved from the chairs to the bed and he made up his mind. Hell, it was a king size bed. It wasn't like there wasn't enough room for both of them, with space to spare.

Not stopping to question his decision, knowing it wasn't a smart one and that he'd change his mind if he thought too long about it, he kicked off his shoes and took off his sweatshirt. Clad in his thin t-shirt and jeans, Nick climbed into the bed next to her, moving slowly so he wouldn't jostle the mattress. He was immediately surrounded by downy comfort and swallowed a sigh of contentment. He turned on his side to face Kayla and watched her for a few minutes, taking comfort in the even rise and fall of her chest,

taking comfort in the warmth of her body next to his.
 Then he closed his eyes, just to rest them.
 Just for a little bit.

Chapter Seventeen

A warm weight settled against his side, soft but solid. Comforting. Nick breathed deeply, full of a drowsy content he didn't quite understand, a content that unsettled him. He shifted and tightened his arm around the weight, holding it more securely against him as it snuggled closer. The sensation was soothing, something he had been missing in his life for entirely too long. He sighed again, thinking he could get accustomed to this.

A minute went by before his subconscious recognized what the weight was, then another minute before his brain registered what his sleeping mind had just acknowledged. Nick opened his eyes to the dimness of the room and looked around, disoriented. The weight next to him shifted again with a sleepy murmur and he came fully awake.

He had fallen asleep in Kayla's bed and she was now curled up next to him, her warm body snuggling against his own. Her head rested in the hollow of his shoulder and her hand was splayed across his bare chest. Funny, he didn't remember taking off his t-shirt. He turned his head to the side and saw the shirt in a puddle on the floor next to the bed. Nick bit back a curse, realizing he must have taken it off in his sleep. A quick check assured him he was still wearing his jeans, something minor to be thankful for since he rarely slept in clothes.

How long had they been asleep? He glanced at the window but could see only a dreary grayness through the lace curtains. Nick couldn't look at his watch without moving Kayla; the same with the alarm clock on the opposite nightstand. His head fell back against the soft pillow as he did a mental rundown of his schedule. Nothing on the agenda for tonight, thankfully. He closed his eyes and took a deep breath, knowing he should get up, or at least get himself untangled from Kayla.

But he enjoyed the feel of her against him too much to move. And what was she going to do when she woke up and realized he had crawled into bed with her, half-naked? Not that being shirtless really qualified as half-naked, but he was pretty sure that's not how she would see it.

Kayla murmured something in her sleep. Nick stopped breathing when her hand moved against his chest, her fingers moving gently up and down in a tender caress. He clenched his jaw against the sensation and reached up, grabbing her hand with his to stop its movement and wondering what the hell he was going to do now.

He needed to get out of the bed. He really, really needed to move away from her. Right now.

Her hand moved again, her fingers twining with his for a second before freeing itself from his and continuing its earlier caress. Nick swallowed.

Damn. He really needed to get out of the bed.

He took a deep breath and tried to ease his arm from around Kayla without waking her.

"Don't leave." The words, barely above a whisper, startled him and caused his heart to jump into his throat. He squeezed his eyes shut, hoping he was dreaming, then opened them and looked down at Kayla. She was looking back at him, her eyes soft with sleep, her expression almost dreamy.

"You're awake."

"For the most part."

"Shit. I'm sorry, I didn't mean—"

"Shh, you're ruining the dream."

That made Nick pause. He stared down at her, wondering if she was talking in her sleep. Her hand continued wandering across his chest, back and forth, playing with the spattering of hair in the center. He reached up to stop her, only to have her push his hand away.

"I always loved playing with your chest."

"I remember," Nick whispered, afraid to move, afraid to say anything more.

"You've filled out quite a bit over the years."

Oh God, he didn't think he could stand it. He grabbed her hand and held it firmly in his, then took a deep breath and stared at her. "Kayla, you're not having a dream. You're awake."

She pushed herself up on her elbow with a small wince and looked down at him for a long minute. A dozen different emotions whirled through Nick while she watched him: curiosity, trepidation, fear, caution. Lust. Definitely lust. He was acting worse than a sex-starved teenager.

"I know I'm awake. But it's easier to pretend I'm dreaming," Kayla whispered. Her soft admission sent an electrifying jolt through him, swift, paralyzing. She let out a soft breath and rested her head against his shoulder once more, shifting closer to him. Her leg tangled with his and another jolt went through him at the contact, freezing him.

"Kayla—"

"Why did you stay?"

"I—" Nick swallowed against the tightness in his throat. "I wasn't sure if you'd need anything. I didn't want you to be left alone if you needed help."

"Thank you."

Two simple words, but they held so much feeling and unleashed so many conflicting emotions that something in Nick's chest squeezed, causing the breath in his lungs to hitch. His arms automatically tightened around her and he dropped a kiss on the top of her head. There was so much he wanted to say to her but he didn't know where to start. And he wasn't sure if she even wanted to listen. He took a deep breath but she spoke before he could say anything.

"I missed you. I hated you for leaving me, but I still missed you. How pathetic is that?"

"Kayla—"

"No, don't say anything. I just want to lay here like this and pretend nothing ever happened. Just for a little bit." She shifted, moving even closer to him, if that was possible. Her hand resumed its gentle circular motion, back and forth against his chest, occasionally dipping lower to brush his stomach. It was torture, but a torture he would gladly bear because she had asked him to.

The rain pattered against the tin roof of the barn and filled the room with a relaxing sound. The whispered hum of the rain and Kayla's soft caresses lulled Nick into a place that was dangerous and comforting at the same time. He told himself he shouldn't let it happen, that he should fight it, but the lure was too strong. And dammit, this was where he wanted to be. Where he'd always wanted to be.

A minute went by, then another. Was it his imagination, or could he feel the hesitant touch of Kayla's lips against his chest, warm and feather light? His muscles tightened under the next soft touch. No, he wasn't imagining it. Kayla was kissing him.

This couldn't be happening. This *shouldn't* be happening. He tightened his arm around her and shifted away. "Kayla."

"Do you know what else is pathetic, Nick? That after all this time, and after everything that's happened, I still want you." She leaned up on her elbow and stared at him, her face only inches from his, her expression serious. "Sometimes I wish...I wish we could go back to the way it was, just for a little bit. To pretend nothing bad ever happened."

Nick swallowed a groan, his body tightening automatically at her words. It took every ounce of self-control not to pull her down against him and kiss her, to willingly take her back to what they used to have. But he couldn't. He wouldn't take advantage of her that way. So instead he reached up and gently guided her head back to his shoulder and held her. Just held her.

Quiet minutes drifted by and Nick was surprised at the contentment spreading through him. Warm, comforting. And, somehow, *right*. Like it was supposed to be this way. For right now, for this minute, it was just the two of them, surrounded by cozy softness and the soothing sound of the rain.

"Don't you ever think about it, Nick? About just going back? What would be so wrong with doing that, just once?" Kayla asked in a soft whisper. Her hand continued its soft caress, growing a little bolder, dipping a little lower with each stroke. Nick clenched his jaw and tightened his hold around her, careful not to squeeze too hard because of her ribs.

"I'm more interested in going forward, Kayla. Who's to say we can't do that?"

She laughed, the sound forced and sarcastic, and lifted her head to look at him. "Because there's too much behind us to move forward. But we had some good times, too, before all that. And we always did have great sex between us, if nothing else."

Nick didn't bother trying to hide his groan. This conversation was leading straight for trouble. The smartest thing for him to do would be to jump out of the bed and run out the door. There were still too many raw wounds, especially for Kayla. The last thing he wanted between them was more pain.

But he didn't want to be smart. How could he, with Kayla laying half on top of him, her body stretched against his? He reached out and ran his hand through her hair, cupping the back of her head as he studied her. "It was more than just sex and you know it."

"No, it wasn't. If it had been, you wouldn't have...it wouldn't have ended like it did. We both know that."

"Are you lying to me? Or to yourself?"

"Neither. I'm just facing reality."

Nick stared at her, trying to figure out where she was heading. He rubbed his thumb along her cheek and finally shook his head. "Your reality, maybe, not mine."

"And your reality is better?"

"I don't—"

"Is it better than this?" Kayla asked, then lowered her head and kissed him, a hungry kiss that immediately exploded. Nick's arms tightened around her as she stretched more fully against him, their bodies touching from lips to toes. The kiss continued, heated and intense. Nick gave into it, for just a minute, just to enjoy the feel of Kayla against him, then he pulled away, his breathing ragged and hoarse.

"Kayla, stop."

"Why? If we had great sex before, imagine how it would be now. Just sex, Nick. No commitment." She lowered her head and ran her lips along his neck, nipping gently at his ear. Nick groaned, part of him wanting to do nothing more than give in to the sensation, to give Kayla what she seemed to be asking for.

With a silent curse, he reached up and grabbed Kayla's shoulders and gently pushed her away, making sure he rolled to his side when he did to keep her from climbing back on top of him. "What do you want, Kayla? A month ago you didn't want to be in the same room with me and now you're propositioning me. Are you playing some kind of game, or trying to prove something?"

Kayla leaned back and studied him, then slowly shook her head. "No, I'm not trying to prove anything, and I'm not playing any game. I'm talking about plain old sex. No strings, no commitments, just two consenting adults."

"You're talking about a one-night stand. Is that something you do now? Just hop in the sack with—"

"I've never done it before, believe it or not. And I figured we both knew each other, knew what it could be like, so why not?"

Nick stared at her in shock, still not quite believing what he heard. If the situation wasn't so sad, he'd laugh. He shook his head, not sure what he should say. The sane part of his mind told him to get out of bed and leave. The reckless part urged him to take Kayla up on her offer, if for no other reason than to teach her a lesson.

"My God, Kayla, do you have any idea how that sounds?"

She rolled on her side so she was facing him and pushed up on her elbow. A minute went by before she reached out and ran a trembling finger down the middle of his chest. "Are you going to tell me that you haven't thought about it at all at any time since September? That you haven't wondered what it would be like now?"

Christ, yes, he had thought about it. Every damn night. And he mentally kicked himself for the thought every time. But not now, not this time. This time, Nick's control snapped. He reached out and grabbed Kayla's hand, pulling it down, holding it firmly against his erection. Emotion flared in Kayla's eyes, sharp and bright, when she looked up at him. "Yeah, I've thought about it. I'm thinking about it now. Is that what you want, Kayla? Just a quick fuck?"

Nick lowered his head and pressed his mouth to hers, deliberately hard and intense, possessive. He wanted to show her this was a bad idea, wanted to scare the stupid idea out of her mind. Two seconds into the searing kiss and Nick was lost. Passion and need, instantaneous and consuming, engulfed him. His hands roamed over her body, searching, caressing. Her own hands trailed along his flesh, igniting a trail of fire wherever they touched him.

Minutes later, her shirt and sweatpants were gone, tossed in a pile with his own jeans. Her hand folded around the length of his cock, stroking and squeezing, sending mindless pleasure racing through him. Nick squeezed his eyes shut, bracing himself against the sensation, trying desperately to remember the point he had foolishly thought he could make.

With a groan he pulled her hand away and rolled so he was lying on top of Kayla, bracing his weight on his forearms so he wouldn't injure her. He stared down at her, waiting for her to change her mind, waiting for her to come to her senses and tell him to stop. Instead she slid her body lower against his and arched her back, lifting her hips, searching.

"Kayla." His voice was hoarse, her name a ragged whisper torn from somewhere deep in his chest. She wrapped her arms around his neck and pulled him closer.

"Nick, please."

He watched her for another second, hoping she would come to her senses, hoping reason would return to him in a flash before they were both lost.

With a silent curse, Nick thrust himself deep inside her, burying himself to the hilt in one quick move.

And one quick prayer that this wouldn't turn into the second biggest mistake of his life.

Chapter Eighteen

Mike bit her lip, trying to silence her moan when Nick pushed himself into her with surprising speed. Her head fell back as sensation tore through her with each of his frantic thrusts. This is what she had asked for, what she had wanted. No, what she *needed*. To feel him deep inside her, thrusting, burying himself.

She lifted her hips and wrapped her legs tightly around him, pulling him even deeper. Her eyes drifted closed and she let herself be swept away, abandoning all thought, wanting—needing—only to feel. The hard length of his body on top of hers, the feel of heated flesh melded together. The taste of his mouth on hers, the touch of his tongue against hers, thrusting, mating, claiming. Mike ran her hands through his hair, her fingers tangling in the damp wavy strands that fell against his neck.

Heat burned her from the inside, searing,

spreading with each thrust, eclipsing the pain of her bruised ribs. She pulled her mouth away from his and dragged her lips across his throat and over his shoulder, arching against him, accepting and demanding more. Harsh breathing echoed around her, his and hers, drowning out the sound of the rain hitting the roof above them. The heat grew, spiraling outward, turning into a promise of more. She buried her face in his shoulder, gasping, reaching, waiting.

"Kayla, look at me," Nick's hoarse voice rumbled in her ear, demanding. She shook her head, not wanting emotion or connection, only sensation. "Look at me."

"No," she muttered, arching her back more, thrusting her own hips to meet him, searching.

"Dammit, Kayla, look at me!" Nick pulled back, easing himself away from her. He reached out and grabbed her hands, pulling them up over her head and forcing her to look at him. His dark eyes blazed with emotion, intense and terrifying as he held her gaze with a force of will she hadn't expected. Slowly, agonizingly, he thrust back into her, watching her as he pulled out. "This isn't a one-night stand."

"Y-yes."

He buried himself, then pulled back, still holding her gaze. "No, it's not."

Mike closed her eyes and moved under him, ignoring his words, seeking only the fulfillment his body promised hers. He pulled away even more, until her resolve shattered. "Nick, please."

"Not until you look at me."

Against her will, she opened her eyes, her gaze immediately trapped by his. He lowered his head and kissed her, hard but promising, then pulled back and looked down at her. "This is not a one-time thing, Kayla."

"Nick—"

"Tell me," he demanded, easing himself back inside her, thrusting twice before pulling away, tormenting her. His gaze still held hers, refusing to let her look away. "Tell me."

"O-okay. Just—please."

His mouth claimed hers again, the kiss nearly violent in its intensity. He broke the kiss with a growl and pulled away, his dark gaze searing as he watched her. As he thrust deeper inside her, harder, faster. Her eyes drifted close as sensation pulled at her, groaned when he stopped moving.

"Look at me, Kayla. I want to watch you, to see you."

Oh God, why had she thought this would be easy? With a groan of frustration, she forced her eyes open and looked up at him. A second of pure torture went by before Nick resumed his thrusting, his gaze holding hers, his body demanding a response. The spiraling inside her twisted then tightened, pausing before exploding in white-hot fragments that tore through her, splitting her apart in numbing sensation.

Nick lowered his mouth to hers and swallowed her cries, thrusting faster, sending shards of pleasure tearing through her already shattered nerve endings. She pulled her hands from his grip and wrapped them around his neck, holding him to her as he shuddered with his own violent release, their mouths still melded together.

Nick gently broke the kiss and trailed his lips along her jaw and neck. His hand caressed her chest and side, the touch soft and light. Mike stiffened under the sensations, wondering why he was still stretched out on top of her, suddenly wanting to be by herself. Nick sighed and pushed himself up, watching her with an unreadable expression. He squeezed his eyes shut and shook his head.

"Dammit, I knew it. Shit." He opened his eyes and gazed at her for another few seconds then, muttering, rolled off her and stared up at the ceiling, his hands clasped behind his head. Mike reached down for the sheet and pulled it over herself, shy and wary as she watched him from the corner of her eye.

"Knew what?"

"I knew this was a mistake, that this was going to happen." Nick sighed and ran his hands through his hair, then abruptly turned to face her, his expression fierce. "I didn't think you'd regret it this fast, though."

"I never said—"

"You didn't have to, Kayla. It's written all over your face." His expression softened. He reached out with his hand and gently caressed her bruised cheek, tucking a strand of hair behind her ear. "Do you want me to leave now? Then you can blame it on the medication in the morning, tell yourself it made you too mellow."

Mike flinched at his words, not because of the gentle way he said them, but because they were true. She had wanted Nick to make love to her but she hadn't wanted to admit it. Not to herself, not to him. She still didn't. And it *had* been a mistake, just like Nick said. But not for exactly the reason he thought.

Yes, she regretted it—but only because she wanted more. She had thought she could take one night. That she could pretend, for one night, that they were back in the past. Only now, she didn't think she could.

Because she wanted more.

And now she wasn't sure what to do. The smartest thing would be to act the charade out to its end. To tell Nick to leave, to pretend nothing had happened, to be cool and aloof the next time they saw each other.

Mike shifted on her side and looked at Nick, noticed the concern etched on his face and the softness in his eyes as he watched her. God, she had been a fool to think she could get near him again and not feel anything, to think she could pretend she didn't care. She bit her lower lip and slowly shook her head. "No, I don't want you to go."

He rolled so he was resting on his stomach, his arms crossed in front of him, his head close enough that he could rest it on her shoulder if he wanted. He watched her for a long minute, the room silent around them, then leaned forward and dropped a kiss on the swell of her breast. "Are you sure?"

No, she wasn't sure. But she nodded anyway. Nick gave her a small smile then reached out and wrapped one arm around her waist, pulling her closer, tucking her protectively against him. Mike stiffened, then finally allowed herself to relax. Maybe she could have just one night. One night of make-believe.

She closed her eyes and let herself drift off, Nick's embrace and her dreams of pretend her only company.

Chapter Nineteen

Mike wandered into the kitchen and poured a glass of water then popped two more pills, wincing against the pull in her side. The ache was a dull throb, beating in time with her pulse and making sleep difficult. She sighed then reached for the bottle of brandy sitting on the counter and poured the dark liquid into the glass, taking a long swallow. Might as well go for complete relaxation, she thought, grabbing the bottle and glass and walking into the darkened living room.

She put the bottle on the table then sat down on the sofa, curling up in the corner and pulling her legs into her chest. Complete relaxation would be nearly impossible, at least for a little longer.

Until Nick woke up and left.

Mike shook her head and took another swallow of the brandy, still not sure how tonight had ever happened. Talk about being a Class A fool. What had ever possessed her to have sex with Nick? Hormones, medication. Loneliness. It had been too long, and she had wanted it. Needed to feel that brief connection, if only for a few minutes. She wanted release and foolishly thought she could use Nick to get it.

Her mistake was thinking she could have casual sex with Nick then act like nothing had happened. With Nick, of all people! Sex had always been great between them, even when they were younger and didn't know what they were doing. At least, she didn't. But Nick had been right about one thing tonight—it *had* been more than just sex all those years ago.

Mike was very much afraid that it had been more than just sex tonight.

She didn't want *more* right now. Not with anyone, and certainly not with Nick. Never again with Nick. It was a disaster waiting to happen. And she had nobody to blame but herself.

"Damn," she muttered, her voice hoarse and scratchy. The word didn't come close to summing up the whole situation. The best she could do was pretend nothing had happened. Just go back to the cool detachment of the last month whenever she saw Nick.

And try to see him as little as possible.

And not think of the heat between them, or the instinctive way her body reacted whenever she was around him.

She took another sip of brandy then frowned, knowing that all of that was easier said than done.

The sound of footsteps drifted down the stairs and Mike tucked herself further into the corner. She wasn't fool enough to think that Nick wouldn't see her, despite the shadows that shrouded her. After all, he was bright enough to notice she wasn't in bed, and there weren't many other places she could go. She drained the brandy and poured another glass, then looked up when Nick finally came into the room.

He leaned against the wall, watching her, though she wasn't sure how well he could see. The night light from the kitchen dispelled enough shadow that she could see him clearly, though, and she wished she couldn't. He stood there, wearing only his jeans, which were unbuttoned and unzipped, calling attention to the one part of his anatomy that she didn't want to notice.

Not that she wanted to notice the rest of it, either. That didn't stop her from looking at him, though. Her eyes drifted up from his bare feet, paused at the opening of his jeans, then continued up. Past the ridges of his flat stomach to his broad chest, tight with muscle and firm skin, dusted with just enough dark hair to run her fingers through.

Mike swallowed, the feel of that naked chest against hers branded indelibly in her memory. She swallowed a groan, hoping he wouldn't hear it, and took another sip of brandy to distract herself from looking at his body.

"Are you okay?" His voice was soft in the darkness, husky from sleep. Mike nodded then realized he may not be able to see her.

"Yeah, fine." She cringed when the words came out as a squeak. Just her luck that Nick sounded sexy and she sounded like a mouse.

He leaned against the wall for another minute, just watching her, then slowly straightened and walked over. He hesitated, almost as if he was trying to decide something, then finally sat down. Mike let out the breath she had been holding when he chose to sit on the loveseat instead of the sofa with her. He stretched his legs out and leaned over to put on his socks and shoes; Mike watched him over the edge of the glass as she sipped, hoping the darkness hid her gaze.

Nick straightened then worked at turning his t-shirt and sweatshirt right side out. He leaned forward to put the shirts on the table then paused. A full minute went by before he straightened and stared at her, his jaw tight.

"What are you drinking?"

"What?" Mike made no effort to hide her confusion, wondering at the flatness of his voice. Before she realized what he was doing, he reached out and grabbed the bottle of brandy from the table and held it up to her.

"Are you drinking this?"

"Yeah."

"Did you take anymore medicine?"

"Yeah. Why?"

"Jesus Kayla. What the hell do you think you're doing?" His voice was cold and angry, accusing. She straightened and stared at him in surprise, not understanding the reason for his sudden change, not like the defensiveness that leaped within her.

"What do you mean, what am I doing? I'm having a drink. You have a problem with that?"

"You're mixing alcohol with pain medication! I thought you were smarter than that. Are you trying to knock yourself unconscious?"

"Excuse me? One or two drinks aren't going to make much difference. It's almost five o'clock in the morning and it's not like I'm going anywhere. And what the hell business is it of yours, anyway?"

Nick stared at her, his expression hard and

unreadable, then he muttered a curse she hadn't heard from him since his wild days. Bottle in hand, he turned and stormed into the kitchen. Mike almost laughed when she heard him drain the contents down the sink then throw the empty bottle into the trash. He returned a minute later and grabbed his shirt from the table, pulling it over his head with jerky movements.

"Do you feel better now?" She asked, not hiding her amusement. He mumbled something from inside his shirt, then finally poked his head through the opening and glared at her.

"Yeah, laugh. It's all one big joke to you, isn't it? And you call me a hypocrite."

"What the hell are you talking about?"

"I'm talking about your drinking. Do you realize that every single time I've seen you these last two months, you've been drinking? Not once have I seen you with anything in your hand besides alcohol."

"Bullshit."

"Really? Think about it. Except for when you're working, you've always been drinking. Don't you think that says something?"

Mike laughed and took a swallow of brandy, then shook her head. "Yeah, Nick, sure. And except for the few meetings we've had, you've seen me what—five times? Six? That really says a lot, doesn't it?"

"Yeah, I think it does. Especially when one of those times, you threw up on me." His voice was flat and calm but Mike could feel the tension oozing from him, so strong that it wrapped around her, suffocating. She stared up at him, honestly confused. Why was he making such a big deal about nothing? He was starting to sound like Jay and the rest of the guys at work. And she was getting a little tired of everyone commenting on her drinking.

"Knock it off, Nick. Just because I've been drinking the few times you've seen me doesn't mean that's all I do. There's nothing wrong with a drink here and there. I'm sure you even have one now and then."

"No, I don't. I told you, I don't drink anymore."

"Yeah, that's what you keep telling me. Excuse me if I have trouble believing that."

Nick lowered his head and rubbed his hands over his face, then let out a long sigh. He looked back up at her, his expression serious. "I'm an alcoholic, Kayla."

His admission hung between them, as loud as if he had shouted it in the silence of the room. Mike stared at him, understanding the words, but not quite grasping their meaning. Nick, an alcoholic? She had trouble putting the image together with the man sitting just a few feet away from her. He watched her expectantly and she realized he was waiting for her to say something. Mike cleared her throat and searched her mind for something, anything, but came up blank.

"Um, okay."

Nick sighed and shook his head, then flopped back against the cushions. Mike took another sip of the brandy and watched him, still having trouble believing him. She stretched her legs in front of her and shifted into a more comfortable position, resting her head against the overstuffed cushion. She had the feeling that there was a specific reason he had made his confession to her, but her thinking was becoming blessedly numb thanks to the medication and brandy.

Unless *that* was why he had said it. Did he think

that she—? She straightened and narrowed her eyes at Nick. "Are you saying you think I'm an alcoholic?"

"What?" Nick raised his head and leveled a cool glare at her.

"I said—"

"I know what you said. And no, that's not what I'm saying. Do I think you drink too much? Yeah. Do I think you could cross that line? Absolutely. But—"

"How dare you! Where do you get off—"

"Forget it, forget I said anything!" Nick yelled, jumping from the loveseat and grabbing his sweatshirt. He didn't even bother putting it on, just tossed it over his shoulder while he searched for his coat. "No matter what I say, you're going to take it the wrong way, so forget it."

Mike slowly stood, swaying slightly with the motion. "Then tell me how else I'm supposed to take that! First you make a comment about my drinking, then you tell me you're an alcoholic. What am I supposed to think?"

Nick found his coat and thrust his arms into the sleeves, the movements short and jerky as he turned to face Mike. Even in the dim light from the kitchen, she could see the flush spreading across his face, see the way he was clenching his jaw. He ran a hand through his hair then exhaled loudly. "That's not why I told you, Kayla."

Mike fought against her own anger, trying to control it like Nick was obviously trying to control his. Except she didn't have his self-control. She stepped around the furniture, steadying herself on the back of the loveseat, then leaned against it, folding her arms across her chest. "Then why, Nick? For sympathy? Hell, it's not like you need sympathy points anymore. You already got what you came for!"

She regretted the words as soon as they left her mouth. It had been a spiteful thing to say, completely uncalled for and totally out of line. And so far from the truth. Mike bit down on her lower lip, hard, before taking a deep breath. "I'm sorry, that wasn't—"

Nick stepped back as if she had slapped him. He held out a rigid hand to stop her, taking another step away from her. The air between them thickened, becoming so heavy that Mike thought it would suffocate her, and still he didn't speak. He just stood there, watching her, his expression hooded and blank. Time stretched, and Mike's nerves stretched right along with it. She pushed away from the loveseat and took a step closer to Nick, wanting to close the distance between them. She reached a hand in his direction then let her arm drop to her side when he remained still.

"Nick, I didn't mean—"

"You know what Kayla? I don't care. Say whatever you want, it doesn't matter. It doesn't matter what you say, or what you think, or what you feel. Yeah, there's a ton of baggage between us, but that— that was uncalled for and one hell of a lot more than I think I deserve." He paused, his steady gaze holding hers for a long minute before he looked away and buttoned his coat with jerky movements. Mike's breath caught in her chest when he looked back at her, unguarded emotion clear in his dark eyes.

She took another step toward him, trying to think of something to say, anything to stop him from saying what she knew was coming next. Because she didn't want him to say goodbye and she knew that's what he was going to do. After everything that had happened between them—all those years ago, the last month, tonight—the bad history didn't matter because she still couldn't bear to hear him say goodbye. But she knew it was coming, could see it in his eyes, in the set of his shoulders and the tilt of his head. And for some inexplicable reason, she knew this would hurt a hundred times more than when he had disappeared from her life without a word ten years ago. "Nick, please, I didn't—"

"I can't stand by and watch you destroy yourself, Kayla. Yeah, I might be responsible for some of it, probably more than I want to admit, but I can't watch it. I had thought...well, I guess it doesn't matter what I thought, now does it?" He paused, watching her for a long minute, then took a deep breath and reached behind him for the door knob. "I'll see you around Kayla."

The door opened, letting in a soft blast of cold damp air, then quietly shut behind him when he walked out. Mike stared at the empty space where Nick had been standing just a second earlier, not really understanding what he had just said, not believing what had just happened.

She leaned against the loveseat and continued staring at the door, grateful for the final numbness brought on by the pain medication. And the alcohol.

Mike blinked her eyes hard several times then pushed away from the loveseat, at a momentary loss for what to do. Her gaze drifted toward the stairs, then over to the kitchen. To the empty bottle of brandy sitting in the trashcan.

She stared at it, frowning. Thinking. Then she shook her head and finally turned toward the steps, slowly climbing the stairs. Returning to her cold, empty bed.

Chapter Twenty

"What the fuck, Mike? What the hell did you do this time?"

Jay's loud voice bounced off the kitchen walls, raking down her spine and echoing in her head. Mike turned from the bulletin board she was cleaning off and stared at him, her eyes widened in shock at his unusual outburst. She looked around, thinking he was yelling at someone else. But no, he had yelled her name, nobody else's. And she was the only one left in the kitchen.

"What are you talking about?" Her voice was calmer than she expected, considering Jay's tone had automatically put her on the defensive.

"This. Have you seen it yet?" He advanced on her, a sheet of paper clenched in his fist. Mike threw the yellowed notice she was holding into the trash, wiped her hands along her pants, then took the paper from him, studying him for a brief second before looking down at it. She scanned it quickly, then went back and read it more slowly, a knot of apprehension fisting in her stomach at the words.

"Oh shit, I am so completely fucked," she mumbled. She closed her eyes and let out a deep breath, trying to come up with an explanation or excuse that would save her hide. Her mind was disgustingly blank.

"Make that doubly fucked when Captain Nelson sees it, especially after that stupid letter you wrote." Jay sat in one of the wooden seats and leaned over the table, watching her carefully. She returned his gaze then sat down herself and rested her head on her folded arms with a groan.

The 'stupid letter' Jay mentioned had been the rough draft, get-it-out-of-her-system, not-intended-for-anyone-to-see venting letter explaining why she could no longer participate in the awareness program at Buckley High, detailing conflict of interest and personal reasons—including animosity between the school's liaison and herself. The letter had been on the bottom of the pile of papers she had tossed on the captain's desk two tricks ago, right before that rescue where she had been clobbered. The only thing that had saved her on that one had been Jay's quick thinking and fancy explanations.

Mike lifted her head and scanned the new letter, her stomach literally turning in fear and apprehension. She was so screwed, it wasn't even funny. She might as well clean out her locker now, because there was no doubt Captain Nelson would have her transferred after this.

Because the letter in her hand was from one Mr. Nick Lansing, politely inquiring if other personnel were available to assist with the awareness program, citing his inability to work with her.

Due to personal reasons and conflict of interest.

An image of her instructional certifications being ripped from her and sucked into a vortex flashed through her mind. She didn't even want to think of the hell Captain Nelson would inflict on her. Fear gripped her again at the thought of being transferred. There was no doubt he'd try. Could he really make that happen? She didn't know but she wouldn't put it past him. He was next on the Chief's list and wouldn't appreciate anything that might mar his reputation—real or imagined. No, he wouldn't put up with this, no matter what she said to refute it.

And no matter how hard she tried, she couldn't think of one single thing to explain away the letter, not when it so closely mirrored hers.

"So what happened? Why would he suddenly write this?" Jay asked, his voice a little calmer. Good for him, since she was anything but calm. Mike looked up at him and laughed, the sound short and brittle.

"I slept with him, then he told me he was an alcoholic."

Jay's eyes widened, surprise clear on his face. He looked away and cleared his throat, then shifted in the chair. A minute went by, filled with more throat clearing, before he looked at her again. "Well, okay. Yeah. That makes a lot of sense."

He looked so flustered that Mike almost wanted to laugh. Almost. Unfortunately, the situation had drained even her warped sense of humor. She leaned back in the chair and stared up at the ceiling, wishing the aging tiles would crumble and fall on top of her. Maybe it would injure her enough that she would be placed off duty until this entire farce was over.

Minutes went by and she knew that all the wishful thinking in the world wasn't going to help. It was too late for that. She mumbled a curse and shook her head, unable to shake the feeling of doom that had grabbed her when she first read the letter.

"Um, Mikey, I don't mean to make things worse, but what you said makes absolutely no sense at all."

"It makes as much sense as the relationship between Nick and me has ever made," she muttered, mostly to herself. She had known he was upset when he left that night, but she never thought he'd do this.

"So when did this, um, you know, um—"

"When did I screw him?"

Jay winced at her bluntness, a faint blush tingeing his cheeks as he nodded, quickly adding, "I don't want the details."

"Three days after the rescue. He came by because we missed the meeting and he wanted to know what was going on. We started talking, he helped me upstairs, one thing led to another and we, well, you can use your imagination."

"No thank you, I think I'll pass on that one." Jay slid the letter across the table and read it to himself, then sat back. "So then what happened? I don't get that part about him telling you he was an alcoholic."

Mike shifted uncomfortably in her chair, unable to face Jay. She took a deep breath for courage, then let the confession tumble out. "Later, I went downstairs for some more medicine, and decided to have a drink. He told me he was an alcoholic and I asked him if he was accusing me of being one. When he said no, I asked why he bothered to tell me because he didn't need sympathy points since we'd already had sex."

Silence filled the room, making Mike even more uncomfortable than she already was. The words, the admission, hadn't come easy, not when she still regretted what she had said that night. She finally looked up at Jay, unable to bear his silence, and saw him frowning at her. Her stomach knotted even more at the look.

"I know it was a stupid thing to say, and I tried apologizing, but it was too late. You don't have to look at me like I'm a total loser."

Jay's expression cleared and he finally shook his head, then reached out and patted her hand in what she supposed was meant as a reassuring gesture. "No, I don't think that. It's just, I'm still confused. I don't get it. I can understand him being angry—admit it, Mike, that was a stupid thing to say, even with your temper. But this," he pointed to the letter, "this seems a bit drastic. I mean, he had to know it would look bad."

"Why would he? It's not like he knows about the other letter, or how things work around here. And with everything that's happened between us, you can't really call it drastic, either. Inevitable, yes. I mean, something like this was bound to happen, especially with our history."

Jay continued looking at her, his confusion evident on his face. He shook his head again and tapped the letter. "But I still don't understand the conflict of interest part. Or what him telling you he was an alcoholic has to do with anything. I mean, he went to a rehab to dry out. It doesn't take a genius to figure out he was an alcoholic."

Mike sat up straighter in the chair and looked up at Jay, narrowing her eyes as she studied him. "What did you just say?"

He pushed back in his chair, looking like he expected her to jump at him. "Uh, which part?"

"The rehab part."

"Oh. Um, yeah. Why?"

"What rehab?"

Jay's eyes widened and he mumbled something under his breath, giving Mike the distinct impression that he just realized he said something he shouldn't have. She fixed him with her sternest glare, making him squirm in his seat. His eyes darted around the room, as if he was looking for something to save him. Unfortunately for him, there was nothing there to help.

"I thought you knew," Jay muttered. He squirmed again, then finally cleared his throat and fixed his gaze on the wall behind her. "Nick went to rehab after your accident. To dry out."

"When did you find this out?"

"Right after we started this thing. The second meeting, maybe? I don't remember." He leaned forward, his gray eyes serious, studying her. "You really didn't know?"

Mike shook her head, too stunned to say anything. Not that there was really anything to say. She looked down at the letter, seeing only blurred black lines as one thought after another tumbled through her mind. Nick had gone to a rehab. But when? And why? For how long? She thought back, but didn't see a reason for it. Yeah, he had definitely known how to drink, and had loved to party, but an alcoholic? It didn't make sense.

Not that it mattered now, anyway. Like Jay had said, she couldn't see a connection. And it didn't concern her, regardless. The only thing that concerned her now was the letter in front of her, and how she could dig herself out of the hole it put her in. She picked the sheet of paper back up and scanned it again.

"How did you get this, anyway?" Mike finally asked.

"The mail just came and I was sorting through it. Why?"

"Because it's the original, not a copy."

"Yeah. He mailed it directly to the station, not through headquarters. Why?"

Mike fingered the letter, thinking. An idea was forming, giving her a slim chance to make things right. Or dig herself an even deeper hole. She looked up at Jay, and knew exactly when he realized what she was thinking.

"The Captain's off this whole trick, right?"

"Yeah. Mike, you can't—"

"That gives me the rest of this trick, plus the four days we're off. Seven days. Did you show this to anyone else?"

"No. Mikey, if you get caught—"

"I'm not going to get caught. I'm just going to see if I can talk to Nick, maybe come to an agreement."

"And what if he mailed a copy to headquarters? Suppose this isn't the only copy floating around? What are you going to do if someone else finds out? Mike, you're taking a big chance."

She folded the letter and tucked it into her pocket, then gave Jay an innocent look. "What chance? Mail gets misplaced all the time. Besides, what's the worse they can do? Suspend me? Transfer me? The same thing could happen when the captain sees the letter. You know how he's strictly by-the-book and wouldn't hesitate to write me up."

"I still think it's a big risk. Suppose Nick pushes the issue? What do you think will happen then? It's too big a chance to take."

"Yeah, well, I have to try. I don't have any other choice."

Chapter Twenty-One

Nick grasped the guitar loosely in his hands and stared down at the sheet in front of him, frowning at the scattered notes. He shook his head, took the pencil from his mouth and made some quick changes, then picked out the new chords. He repeated them then nodded to himself, satisfied with the sound. Mellow, a little bluesy, perfectly matching his mood. Just for good measure he plucked the notes of the song from the beginning, listening critically. Not too bad. Needed a little tweaking, but getting there.

He leaned the guitar against the sofa then stood and stretched, feeling his back pop with the movement. He walked over to the stereo and popped in a CD then moved to the kitchen to fix dinner, the sounds of Kenny Wayne Shepherd following him.

Nick just finished fixing his plate when the doorbell rang. Sighing, he looked at the clock on the microwave and muttered to himself, covered the plate, then went to answer the door. The bell rang again as he walked down the short flight of stairs of the split-level, and he bit back a comment about patience.

"Yeah?" He opened the door, already planning on getting rid of whoever was there, then paused. Kayla was standing on the front porch, dressed in her uniform, her face expressionless. Nick braced his arm against the doorframe, effectively blocking her from entering, and stared at her. "What do you want?"

She eyed him warily, her gaze taking in his unwelcoming posture, and shifted her weight from one foot to the other. "I was wondering if we could talk."

"I really don't have anything to say."

Kayla paused, obviously not expecting to hear him say that. She cleared her throat and looked over at the driveway, then leaned to the side to look past him. Nick eased the door closed a fraction, just enough to block her view. Kayla straightened and looked directly at him then quickly looked away, her shoulders slumping just a bit.

"Then would it be okay if I talked to you?"

"What about?"

She muttered something under her breath and Nick instinctively knew she hadn't expected a hard time from him. And why should she have? After all, he had been the one pursuing her, approaching her, trying to get closer to her. Kayla mumbled something else then reached into an inside jacket pocket and pulled out a folded sheet of paper, holding it out to him. He reluctantly reached out and took it from her then opened it.

"Where did you get this?"

"Could I maybe come in so we can talk about it? In case you haven't noticed, it's a little cold out here."

Nick watched her for another minute, his expression carefully blank, then handed the letter back to her and stepped aside, motioning for her to come in. She mumbled a thank you then followed him up the stairs. He walked through the living room and into the kitchen, Kayla a few feet behind him. He placed the plate in the microwave, set the timer and then hit the start button before turning around to face her.

"So what do you want?"

She looked noticeably uncomfortable, shifting awkwardly as he watched her. Her gaze darted around the kitchen, finally settling on something behind him as she took a deep breath. "I'd like you to reconsider what you said in the letter."

"No." Nick turned when the timer went off and removed the plate from the microwave, gave the contents a quick stir, then replaced it and reset the timer. Kayla was still staring at him in surprise when he turned back around.

"Why not?"

"Because we can't work together. You know it. I know it. If we keep working together, the program will fall apart. I can't let that happen."

"What do you mean, the program will fall apart? That's a crock of shit and you know it."

"No, I don't know it."

Kayla looked away from him and shook her head in disbelief, obviously thinking she had been going to change his mind. Nick removed his dinner from the microwave and put it on the island counter, then pulled a bottle of water from the refrigerator. The only sound in the room was the bluesy rock drifting in from the stereo, which suited Nick fine. He took a seat at the counter and started eating, resolved to ignore Kayla.

"So how did you get the letter?" Nick finally asked after several long minutes and a few bites of food. He hadn't planned on asking her, was going to ignore her until she left, but it wasn't as easy as he thought it would be. Not with her standing there watching him, something close to desperation on her face.

"It came in the mail at the station and I opened it."

"Funny. I don't remember addressing it to you."

She ignored him, looking at a spot above his shoulder. Nick sighed and resumed eating, the leftover sweet and sour chicken and fried rice now tasting gritty and too tart against his tongue.

"I don't understand it, Nick. One thing shouldn't have anything to do with the other."

Nick dropped his fork on the plate with a clang and pushed it away, his appetite gone. He propped his elbows on the counter and fixed her with a steady look. "And what one thing would that be, Kayla?"

She motioned with her hand between them, her discomfort obvious. "You know, the other week. And what happened."

"No, tell me. What exactly happened? The no-strings fuck you asked for, or our little discussion afterward?"

Her face paled but she didn't look away, which is what Nick had expected. He continued watching her, waiting for her to say something, wondering what excuse, what story she would come up with. But she didn't say anything, just finally sighed and hoisted herself on the stool across from him, easing off her jacket when she got settled. He noticed the small wince when she did, only because he was looking for it, and almost asked if she was feeling any better.

But he didn't, just raised an eyebrow in her direction, half-tempted to remind her that he hadn't invited her to stay. He opened his mouth to say just that but she spoke up first.

"Did you really go into rehab?" Her question was hesitant, her voice barely above a whisper, and she didn't look at him when she asked it. It caught him so off-guard that Nick's pulse actually stopped for a few seconds. He wondered how she had found out, but as soon as the question entered his mind, he knew the answer. Her buddy at work, Jay.

Nick muttered a curse and stood up so quickly the stool rocked backward. He caught it before it fell then grabbed his plate and dumped it into the sink, scraps and all. He didn't have a problem with Kayla knowing but he didn't feel up to the sarcastic comments he was sure she would make.

"Were you?" She asked again, her voice still quiet. Nick leaned against the counter and folded his arms across his chest, studying her.

"Yeah, I was."

"Why?"

"Now why do you think? For the same reason most people go into rehab. Because I had a drinking problem, that's why."

Kayla didn't say anything, just sat there on the stool, drawing an invisible circle on the island countertop with her finger. She finally stopped her imaginary doodling, took a deep breath, and looked up at him. "But you didn't have a problem."

"Yeah, Kayla, I did."

"How? And when? I don't remember you drinking that much."

Nick gabbed the bottle of water from the counter and took a long swallow, watching her closely, wondering why she was suddenly so interested. Was it merely curiosity? Or something more? He recapped the bottle then hoisted himself up on the counter, leaning forward so he wouldn't bang his head against the cabinets behind him. His hands gripped the edge of the counter as he thought about how much to tell her.

How could she not remember? Life had been one endless party. Beer. Whiskey. A little pot. Music and sex. That was all that had mattered. Nothing else. Getting drunk, maybe high. Playing his music.

Spending time with Kayla.

Every day. Day after day. How could she not remember?

"Kayla, I drank all the time. *All* the time. Between the alcohol and the occasional pot, I was stoned more than I was sober. Are you honestly going to tell me you don't remember that?"

She bit her lower lip and slowly shook her head. "Not really, no. I mean, yeah, you partied a lot, but you were, what? Eighteen? Nineteen? Everybody parties at that age."

"Partying? Is that what you think I was doing?" Nick paused then took another sip of water, shaking his head. "It was one hell of a lot more than partying, Kayla. What did you think I was doing while you were in school? Do you think I waited to start drinking until I picked you up at night?"

"No. I don't know. I guess I never thought about it."

"Yeah, I guess not. Do you want to know what I did that night after the accident? After leaving the hospital and after the police got through with me? I went out and got drunk, and I got stoned, and I pretty much stayed that way for several days straight. Right after the accident. Right after I damn near killed you." His voice broke and he swallowed against the sudden thickness in his throat. He closed his eyes and rested his head against the cabinet, trying to banish the memories, trying to breathe against the despair that threatened to drown him.

He took a deep breath then grabbed the water bottle and took another sip, almost wishing it was something stronger. Kayla was silent. He looked over at her, surprised to see that she was just sitting there, her face expressionless, still doodling on the counter with her finger.

Minutes ticked by, filled with nothing but the music coming from the stereo. The last song on the CD faded and Nick heard the faint click of the disc changer as it chose a new CD. He inwardly groaned when he recognized it as one he burned himself, full of older slow rock songs that were popular when he and Kayla had been dating. Quite a few of them held more than just a casual memory, too. Perfect. Just what he needed, tonight of all nights. Nick spared a glance in Kayla's direction but she didn't seem to notice.

Her silence was beginning to make him uncomfortable, because it was too unlike her. At least, what he knew of this new Kayla, which wasn't a whole lot once he stopped to think about it. She had been right the other night when she said that, except for the meetings they had been forced to have, they had only seen each other personally several times in the last two months. And with the exception of the other night, none of those encounters had lasted very long, or amounted to much.

God, had it really only been a few times? And only a couple of months? It felt like so much longer. It felt like the last ten years had never happened, that they had never spent time apart.

But that didn't make things any easier, not with the history between them—because the last ten years *had* happened and they really didn't know one another, not any more. Nick sighed and finished off the water, then recapped the bottle and sat it on the counter.

"So why did you write the letter?" Kayla's question penetrated the silence, startling Nick. He turned toward her to see that she was standing now, leaning against the counter with the letter in front of her. He took a deep breath and let it out, then leaned his head against the cabinet, wondering if it would be better to stay where he was, or to get down off the counter and stand instead.

Nick ran a hand over his face then hopped off the counter and threw the empty bottle in the trash can. He turned to face Kayla, crossing his arms in front of him. "I wrote it because I really don't think we can work together, Kayla. Not on this. The first presentation is supposed to take place in two weeks, and right now, it's the furthest thing from my mind. There's too much tension between us, Kayla. Even you have to be able to see that."

He paused to see her reaction but she just stood there, watching him with a blank look. She finally shook her head and glanced back at the letter in her hand.

"Tension or not, this was a bit drastic, don't you think? I mean, we're both grown adults. We should be able to work around it."

"Kayla, I have too much riding on this program. I can't afford to have it get messed up."

She looked up at him, a spark flashing in her eyes. "You're not the only one who has a lot riding on it. If I get pulled from this, our captain will go ballistic. At best, he's going to write me up. At worst, they could yank my certification or transfer me. Knowing Captain Nelson, I wouldn't be surprised if he tried to have me suspended."

"I'm supposed to believe that? After you already told me that Jay was the one who was supposed to be doing everything?" Nick leaned against the counter, making no attempt to hide his suspicion.

"Yeah. Jay *is* supposed to do everything, and he will because he needs this for his next level. But he can't do it without someone else overseeing and evaluating. I'm the only one on our shift with the qualification to do that. Our captain wants this project to stay on our shift, because it'll look good for him when promotions come up." She held up the letter and waved it in Nick's direction, the movement sharp and angry. "If I get yanked, Jay will get probably get yanked, which will make our captain extremely unhappy."

"Kayla, I don't—"

"Come off it, Nick. There's got to be a way to work around this." She paused, looking him squarely in the eye, beseeching. "Please."

The sincerity in her voice and the pleading in her eyes did him in. He bit back an oath and shook his head, knowing that somehow, he was going to regret what he was about to do. Taking a deep breath, he moved the two steps to the counter island and grabbed the letter, then tore it in half, and half again. "There. It's done. Is that what you wanted?"

Kayla sighed and closed her eyes, her lips moving silently. Nick couldn't tell what she had muttered to herself, but the relief was evident in her eyes when she reopened them and looked at him. "Thank you."

Nick was silent for a minute, then fixed her with a hard look, stepping closer to her. "Don't thank me yet, Kayla. If we're going to do this, we're doing it my way. No more battles, no more tension, no more butting heads. Can you do that?"

"I—"

"Can you? Because if you can't, tell me now and that'll be it. I'll send another letter, and I'll make sure you can't get to it first. Do we have a deal?"

A range of emotions flickered across her face, from surprise to resentment to reluctant acceptance. She pursed her lips and nodded, a quick jerk of her head. "Fine. But what is it you want to do differently?"

Nick studied her, then stepped away, putting a safe distance between them. "I'll get in touch with Jay and let him know."

"Fine."

"Good."

They stared at each other, awareness and tension pulsating between them. Kayla finally looked away and grabbed her jacket, pulling it on and zipping it with surprising speed, like she couldn't leave fast enough. She cast a quick glance at Nick and took a deep breath. "Thank you."

Nick nodded his acknowledgment and watched as she walked out of the kitchen. He followed her as she made her way to the door. "Kayla," he called.

She paused at the door and looked up at him. "Yeah?"

"What would you have done if I had said no? If I hadn't changed my mind?"

Her shoulders slumped and she looked away for a minute, considering. She opened the door then looked back at him, her face carefully blank, her eyes not quite meeting his. "I don't know."

Nick continued standing there after she left, staring at the closed door, and wondered if she had told him the truth.

Chapter Twenty-Two

"Tell me again why we're here," Mike said to Jay when he pulled his truck into the parking lot of a bar and grill. Jay turned the engine off and got out, not bothering to wait for her. Mike rushed to catch up to him, wondering why he seemed to be in such a hurry.

"Because this is where Nick said to meet him. Other than that, I have no idea."

"This is ridiculous. How are we supposed to work in here?" Mike asked when they walked through the door. It was close to five o'clock and the happy hour crowd was starting to thicken in the bar, the noise a raucous symphony around them. Jay paused at the entrance and looked around, then turned to face Mike, his expression serious and unforgiving.

"Ridiculous or not, you just better be grateful Nick reconsidered. You have one hell of a lot more to lose than I do, so you better just keep the remarks to yourself."

Mike bit back the retort she wanted to make, knowing that Jay was right. For the moment, they were at Nick's mercy. Or rather, she was. It wasn't a position she enjoyed. Worse, she couldn't figure out what Nick had in mind. Because there was no doubt he had something planned, and she was sure she wasn't going to like it one bit once she figured it out.

"There he is." Jay pointed to a table in the far corner of the restaurant side and threaded his way through the crowd, dragging Mike with him. They reached the booth and Jay motioned for her to slide in first then he followed, setting his bag containing the files on the floor next to him. Mike slid further into the corner, doing her best not to look at Nick, which was difficult since his gaze was focused directly on her.

"Did you guys want to eat first?" Nick asked, finally pulling his gaze away from her. She breathed a sigh of relief and stretched out more comfortably, straightening her legs in front of her.

"Maybe just something light, I can't stay long."

"What?" Mike turned and stared at Jay, not believing what he said. "What do you mean, you can't stay long?"

"Just what I said. I have a date later."

"Date, my ass. Why didn't you say something earlier? Just how am I supposed to get home? You're the one who drove!"

"I'll drop you off."

Mike turned to face Nick, not bothering to hide her anger. The vague uneasiness she had felt ever since Jay had told her about this meeting solidified with the suspicion that she was being set up. She turned her look on Jay, narrowing her eyes at him. "You had this planned, didn't you?"

"Actually, no. I was planning on dropping you

off before my date, but this will work out, too."

"The hell it will—"

"Mikey, we're wasting time. Let's just grab something quick so we can get on with this." Jay's voice was calm, but far from reassuring. She studied him, looking for some sign that he was lying. His face was a picture of perfect innocence, which only made her even more suspicious. She bit the inside of her cheek to stop herself from saying anything and leaned back in the corner, nodding her silent acquiescence against her will.

A waitress showed up at their table less than a minute later, her attention called by Nick. She smiled down at him and Mike rolled her eyes at the obvious interest on the girl's face. Nick and Jay agreed to split a large serving of nachos, then Nick looked at her expectantly.

"Nachos are fine. And a margarita," she added. "On the rocks, no salt."

"No alcohol."

"Excuse me?" Mike stared at Nick, her expression clearly telling him what she thought.

"No alcohol. That's one of the conditions."

Mike glared at him, silently stewing at his high-handedness. So this was what he was up to. Fine. Like it really mattered to her. She waved her hand at the waitress, who was watching them with undisguised curiosity. "Whatever. I'll have an iced tea then. No big deal."

The waitress left with their order and Mike sank further into the corner when Jay pulled out a stack of files. Nick rearranged the table to give them more room and the two of them got down to business, planning in more detail what should happen with the first presentation. Mike tuned them out, not interested, still steaming from the obvious set-up.

"So what do you think, Mike?"

"Huh?" She looked up at Jay, who was watching her expectantly. "Think about what? This isn't my show, remember? I'm here to observe and evaluate and sign off, that's it."

"Not anymore. That's another condition. From here on out, you're taking a more active role in this," Nick said, his tone of voice telling her that it was a demand, not a request. She stared at him, clenching her jaw and doing her best not to say anything. Her effort collapsed after five seconds, and she slapped her hand down on the table.

"That's it. This is such bullshit. Let's get something straight, Nick. This isn't my project. It never was. I'm not *supposed* to have anything to do with this. And for you—"

"Mike, take it easy." Jay rested a hand on her arm and tried to ease her back into the seat. She shook his touch off, not even sparing him a glance.

"No. For you to sit there and start making demands—ridiculous demands. This is outrageous Nick, and you know it. You have no right to do this!"

Jay stiffened next to her and mumbled something but she paid him no attention, instead focusing on Nick. He sat up straight across from her, his dark gaze intense as he studied her. A minute went by before he reached into the pocket of the blazer he was wearing and pulled out a sealed envelope. He held it in his hand for a second, then slowly reached across the table, holding it out for her to take. She looked down at the envelope, noticed the address of fire department headquarters neatly typed across the front, and felt her stomach sink.

Nick held the envelope out for another second then, when she made no move to take it, placed it in the middle of the table and pushed it toward her. "We made a deal the other night when I told you that I was going to change things. This is part of that deal. Now you can either go along with it, or I can mail this letter. And you can be sure it's not going to go where you can get it first."

Mike slumped back in her seat and stared first at Nick then at the letter, trying hard to rein in her temper. A tense silence fell over them, a silence that wasn't even eased when the waitress returned with their order and quickly placed it on the table in front of them.

"Mikey." Jay's voice was a tense whisper, holding a warning in that single low tone. She turned to face him, staring, looking for help in his gaze. What she saw didn't ease her mind at all. Instead of help or even reassurance, she saw warning—and even impatience. She looked away from Jay, not liking the feeling that she had just lost support from her best friend, then took a deep breath and faced Nick, speaking in an angry hiss when the waitress left.

"This is blackmail, Nick. And really low."

Nick shrugged then scooped some nachos from the plate and took a bite. He chewed the food, then fixed her with a steady gaze. "I never said I wouldn't stoop to low tactics."

Mike ran her hands through her hair and fought the very strong urge to bang her head against the table. She let out a deep breath and turned back to Jay. "What do you think?"

Jay returned her look, that same expression on

his face. He reached under the table to give her leg a reassuring squeeze. "I don't think you have a choice."

Chapter Twenty-Three

More than three hours later, Mike was still stuck with Nick, completely against her will, and totally alone. Jay had abandoned her two hours ago, leaving for his date, handing the files over to Nick so they could continue to tweak the first presentation. To Mike's surprise, Nick had put the files away and suggested they order dinner, which she reluctantly agreed to. There was no sense in starving herself just to prove a point.

The surprises continued when Nick then suggested they continue work at his house once they finished eating, using the noise and crowd as an excuse. Mike said absolutely nothing, just shot him numerous dirty looks when they left the restaurant and drove to his place.

And now here she was, sitting on the leather sofa in his living room, seething with anger while Nick went to change. Mike glanced at her watch and wondered how long this charade was going to last. It was already after eight o'clock. Surely Nick would want to call it quits soon since it was a weeknight and she was certain he had to work in the morning.

All she wanted to do right now was go home, change into her flannel pajamas and a t-shirt, and have a drink. A nice, stiff drink. She was sure Nick would turn *that* one around to mean something menacing if she told him.

And speak of the devil, here he came. She looked up as Nick came down the hallway from his bedroom and wished she had that drink right now. He was barefoot, wearing a pair of loose, low-slung sweatpants and a ratty old tank shirt. Mike swallowed a groan and tried to look like she wasn't interested in the change of scenery.

"It's a little cold to be wearing a tank shirt, isn't it?" She didn't bother to hide the sarcasm from her voice. Sarcasm was ten times better than letting him think, even for a second, that she was effected by the sight of his broad shoulders and sculpted arms. Nick paused to stare at her as if she was crazy, then walked over to the built-in entertainment center.

"Did you need me to turn the heat up?" His voice was laced with insincere hospitality and Mike bit back another sarcastic comment, knowing he would only turn it around like he did with the shirt comment. He raised his eyebrows at her silence, the barest hint of a grin teasing the corners of his mouth, then turned away and sorted through a collection of CD's, inserting them into the stereo. Mike watched him, noticing the play of muscles in his back and arms. Her eyes widened when she noticed the tattoo high up on the back of his right shoulder.

"When did you get the tattoo?" She immediately regretted the question and wished she could take it back. Shouldn't she have noticed the other night when they were together? When she had been in bed with him. Naked. Not that she had been paying any attention to his back.

Nick hit a button on the stereo then turned to face her. "When did you get yours?"

"How did—never mind." Mike looked away, cursing the blush heating her face. Nick walked over to the sofa and sat down next to her, entirely too close. She edged away from him, only managing to move a few inches because she was already sitting as far over as she could go. Any further and she would be sitting on the arm of the sofa. Or the floor.

"I guess I was the only one paying any attention to the details the other night, hm?" Nick draped his arm across the back of the sofa, his hand grazing her shoulder, and watched her in silence. Mike closed her eyes and barely refrained from groaning out loud, both at his nearness and at the realization he must have been awake when she got out of bed the other night. That was the only way he would have been able to see the small dolphin tattoo in the middle of her lower back.

"So, um, why don't we just finish up with this presentation? Where did you put the files?" Mike looked everywhere but at Nick, needing to change the subject before she embarrassed herself even more. He shifted next to her, stretching his legs out and propping them on the glass coffee table in front of them. He was so close, she could feel the heat of his legs next to hers. The heat of his arm where it barely touched her shoulders.

"Actually, I think we did enough for tonight. We can give it a break for now."

Mike clenched her jaw and turned to stare at him, not trying to hide her surprise or her anger. "Then what the hell am I doing here? I thought the whole point was to do some more work."

"I changed my mind."

"Yeah, right." Mike watched him for another second then abruptly stood, her fists clenched at her side. Anger coursed through her and she welcomed it, knowing it was better than the other emotions warring within her, unwelcome and confusing. "I want to go home. I mean it, Nick. I don't know what game you're playing, but you can count me out. Now take me home."

If she had been expecting a reaction, she was going to be disappointed. He didn't move, not even to raise an eyebrow at her demand. Nick just sat there, looking too relaxed and too comfortable, his legs stretched out in front of him and his arm still draped across the back of the sofa. He watched her, his dark eyes intense, piercing. Long minutes went by, filled only with the music coming from the stereo. Mike recognized it as the same CD that had been playing the other night when she stopped by, the one filled with songs that held too many memories. Watching Nick sit there, looking at her with that dark intense gaze, she wondered if it had been a deliberate choice. If the music meant to him what it did to her, or if it was nothing more than a casual coincidence.

Nick stood suddenly, his lean body unfolding from the sofa with a powerful grace that made Mike take a step backward. He closed the distance between them, tension radiating from him in suffocating waves that froze her in place. He stopped an inch in front of her, staring down at her, holding her in place with nothing more than a look. Mike swallowed her sudden uncertainty and forced her gaze away from his, needing to break the hold he had on her. How was that possible, after all these years?

"Nick, please take me home." Her voice was just above a whisper, pleading. But she didn't care if it made her sound weak. She was weak, where Nick was concerned. She had always been weak with Nick. And she wanted—needed—to leave.

But Nick said nothing and she wondered if he had heard her because he just stood there, looking at her, his expression unreadable. Slowly he reached out for her, his hand gently closing around her arm and pulling her to him. His other arm wrapped around her back, tucking her body against his in a tentative embrace. Mike stiffened and placed her hands against his chest, trying to push away, only to have him tighten his hold. "Nick, take me home."

"Not yet," he whispered. His hand drifted up her back and behind her neck, then cradled her head and guided it to rest on his shoulder. His body began swaying to the music, so slow at first that Mike didn't realize what he was doing. Her eyes closed and she swallowed, not wanting to follow his lead but doing it anyway. "Remember when you said you wanted to go back, just for a little bit? To pretend like nothing happened?"

Mike nodded, not trusting her voice, wondering where Nick was heading. His arm tightened around her waist, pulling her even closer, and his lips grazed her temple, a fleeting touch that was there and gone before Mike could react.

"That's the final condition. While we work on this, we pretend the last ten years never happened,"

Nick explained, his voice a soft breath against her ear. The words, wrapped in the seductive whisper of his voice, sent a shiver through her. She leaned forward, melting against him. It was too easy; it felt too good, even though her mind was screaming *no*. "We pretend to go back, just for a little bit."

Mike pulled away, but not hard enough to break his hold on her. Anger flared then stilled, disappearing just below the surface, replaced for a brief moment by fleeting hope. She bit down on her lower lip and rested her forehead on his bare shoulder, just for a second before reality crashed over her. She pulled back again, still not breaking Nick's hold, but no longer leaning against him.

"That's impossible, Nick, and you know it. You can't make it a condition. It'll never work."

"How do you know?" He studied her with a quiet intensity that disturbed her because she didn't understand it. His eyes searched hers, silent and dark as his fingers gently rubbed the back of her neck. Nick's right arm was still wrapped lightly around her waist, leading her in the gentle sway of the music. Mike closed her eyes, no longer able to meet his gaze, tempted to give in to the hope he waved in front of her.

Tempted to give in to *him*.

But what he was suggesting was impossible. She could never forget; she wasn't sure if she could ever forgive. For all that she missed what they had before, they could never go back. They were two completely different people now.

"Kayla, look at me," Nick whispered. Reluctantly she did as he asked. Her breath caught in her throat at the look in his eyes and she had to fight to hold on to the reasons she had just given herself. "I'm not saying forget. Too much has happened for either one of us to do that."

"Then what are you saying?"

"I'm just saying that while we're doing this program, we pretend like nothing is wrong between us. That we spend time together, that we act like normal people. No animosity, no tension." He held her tightly against him, his hand rubbing circles on her lower back, distracting her. So much for the 'no tension', she thought. Mike closed her eyes, trying to concentrate, trying to remember why Nick's idea was a bad one.

"I don't think it's going to work."

"Will you at least try?"

She knew she should say no. There was no doubt that there was at least one ulterior motive behind his plan, probably more. Not to mention everything that could go wrong. But a small part of her, someplace deep down where she kept her secrets, wanted to say yes. To take just this small slice of time, this little bit of make-believe, and make it hers. To pretend there was no bad history between them. To pretend things were the way they used to be.

Mike took a deep breath and let it out slowly, then nodded. "Okay, I'll try."

It was probably her imagination but she thought some of the tension left Nick at her words. His arms tightened around her once more and she let go of the hesitation holding her back, allowing herself to lean against him, to wrap her arms around his waist.

Music drifted around them as they swayed in each other's arms, not saying anything. She had been wrong, she realized. There was still tension between them, but not like she thought. This was something completely different, heat flaring to life with awareness—and with her body's reaction to the nearness of his. As close as she was to Nick, pressed against him, it was obvious he felt it as well. Her breath hitched in her chest as her pulse soared, awareness and excitement building along with apprehension. Nick's lips trailed a light path along her jaw to her temple. Mike closed her eyes and tilted her head, her mouth seeking his and finding it.

The kiss was tentative at first, slow and searching, innocent and inquisitive. Nick's mouth opened under hers and their tongues met. The kiss exploded, detonating the desire within her. She leaned against him, her arms moving up and wrapping tightly around his neck, her body seeking to get closer. Nick moved quickly, backing her against the wall, cupping her face in his hands while his tongue invaded her mouth, doing dangerous things to her mind and body.

And to her soul.

His body pressed closer to hers. Her hips arched against him, rubbing against the hard length of his erection as her hands reached under his shirt and moved up his chest. A groan broke free from her, only to be swallowed by Nick's mouth, still ravenous on hers, hot and wet. Frantic.

Mike broke free from the kiss with effort, trailing her lips along his jaw and down his throat, nipping. She pushed his shirt up, exposing his chest, and trailed hot kisses along his heated flesh, feeling the rapid beat of his heart under her lips. He reached up and lightly gripped her chin, tilting her head back to claim her lips again, opening her mouth under his. The kiss slowed, then stilled, and Nick finally pulled away with a soft moan.

"I think it's time for me to take you home," he said in a ragged whisper. Mike shook her head to clear it, not grasping the meaning of his words. Her body was still anchored between him and the wall, and there was no denying that Nick was effected by their physical contact. She tilted her hips slightly against his and let out a moan of frustration when he pulled away.

She opened her eyes and looked up at him, at the heated desire burning in his gaze, and knew she hadn't heard him correctly. She leaned forward, only to have him pull away a little more. His thumb gently caressed her cheek as he stared down at her, leaving her confused. And frustrated.

"I need to take you home, Kayla," he repeated.

"Why? I don't—"

With a sigh, he stepped away, leaving her feeling cold and empty. She cursed her body's reaction to him, to the loss of him, even as she stared at him in bewilderment.

"Because I don't want you to think this is about sex. And if we keep this up, if we finish this, that's exactly what you're going to think."

Mike uttered a colorful curse in frustration. She ran her hands through her hair and clenched her jaw so tightly her back teeth were grinding. Did he really think he was doing either one of them any good by stopping? "God, this is so stupid! That is the stupidest thing I have ever heard! First you get me to agree to this stupid game, then you start something, and now you're telling me to stop! You're not making any sense, Nick."

"Yeah, I am. Look at me Kayla."

She waved him off and continued her frustrated pacing. She didn't know whether to laugh, cry, or scream. Or just run over and jump him and finish what he started. The choices made her even more frustrated, which increased her agitation.

"Kayla, stop and look at me."

"No. No, no, no. This is stupid, Nick. So stupid."

"Is it?" He finally grabbed her arm and pulled her into his embrace, a glint in his eye as he looked down at her. One corner of his mouth twitched and she realized he was trying not to laugh. She bit down on the inside of her cheek and tried to pull away, only to have his arms tighten around her.

"Let me go, Nick. I don't believe this! How can you stand there and laugh? This isn't funny!"

"You're right, it isn't. C'mon, hold still and listen to me." A smile briefly curved his lips before his expression turned serious again. He rocked his hips against hers, just once, leaving no doubt that his body, at least, wanted her. "Kayla, there is nothing more that I want than to take you right now, to make love to you all night long and then some."

"Then let's—"

"No. Because if I do, you're going to convince yourself that this is about sex, that that's all I want from you, and it's not. And then you're going to regret it, just like you regretted it the other week."

"I won't regret it, really."

Nick offered her a small smile, his arms briefly tightening around her waist. "Yeah, you will. And then you're going to pull away again and shut yourself down, and convince yourself it was another mistake. I don't want that to happen, not this time."

Mike squeezed her eyes tight, trying to contain

her frustration. He was being ridiculous and she searched her mind for a way to convince him of that. But every argument fell flat because at least part of what Nick was saying made sense—and it pissed her off that he could still know her so well, even after all this time. Because he was right, she *would* convince herself it was all a big mistake, and blame it all on Nick.

Which didn't say a whole lot about her. Did it make her just as crazy as he was, actually seeing the logic of his argument? She let out a loud sigh and eased away from his arms, part of her cursing the ease with which Nick let her go. She opened her eyes and watched him for a long minute, then took another step back, finally nodding.

"Alright, you win this one. Now take me home before I say something just as stupid as your insane idea."

"Insane, huh?"

"Yeah, insane." Mike turned away and grabbed her coat from the recliner where she had tossed it then shrugged it on, careful to keep her gaze averted from Nick. Outside she might look calm and reasonable, but inside she was shaking. The depth of her body's response to him scared her. The emotions that lurked beneath the surface terrified her. She refused to look at them too closely, afraid of what they might be. Worse, she was afraid of what she wanted them to be.

"Kayla." She jumped at Nick's whisper, surprised to realize that he was standing so close behind her. His arms wrapped around her waist from behind and he held her, resting his chin on top of her head. "Are you mad at me?"

She stiffened in his arms for a brief second then let herself relax as she shook her head. "No, I'm not mad. I do think you're crazy, though." She took a deep breath and forced herself to laugh, glad that her back was to him so he couldn't see her face—and the emotions she was sure were clearly written on it. "Now take me home so I can jump in a cold shower."

***

Nick watched from the warmth of his car as Kayla walked into the house, briefly waving at him before she closed the door. He had wanted to walk her in, felt bad about waiting in the car, but she had insisted. And in that she had been right, because if he had gone in with her, he wasn't sure if he would have left. It had been hard enough pulling away from her once. Twice would have taken more resolve than he possessed.

Because tonight had been, with a doubt, the dumbest thing he had ever done. He needed his head examined for turning Kayla down, especially since she was as hungry for him as he was for her. But his conscience wouldn't allow it, no matter what his body wanted.

And his sexual frustration aside, he was happy with the way tonight had gone. He had expected more of a fight from her when he mentioned each condition, especially the last one. Part of him still couldn't believe she had actually agreed. But she had, for which he was grateful. If he could just get her to let go of the past, even for a little bit, it would give them each a chance to get to know each other again. Not who they were back then, but who they were now. And if they did that...

Nick hoped it would be enough to convince Kayla to at least think about moving forward. That, more than anything, was what he wanted. He still had feelings for her, deep feelings, and all he wanted was a chance to see what they might be together now, without all the baggage from their past weighing them down.

He watched as the downstairs lights went off, followed by a dim glow from the upstairs window. A few minutes later and that, too, went dark. Nick sighed and put his car in reverse and slowly backed out of the driveway, feeling too much like a stalker watching the dark house.

Yes, Kayla's agreement had been a complete surprise and he was afraid to read too much into it. Part of him wanted to think that she only needed an excuse, no matter how weak, to spend time with him. That maybe part of her was willing to look forward to what they might be able to have together. The other part of him, the part rooted in reality, knew that her friend Jay probably had more to do with her agreement than anything else.

He sighed and cast one last glance at Kayla's darkened house, then drove away, wondering at all the things that could possibly go wrong.

Chapter Twenty-Four

"So how do you think it went?" Nick leaned against his desk and watched Jay and Kayla, waiting for their answer. Jay shrugged, his brow creased in thought as he began collecting the leftover pamphlets that littered the desks.

"I don't know. Okay, I guess. I mean, it could have gone worse. I think for the first one, it wasn't too bad. We weren't aiming for perfection the first time around, were we?" Jay's rambling was unusual, the words spoken quickly and as close to emotionless as possible without being completely flat. Jay continued picking up the pamphlets—most of them had been left behind—but said nothing else. His face was carefully blank and he wouldn't meet Nick's eyes—which made him wonder exactly what he was trying to hide.

"Hm." Nick looked over at Kayla. She was still sitting at the back of the room, her elbows propped on the desk, her chin resting on her folded hands. Her expression was one of sheer boredom and it reminded Nick, unfortunately, of the expressions on the students' faces during most of the presentation. "Well, Kayla, what do you think?"

She sat up straighter and slowly stretched, her uniform shirt pulling tight across her chest. Nick looked away, his mouth suddenly dry as he wondered how she could look so appealing dressed in that shapeless, unflattering uniform. For the thousandth time in the last few weeks, he questioned the wisdom of his self-imposed celibacy. And for at least the hundredth time since then, he wondered if Kayla had acted to deliberately get his attention.

"I think you lost them after the first five minutes," she finally said, her voice matter-of-fact. Nick let out the breath he had been holding, realizing he had expected an answer like that from her. The worst part of it was, she was right.

The students had let it be known, clearly and without having to say a word, that they weren't interested in the topic. And not only were they *not* interested, they resented being forced to sit still and listen to it for forty minutes.

The reception to this had been worse than his class on the symbolism of the evils of humanity in *The Scarlet Letter*.

Jay tossed the stack of pamphlets on the nearest desk then leaned against it, his arms crossed tightly in front of him. The muscle in his clenched jaw twitched as he stared at Kayla. Nick realized that the man was upset about the less-than-successful program that had just ended. Or maybe he was upset with Kayla's blunt assessment. "So do you have any better ideas?

"Don't go copping an attitude with me, Jay. It wasn't anything you did, okay?" Kayla's voice was mellow and reassuring and Nick was amazed to see how quickly Jay's anger faded. Kayla stood and reached for a pamphlet, flipping through the colored handout with mild interest. "They're seniors. Seventeen and eighteen years old. They're invincible, remember? We all were at that age." Her gaze slid to Nick and rested on him briefly. He shifted, understanding her meaning all too well.

Kayla paced around the room, stopping at the blackboard where bulleted items were listed, a visual aid to the lecture that had just ended. She reached up with one finger and tapped at each one, blurring the chalky words. "They think that nothing is going to happen to them. Lecturing them isn't going to change that, and that's essentially all this was—a lecture. They know that drunk driving is dangerous—just not for them. Invincible, remember? Preaching just makes them tune out."

She turned back around and faced both of them, her gaze fixed on Nick for a long minute before moving to Jay. "Did you drink in high school?"

Nick straightened, an automatic defensiveness surging to the surface at her question until he realized that it had been directed at Jay, not him. Jay tossed an uncomfortable glance his way then faced Kayla, shrugging.

"Of course. Who didn't?"

"Exactly. And if some official authority figure came in and lectured you on the evils of drunk driving, what would you have done?"

Jay studied Kayla for a long time then looked at the notes on the blackboard and the pamphlet in his hand. He let out a loud sigh and sank further against the desk. "Laughed at them."

"Bingo." Kayla picked up the eraser and cleaned the blackboard then sat in Nick's chair, her leg brushing his as she propped her feet on the corner of the desk. "Next time, don't lecture them. We know they're going to drink. They know they're going to drink. Be up front about it, let them know it's not about not drinking, but about not driving drunk. There's a difference. We just need to show them that difference. And then show them the reality of driving drunk."

More discomfort surged through Nick and he looked down at Kayla, expecting her to be pointedly staring at him. Instead, she was looking at her lap, picking at a spot on her dark blue uniform pants. He straightened and looked from Kayla to Jay, then back again. "Wait a minute. You're not saying that you want to tell them that it's okay to drink, are you?"

"No, I'm saying stay away from the 'don't drink' angle. The more you preach, the more they're going to tune out."

"Then what about showing them the reality? How do you plan on doing that?"

Kayla finally looked up at him, her eyes carefully hooded. She took a deep breath and blew it out, the sound one of pure frustration. "With pictures, Nick. Next to the real thing, that's the best we can do. But instead of preaching with the pictures, you toss them up behind whoever is talking. You don't even mention them, just use them as background. They'll focus more that way."

"What, those same pictures you showed me before? I already told you I don't think we can use them. They're too graphic."

"I don't know, Nick. I think she has a point. You

saw how they were today. We weren't getting through to them." Jay moved around the room, collecting the handouts and his outline, then tossed everything in his briefcase. "Think about it. At this point, it certainly can't hurt."

"I don't know. I think the pictures are too much," Nick said, shaking his head. Jay shrugged, snapping the briefcase closed and straightening, then moving toward the door.

"Well, we have time to figure something out. There's a couple of weeks before the next presentation." He paused and faced Kayla. "Are you going to finish the paperwork here, or at the station?"

"I'll get it Sunday when we go in." Jay nodded then walked out of the room, closing the door behind him with a soft click. Nick looked over at Kayla, surprised she hadn't left with Jay. She was still sitting in his chair, leaning back with her feet propped up, her hands laced behind her head as she studied Nick. He looked at her for a minute then walked around the room, straightening a chair here, picking up a scrap of paper there.

Kayla sighed and lowered her feet from the desk, then stood with a small groan, stretching some more. Nick watched her twist from side to side, then he quickly looked away when she focused her gaze on his.

"So what's the big deal about the pictures, Nick? Why are you so against using them?"

"I don't think they're appropriate, and I didn't think we'd have to resort to shock therapy to get the point across." He rested his hands on the back of one of the chairs, his fingers curling over the wood. "I'm a teacher, Kayla. I have to think of the welfare of the students. And I don't think the pictures are a good idea."

Kayla studied him for a long minute, her face blank of all expression. Then she shrugged, the motion slow and careful, almost too casual. "Listen, you asked what I thought, I told you. If you don't want to use them, then don't. It doesn't matter to me one way or the other." She glanced at her watch, then reached for her jacket. "I have to run."

"Kayla."

"Yeah?" She paused, one arm in a sleeve, the jacket hanging loosely by her side as she faced him. Nick took a deep breath and stepped closer to her, but not too close. She had kept her word and lived up to his conditions over the last few weeks, but he couldn't shake the feeling that she was still holding something back.

"Did you want to get together tonight? I was thinking—"

"I already had plans, sorry." She finished putting on her jacket then picked up the thick file folder she had brought with her. "Besides, I thought you usually played on Friday nights."

"We do. I thought maybe you'd want to go with me. We were playing at Duffy's again and—"

"Duffy's?" Kayla whirled around and stared at him, her mouth opened in surprise. Irritation flickered in the depths of her eyes before she had a chance to hide it.

Nick folded his arms and watched her, his jaw clenched. He didn't need her to tell him that her plans had included going to Duffy's, and that his being there was going to interfere. "Why do I get the sudden feeling that you're not happy to hear that?"

"No, I just—you caught me off guard. I didn't know Grant had planned on having you guys back." Kayla walked to the door then paused, studying him. She finally offered him a faint smile and shrugged. "In that case, I guess I'll see you tonight."

Nick watched her walk out the door, wondering if she would find some excuse not to show up.

Chapter Twenty-Five

"Brian, I need you to do me a favor." Nick placed his guitar on the rack and stepped off the stage.

"Depends. What do you need?" They walked over to the bar, pushing their way through the crowd until they could lean against the wooden railing. The barmaid immediately came over to them and took their order, and Nick made a mental note to thank Jay for making the service arrangements. Soda in one hand and a glass of iced tea in the other, Nick turned and scanned the crowded room, his eyes automatically resting on Kayla. She was seated at the back table with some of the guys she worked with, laughing.

"I need you to take over the vocals and lead for the first song during our next set." Nick explained why, drawing a look of skepticism from Brian in addition to his reluctant agreement. Nick thanked him then threaded his way to the far side of the room, barely acknowledging the greetings and comments he received. Kayla looked up when he was a few feet away, her gaze locking with his as he approached. She stiffened for a split second, her smile faltering when he stopped next to her.

"Nick. Um, nice set. You guys are pretty good." Her voice was too bright, her new smile too forced. Nick raised an eyebrow at her then took the seat someone held out for him, purposefully scooting closer to her when he sat down. He sat both cups on the table in front of him then turned and watched Kayla, his eyes studying her, noticing the slight flush that fanned across her cheeks. Embarrassment? Or something else?

She stiffened and looked everywhere but at Nick. With another smile that was obviously forced, she finally shrugged then reached for the pitcher of beer in the middle of the table to top off her drink. But before she could fill her cup, Nick reached out and took it from her, making sure he placed it in the middle of the table, out of her reach.

He knew he was drawing strange looks from a few of her coworkers but he ignored them, focusing solely on Kayla and the furious blush that now colored her face. He said nothing as he grabbed the glass of iced tea and held it out to her. A tense minute went by as she stared at him, anger clearly reflected in the deep green of her eyes. She made no move to accept the glass from him so he placed it directly in front of her and leaned over, his voice low so only she could hear him.

"No alcohol. Remember?"

His gaze held hers for another minute before she finally looked away, her jaw clenched. Yeah, there was no doubt she was furious. And he had no doubt that she thought his condition had only applied only to that one time. Well, let her be angry, he thought. She needed to know he was serious.

He slid his chair even closer and crossed his legs, resting his right ankle on his left knee, and leaned toward Kayla. She shifted away, quickly, as if she had been hit by something, and knocked into Jay's arm, spilling some of his drink.

"Hey! Dammit Mikey, watch what you're doing." Jay grabbed some napkins and dabbed at the spilled beer. The blonde sitting on his other side immediately started fawning over him, shooting Kayla a dirty look. Kayla rolled her eyes then reluctantly turned back to Nick, a comical expression on her face. The iced tea sat in front of her, ignored.

Nick watched the byplay with interest and wondered if he had merely imagined the tension between Kayla and the blonde—and between Kayla and Jay. He studied Kayla for another second then turned his attention to Jay's date, who was now sitting in his lap, her arms wrapped protectively around his neck. Nick took a sip of his soda but said nothing as the tension around him grew thicker.

"Don't you have to get back up there or something?" Kayla asked, eyeing him with impatience. He shifted closer to her and shook his head.

"Not yet. I thought I'd come over and talk to you for a while. Or didn't you want me to?"

"No, I..." Kayla trailed off, shifting in her chair. She finally grabbed the glass of iced tea and took a long swallow, keeping her gaze averted. They sat in silence while all around them laughter and conversation mixed and overlapped, occasionally drowned out by music from the jukebox. Kayla glanced at Nick then looked away, taking another drink. He reached out and took the glass from her and sat it on the table, then grabbed her hand in his.

"What—"

"C'mon, I want to dance." He stood up, pulling her with him and leading her onto the crowded floor before she had a chance to say no. He turned and wrapped her in his arms, holding her stiff body tight against his so she couldn't pull away. The music was barely audible above the din of the crowd but that didn't stop anyone from joining in, and they were jostled a few times by other dancers.

"Nick, I don't think this is a good idea." Kayla's words were muffled against his chest, but at least she didn't try to pull away. He elbowed an enthusiastic couple away from them then looked down at her.

"Why not?"

She shrugged, not meeting his eyes. Nick sighed and tightened his hold, moving in a smaller circle to avoid being bumped. Kayla didn't lean into him but she did relax her body, not holding herself quite as stiffly in his arms.

"You better get going. It looks like they're setting up again," Kayla finally said to him. Nick glanced at the stage and saw the rest of the band getting ready. He turned back to her, making no move to stop dancing.

"I get to sit the first one out."

Kayla eyed him warily, caution flitting across her face as the sound of instruments warming up floated across the crowd. She tried to pull back but Nick tightened his hold around her waist, keeping her against him.

"I didn't expect you to show up tonight, you

know. I thought you'd come up with some excuse to go somewhere else."

Kayla's footsteps faltered and Nick felt her sigh rather than heard it before she spoke. "I almost did. I was outvoted, though."

"Outvoted? You could have still gone somewhere else."

"It wouldn't have been much fun by myself, though, now would it?"

Her statement momentarily stunned Nick, until he realized she had no idea how much it revealed. The guys she worked with had decided to come here, so she had to come here, too. Because she'd be by herself if she didn't. It made him realize again how little he really knew about her. He thought about asking if she ever did anything without the guys from work, then quickly decided it probably wasn't the smartest question he could ask.

"So, are you having fun?"

Kayla looked up at him, again eyeing him warily, pausing as though she were considering her answer. She finally looked away and shrugged. "I've had worse times, if that's what you mean."

"I guess I could take that as a good sign," Nick muttered. The jukebox suddenly went quiet and the crowd around them thinned as people moved back to their tables or to the bar. Kayla stopped dancing as well and tried to move away. "No, not yet."

She looked up at him, confusion clear on her face. Nick glanced quickly at the stage and saw Brian sling the guitar over his shoulder and step to the mike to do a sound check. He turned back to Kayla and grabbed her hand when she would have walked away, pulling her back into his arms.

"Were you guys staying here the rest of the night, or going somewhere else?"

"I don't know. Staying here, I guess. Why? What are you up to?"

"Up to? Nothing. I was just wondering."

"Nick—"

She didn't get a chance to finish whatever she was going to say because Brian started the intro for the next set. Nick watched Kayla's face closely for any reaction when the first song started. It was an original slow rock number, one that Nick had written more than a decade ago. With her help.

Kayla froze, the color draining from her face as soon as recognition struck. Nick tightened his arms around her and swayed to the soft notes, leading her in a gentle circle. Color rushed back to her cheeks and she looked up at him, her eyes wide and dazed, shining a little too brightly in the soft lights. "I had forgotten all about this."

"I didn't," he whispered. Nick's gaze held hers for a long minute before he slowly lowered his head and brushed his lips against hers in a brief kiss. He tucked her head against his shoulder and softly sang the lyrics in her ear, his eyes closing when she relaxed against him. For a minute everyone else around them disappeared and it was just the two of them on the dance floor, alone. Kayla's hand tightened around his. Was it his imagination, or were her fingers trembling the tiniest bit? Emotion thickened his voice and he stopped his whispered singing, pulling back to look down at Kayla.

Her eyes were still closed and Nick thought he saw a dampness on her dark lashes but he wasn't sure. He tipped her chin up with his finger until she slowly opened her eyes and looked at him. Bare emotion filled her eyes for an unguarded second, causing Nick's heart to pound painfully in his chest. He lowered his head and caught her mouth with his, kissing her. Hot, sweet, frantic.

Somewhere in the recesses of his consciousness he heard the last notes of the song fade and he slowly pulled away from Kayla, ending the kiss entirely too soon. She lowered her head, resting it on his shoulder with a heavy sigh as he hugged her more tightly.

Nick reluctantly released her from his arms and cleared his throat. "I need to get back up there. Will you let me know if you guys decide to leave?"

"Um, yeah." Her voice was quiet and subdued, almost as if she wasn't sure what was going on. Nick knew how she felt exactly: it was if something had happened during the song, as if the balance had changed and shifted between them.

Nick studied her for another quick second then leaned forward and placed a quick kiss on her lips before heading to take his place on the stage. He watched as she made her way to the table and sat among her friends, surprised that she didn't pour herself a fresh beer since he was no longer there to take it away.

He said a quick prayer that it hadn't been his imagination—that something *had* shifted between them. But only time would tell if he was right.

Chapter Twenty-Six

Mike leaned back in the chair, the now-empty glass of tea held loosely in her hand. She looked down at it, wondering again why she had let Nick demand that she drink tea instead of beer. Did she really care about his conditions? No, she didn't. What she did during her own personal time was just that: personal. So why had she listened to him?

She let out a heavy sigh and placed the empty glass on the table then turned to watch the last few remaining patrons gather their things and head out the door. The bar lights had been turned up, the jukebox was dark and silent against the wall, and the band was packing up their assorted instruments and gear. Her eyes focused on Nick, standing with his back to her, taking apart the microphones.

"Shit," she muttered to herself, closing her eyes to block out the sight of his broad back and trim waist and firm ass. Yeah, she didn't need to be watching him. What the hell had happened on the dance floor earlier? She had no idea, knew only that it filled her with apprehension and made her uncomfortable. Sighing, she opened her eyes to find Jay standing in front of her, watching her curiously. "What?"

"Are you okay?"

Well, that was a loaded question. Was she okay? Not for the first time that night, she wondered the same thing. Mike gave a short laugh and shook her head, which only made Jay frown down at her. She waved at him and nodded. "Yeah, I'm fine."

"You sure? You're okay to drive?"

"Yes, Jay." She couldn't keep the impatience from her voice. Hadn't he noticed that she'd been drinking iced tea most of the night? Ever since Nick had come over, ever since that dance. That song. That damn song.

He frowned then glanced over his shoulder at the stage before looking back at her. "What about, you know? You okay with all that?"

Mike looked down at her hands, clasped loosely in her lap, and thought about how to answer the question. Was she okay? Hell if she knew. Everything had been skewed since that one dance and she didn't know what to make about any of it. She thought about talking it over with Jay, since he knew something wasn't right, but when she looked up, his date was standing next to him, hanging over him impatiently while glaring at Mike.

"Yeah, I'm fine. With everything. Just go, have fun." Mike forced a brilliant smile in their direction while mentally rolling her eyes at Jay's date. He frowned at her then finally shrugged and left, his arm draped around the blonde's shoulders.

Mike looked around and realized that she was

now the only person left, with the exception of the band. She looked over at the bar, watching Grant and Angie cleaning up. No, not quite. Grant was cleaning up. Angie was watching Jay leave, a frown on her face. Mike blinked, wondering if she was seeing things. No, Angie was definitely watching Jay, with an expression she recognized all too well. It was the same look Mike was certain was on her own face whenever she looked at Nick, when she was sure nobody was watching.

She wanted to tell Angie to let it go. Jay would never settle down. And he would certainly never ask Angie out, not when he worked with her brother, Dave.

Mike sighed, telling herself it wasn't her business, that she was probably imagining things, then looked around the empty bar again. Why was she still sitting here? She wasn't sure, didn't want to look too closely at the reason. She blew out a quick breath then stood up and grabbed her jacket from the back of the chair.

"Hey Nick, I'm leaving." She pulled the jacket on then headed for the door, afraid to stop, afraid to hang around any longer. She didn't even know why she had bothered telling him she was leaving. It wasn't any of his business, even if he had asked her to let him know. Mike was a few feet from escape when Nick caught up to her, stopping her with a hand on her shoulder.

"Whoa, hold up. What do you mean, you're leaving?"

Mike turned and faced him, careful not to look directly at him. Her emotions and thoughts were still in turmoil, still swirling through her mind like some crazy tornado, and she was afraid it was clearly written on her face. "Just what I said, I'm leaving."

"Who's driving you home?"

"Me."

"But you've been drinking."

Mike sighed and finally looked up at Nick, letting her irritation show, hoping it was enough to mask anything else that might be visible on her face. "No, Nick, I haven't. I've been drinking iced tea. I am fine to drive. If I had known this was going to happen, I wouldn't have bothered letting you know I was leaving."

Nick watched her for a silent second, his gaze intense and studying. He loosened his hold on her shoulder and shifted so that he was a little closer to her. "Why don't you let me take you home?"

The offer hung in the air between them, quiet and casual. Just one friend looking after another. Or was it? Mike finally met his gaze. Her stomach did a sudden roll at the look in his eyes and she immediately attributed it to the confusion that had been consuming her since Nick had asked her to dance. She swallowed and looked away, part of her wanting to accept his offer.

And part of her wanting to run away.

And that was the issue, right there. That part of her wanted to accept his offer. Why? What had happened to change her mind, to change her thinking? Why did this one man have the ability to confuse her and drive her crazy and make her *want*? Nobody else had ever come close to doing what Nick did to her, to making her think and feel and want the way Nick did.

To make her *need* the way Nick did.

Mike knew she was fine to drive. Perfectly fine.

But if it had been anyone else offering, she wouldn't have hesitated to accept, just for company if for no other reason. But it wasn't anyone else. It was Nick.

And she was suddenly afraid of being alone with him.

"I don't think that's a good idea," she finally muttered, taking a step back to put more space between them. Nick kept watching her, a frown creasing his forehead. The frown disappeared, replaced by a look of mischievousness. There was a glint in his eye when he finally shook his head and stepped back, reaching into his pocket for something. Mike's mouth dropped open when he pulled out her car keys. "How did—"

"Either I drive you home, or you can walk." He waved the keys in front of her, then deftly pulled them out of her reach when she tried to grab them. She narrowed her eyes at him, her mind racing, trying to think of something to do. This was ridiculous. She didn't need a ride home, and she certainly didn't want to be alone with Nick. But he kept looking at her, amusement and something else—something she didn't want to see, didn't want to accept—deep in his eyes.

Part of her considered the possibility of just tackling him and grabbing the keys, but only for a second. She didn't think for a minute that she would have any luck succeeding at that. Another part of her actually considered walking. But again, that thought was quickly dismissed. It was late, it was dark, and home was a good six miles away on a back country road.

If she hadn't been so completely lost in thought, she wouldn't be the last to leave, and she wouldn't be in this predicament. From the small smile on Nick's face, he knew it—and was taking full advantage of it.

Mike crossed her arms tightly across her chest and leveled a dirty look at Nick. "Fine. You can take me home."

His eyes lit up with satisfaction and Mike had a hard time resisting the urge to kick him, just to wipe the look off his face. Nick walked back to the stage setup and said something to the guys there, then grabbed his leather bomber jacket and returned, guiding her out the door. Mike paused as the cold air hit her, realized Nick's hand was now resting on her back, the warmth of his touch reaching her through her jacket and sweater. She shivered and hoped that Nick didn't notice. Or, if he did, that he would attribute it to the chill in the air.

They walked to her Jeep in silence and Mike climbed in, huddling against the cold as Nick started the engine and pulled out of the driveway. The trip was a quiet one, the interior of the Jeep filled only with music from the stereo. She may have nodded off during the ride, or maybe she was just completely engrossed in her own thoughts, because they made it back to her place faster than she expected. Mike mumbled a thank you to Nick then stepped out of the Jeep, not realizing he still had the keys until she tried to open the locked door.

Biting back a curse, she turned to get Nick's attention, only to run straight into his solid chest. He reached out and steadied her with his hands. The touch did something funny to her pulse rate and she had trouble catching her breath until she stepped away from him. Mike closed her eyes, cursing the effects he had on her. And she wished, fervently, that she had been drinking beer instead of tea all night, because alcohol would have muted her awareness of him. At least, that's what she tried to tell herself.

Nick gave her a funny look then reached past her and unlocked the door, leading the way inside. Mike stepped over the threshold and took a deep breath, grateful to be home, anxious for Nick to leave. She flipped on the living room light and pulled off her jacket then walked straight into the kitchen, thinking she could have a drink now, that it wasn't too late to try and dull her awareness of him. Nick followed her, stopping right behind her as she rummaged through the refrigerator.

Her hand closed around a bottle of beer but she stopped, not pulling it out. Maybe it was because Nick was standing so close behind her. Maybe it was because she worried about what he would say, or about that stupid asinine condition of his. Whatever the reason, she released her hold on the beer and grabbed a bottle of water instead.

"Mind if I have one?"

Mike closed the refrigerator door, water bottle in hand, and faced Nick, surprised at the jumping of her pulse when she looked at him. She swallowed and forced a bored expression on her face. "Don't you need to leave now?"

Nick stepped even closer and she felt a brief moment of panic when she realized there was no place for her to go. She was backed against the refrigerator, with Nick mere inches in front of her, trapped. Her mind fought the sensation, but her body turned traitor and quickened at his nearness. Nick reached out and gently pulled the bottle from her hand, then leaned over and placed it on the counter before turning back to her.

"I can't leave, because my car isn't here."

Mike's jaw clenched at his words, at the realization that he was right. He had brought her home in her Jeep, and she had given no thought whatsoever to how he would get home. The crazy thought that she could let him use her Jeep entered her mind but she quickly banished it. Nobody borrowed her Jeep. Nobody. Which meant he would just have to call someone to pick him up, maybe one of the guys who played in the band with him. She was ready to make that suggestion when Nick suddenly stepped away from her and turned toward the living room.

"I'll just sleep on the sofa, and you can take me home in the morning."

Chapter Twenty-Seven

I'll just sleep on the sofa.

Nick's words came back to haunt him for the hundredth time as he rolled over on the couch and tried to get comfortable. He groaned and readjusted the quilt, covering his bare shoulders only to have his feet peek out. He sighed and ran a hand through his hair, staring up at the ceiling in the pale light that came from the kitchen.

He had no idea what he had thought to accomplish by saying he'd sleep on the sofa, but continuously rolling over in frustration certainly hadn't been it. And Kayla. The look on her face when he had opened his mouth was almost comical. She stood there in the kitchen, backed against the refrigerator, her eyes wide with surprise. Then, as if something had exploded inside her, she grabbed the water bottle off the counter and flew through the living room and up the stairs, telling him there was a quilt and pillows in the closet.

That had been over an hour ago. By now, she

was no doubt snuggled in the feathery comfort of her bed, sound asleep, while he was down here on the sofa, calling himself the worst kind of fool while his mind moved from one thought to another to another. Yet no matter which way it turned, it always ended back on one thing: the guitar he had seen in the closet when he took out the quilt and pillows.

With a frustrated sigh Nick sat up and tossed the covers aside, then walked to the closet and pulled out the guitar. It was Kayla's old acoustic, still in good shape. He sat back on the sofa and pulled it across his lap, toying with the strings, surprised to see it was well-tuned. Maybe she still played once in a while. Or maybe not.

Nick leaned back and closed his eyes, his fingers alternately strumming and picking the strings, turning the solitary notes into soft music. He lost track of the minutes as he played, lost track of everything as the music flowed through and out of him, comforting, soothing.

He wasn't sure how much time had passed before he became aware of a subtle difference in the air around him, a change in the solitude cloaking him. His fingers slowed then stopped, the music drifting to a silent finish as he opened his eyes. Kayla was standing at the base of the stairs, silhouetted in shadows, wearing an oversized t-shirt. Nick hesitated before setting the guitar off to the side.

"I didn't mean to wake you up."

"I wasn't sleeping." Her quiet words penetrated the silence, a soft whisper in the still room. Nick stared at her, unable to see her face and wishing he could. A long minute went by before Kayla took a hesitant step forward. He grabbed the quilt and drew it over his lap, holding out one hand to stop her.

"Kayla, I'm not really dressed."

She paused for just a split second then continued walking, her steps slow and unsure, not stopping until she was less than a foot away from him. The light from the kitchen fell across her face, revealing an expression of heartbreaking loneliness and uncertainty. Nick watched her, his breath held, afraid to move, afraid to speak.

"I want you to hold me." Her voice was shaky, the words barely a whisper in the stillness surrounding them. Nick swallowed, still staring up at her, trying to see her eyes more clearly. He held out his hand palm up between them, not daring to breathe. Seconds ticked by, quiet and tense, before she reached out and took his hand in her own, lacing her fingers with his.

Nick slowly stood, his heart beating heavy in his chest, his breath catching in his throat. He wanted to pull her to him, to wrap his arms around her and hold her tight against him. But he didn't move, didn't touch her except for where their hands joined, knowing somehow that this was something she needed to do on her own.

Kayla hesitated, staring up at him with wide eyes, then slowly stepped closer and wrapped her arms around his waist. Nick took a deep breath, almost afraid to move, then brought his arms around her and held her tight, feeling her body press against him as she rested her head on his shoulder. A knot tightened and rolled in his stomach and he took a shaky breath to calm it. "Kayla, are you okay?"

"No. Yes. I don't know." The words were mumbled against his neck, her breath soft and warm on his flesh. "Just hold me."

Nick squeezed his eyes shut, not sure what to say or do. He tightened his arms around her, his hand gently rubbing small circles on her lower back as he waited. The tension coming off Kayla was thick enough to wrap around both of them and Nick wondered how long it would be before it broke.

Several long moments went by before Nick noticed a droplet of moisture on his shoulder, followed by another and another. Kayla's breathing hitched and became irregular, and Nick realized she was crying. Something painful squeezed in his chest and he wrapped his arms more securely around her, gently rocking her. He reached up with one hand and cradled the back of her head, threading his fingers through her hair.

"Kayla." He stopped, not sure what else to say. Nick eased away from her a fraction of an inch and looked down, surprised when she raised her head to look up at him. Her cheeks were damp with moisture, her eyes wide and uncertain. Nick reached up and gently wiped at her cheek with his thumb, surprised to see that his hand was trembling. "Talk to me, Kayla."

She continued watching him, that look of uncertainty and vulnerability still in her eyes. She finally closed her eyes and rested her head on his shoulder again. "I'm scared, Nick. I don't know what's happening anymore."

"Scared of what?" Nick whispered the question into the quiet air, his arms still tight around Kayla. She was pressed so firmly against him that he could feel her heart beating hard and fast in her chest, a rhythm that said even more about the tension thrumming through her than her words. "C'mon Kayla, talk to me. Why are you scared?"

She was quiet for a long time, so long that Nick thought she had changed her mind, that the chance to have Kayla open up was gone. Then suddenly she loosened her hold on him and looked up, her deep eyes holding his gaze with a penetrating look. Kayla licked her lips and looked away, still holding him but not as desperately. She took a deep shaking breath, almost as if working up courage.

"I...I still want you, Nick. After all these years. And I don't know why and it scares the hell out of me." Kayla pushed away from him and began pacing, small hesitant steps back and forth as Nick fought to catch his breath, still shocked at her words, shocked at the anguish in her voice. He opened his mouth to say something, only to shut it again when she continued speaking. "I use to hate you for what you did. Up until a few months ago, I would have sworn that I still hated you. But I don't think I do. How could I still hate you and want you as much as I do? And it hurts."

Her voice broke on her last words, releasing Nick from his paralysis. He closed the distance between them and took Kayla in his arms, holding her and rocking her as she sobbed quietly, her arms entwined around his waist as if he were a lifeline. "Kayla, it's going to be okay."

"No, it's not. I'm not used to feeling anything anymore, Nick. I haven't felt anything for a long time, and then you come back and now suddenly...and I don't know what to do anymore, and I'm scared."

Nick squeezed his eyes closed, swallowing against the pain twisting inside him, a razor sharp slicing that didn't even compare to the pain racking Kayla's body as surely as her sobs. He wasn't sure why she was suddenly opening to him, admitting all of this to him. And he was terrified of saying the wrong thing, of doing something that would only make her pain worse. Something that would drive a wedge even more completely between them.

In the end, the only thing he could do was follow his instinct. He cupped her face gently in his hands, his touch feather-light as he traced her tears with his thumbs. "Shh, I'm here. We'll figure something out."

Kayla blinked up at him but said nothing, only watched him in silence for a long minute, her wide eyes bright with moisture. Then she slowly leaned forward, pressing herself closer until her lips met his in the barest of touches. Soft and hesitant at first, then firmer, more demanding, exploring. Sensation exploded inside Nick at the first touch and he opened his mouth under hers, quickly taking over, threading his fingers through her thick hair and holding her.

A shred of sanity flashed through his mind, as quickly as the initial explosion. Nick groaned his frustration and gentled the kiss, trying to ease away from Kayla. Her own groan trembled against his lips, making it even harder to pull away.

"Kayla, this isn't—"

"Make love to me, Nick, please. I need to feel again." She paused, naked emotion clear in her eyes as she reached up with a trembling finger and caressed his lower lip. "I need to feel *you*."

Nick made no effort to hide his groan as he struggled to maintain a grip on the thin thread of sanity holding him back from giving her exactly what she wanted. He took a deep breath, trying to ignore the touch of her finger against his lip. "God, you're driving me crazy, Kayla. I'm not superhuman, I don't know how much more of this I can stand."

"Then stop fighting it, Nick." She lowered her hand, sliding her finger across his throat and down his breastbone. She rested her open hand in the middle of his bare chest, directly over his pounding heart. Nick took another deep breath, this one shaky, and stared down at her, at the emotion and desire so clear in her eyes. The thread of sanity snapped and he lowered his head, claiming her mouth with a fierceness that took the breath from both of them.

He forced her mouth open with one swipe of his tongue then delved deeper, his tongue meeting hers in a wild frenzy. His hands roamed over her body, hungry for the feel of her silky skin. He grabbed the hem of her nightshirt and dragged it upward, his knuckles grazing the curve of her bare bottom, the swell of her hip, the smooth arch of her back. She broke the kiss and stepped back, raising her arms over her head so he could completely remove the cotton shirt. He tossed the wadded material to the floor and stared at her.

Nick's heart swelled at the sight of her, standing naked and proud in front of him. He reached out with one hand and trailed a shaking finger across her collarbone then down, tracing the swell of her breast, circling the rosy nipple until it was a taut peak under his touch. Kayla's breathing hitched as her head fell back, a soft sigh escaping her parted lips.

He stepped closer, watching her body's response to his touch, then lowered his head and closed his mouth over one taught nipple, sucking, teasing the rigid flesh with his tongue. She wrapped her fingers in his hair and held him to her, her back arching to give him better access. A moan tore through her, shaking him to his core. Nick lifted his head and straightened, watching her, then leaned forward and claimed her mouth once more, drinking her in, taking as much as she could give, giving the same back.

Kayla pressed her body even closer, arching her hips against him as her hands traveled downward. Her fingers eased into the waistband of his boxer briefs and tugged at them, easing them down over his hips until his erection popped free against her. She moaned and rubbed against him, breaking the kiss and letting her head fall back as she reached between them and cupped him firmly with one hand.

Nick groaned at the sensation, his muscles clenching at her touch. Her hand squeezed around him gently, then slowly began stroking him, back and forth, an exquisite torture that turned him inside out. He allowed himself to enjoy her touch for another minute before biting back an oath and reaching between them to still her hand. With a swift move he bent over and picked Kayla up, cradling her in his arms long enough to turn around and gently lay her on the sofa.

She looked up at him as he leaned over her, her eyes glazed with passion and desire. Her arms reached out and wrapped around his neck, pulling him down so their mouths met, wet and hungry and wild. His hands moved over her, touching her, sliding down her body until his fingers found the opening at the juncture of her thighs. She sighed into his mouth, a breathy sound that tore through him as she arched her hips more fully against his hand.

"Nick." Kayla whispered his name, her voice

pleading as she eased her hands along his shoulder and back, lower still to push his briefs further down his legs. Nick pulled back and stepped out of his underwear, kicking them away before easing himself on top of Kayla. She sighed again, reaching for him, her teeth nipping at his shoulder.

"Are you sure this is what you want, Kayla?"

She opened her eyes and looked at him, her honesty clear as she nodded. "Yes, Nick, please."

He groaned and claimed her lips in a quick kiss, then pulled away. "Not yet," he whispered. He lowered his mouth to her neck, nipping and kissing, trailing his lips down along the smooth silkiness of her skin, stopping to suckle at each breast. Her body writhed under him, her breath coming in short gasps from her parted lips. Nick continued further down her body, his hands caressing every inch of her, his lips and tongue skimming the flat of her stomach, his mouth gently caressing the marred flesh of her skin, moving even lower.

He shifted on the sofa and settled himself more fully between her legs, draping each long limb over his shoulders. Nick lowered his mouth, pressing his lips against her hot opening, licking, reveling in the tangy taste of her. Kayla called his name, a hoarse demand as her body came to life under his touch. But he showed her no mercy, caressing her inner thighs with his hands, caressing her softness with his mouth and tongue until she shattered under his touch.

Kayla reached out, searching for him, pulling him toward her. Nick lifted himself over her, still touching her with one gently teasing finger as she continued reaching for him. He held himself still, staring down at her and softly demanding that she open her eyes and look at him.

"I've never forgotten you, Kayla. Never," Nick whispered, his voice hoarse with emotion and restraint. He lowered his mouth to claim her lips in a possessive kiss as he entered her, slowly, feeling her open even more to accept his fullness. She breathed into his mouth, a deep sigh as her hips arched to meet his, her legs wrapping tightly around his waist.

Nick thrust fully into her softness, burying himself to the hilt, groaning as she squeezed around him, tightening then releasing. He continued thrusting, in and out, trying to keep a thin hold on his control. Kayla threaded her fingers in his hair, holding him to her, alternately nipping his shoulder with her teeth then kissing him.

Their movements became more heated, their joining more frantic as sensation spiraled then erupted between them. Nick braced himself on his hands, holding himself above her, thrusting even deeper. He clenched his jaw and groaned, reveling in the small sounds coming from Kayla, in the feel of her tightness around him, holding him.

Nick pushed himself to his knees, sinking deeper into her as he grabbed her legs and held them against his chest. Kayla's head fell back, a long moan escaping her as he drove into her, over and over. Her head twisted from side to side, her hands reaching out for him, his name a soft whisper on her lips. Nick thrust again, and again and again until she tightened around him then shattered, squeezing him over and over, driving him to his own pulsating climax. He groaned her name and pumped himself into her, feeling every muscle go liquid at the powerful release.

Nick collapsed on top of her, raining kisses

against her heated flesh as her arms wrapped around him and held him to her. There was a long moment of contentment, then soft surrender as they disappeared into oblivion, holding on to each other.

Chapter Twenty-Eight

Nick woke a little time later, curled against Kayla on the sofa. He shifted with a small sigh and smiled when she snuggled even closer to him. He looked down at her, at the peaceful expression that claimed her face in sleep. His hand glided along her arm and side, gently touching her, needing to touch her, enjoying the softness of her skin.

He had forgotten this part, how it was between them. But the memory was clear now, how much he had always enjoyed just touching her, how they had often lain together, their hands roaming each other's bodies, not quite able to get enough of the other. Nick used to swear that even if they could never have sex again, he would survive as long as he could just touch her.

Had he really forgotten this? Or was it something he had just buried deep in his mind, unwilling to remember, unwilling to bear the pain of the memory?

It didn't matter, not any longer. Because, even after all these years, he still felt the same. That deep desire to just hold her, to touch her. It was an intimacy he had never felt with anyone else, not in his limited experience before Kayla, and certainly not after. And it was something he didn't want to examine too closely; he was just grateful that it was still there.

Kayla stirred under his touch then settled deeper into the sofa. Nick reached down for the quilt and drew it over them, tucking the edge of the soft material around her before dropping a kiss on the curve of her shoulder. He curled his body around hers, draping his arm around her waist and laying back with a sigh.

They would need to talk later, about tonight, and about what else was between them. It wasn't something he was looking forward to, knowing already that Kayla would fight against it. Nick had no doubts that getting her to talk would be difficult. Something had happened with her tonight, though, something that had made her open up to him, however briefly. He only hoped that she wouldn't regret it, that she wouldn't blame him for it. And he hoped that she wouldn't try to rebuild the emotional wall around her that was breached, however briefly, tonight.

What was it she had said? That she didn't feel anything anymore and hadn't for quite a while. That the only time she felt something was with him. Nick had no idea what that meant, or what he was supposed to make of it. Part of him was afraid to examine it too closely. His Kayla—the Kayla from his youth—had never been unable to feel. In fact, she had always been able to see and feel things that others couldn't. She had always been able to look deeper than the surface, to see what most people couldn't see. Or wouldn't see.

Nick couldn't believe that any of that had changed.

Nick didn't want to believe that any of that had changed.

Because if it had, that meant *he* was responsible. As responsible for that as he was for the scar that marred her flesh, the scar that marred her heart. And he couldn't bear that responsibility.

He swallowed against the emotion clogging his throat then turned his head and looked down at Kayla's sleeping profile. Her long lashes were dark crescents against her pale skin, her lips full and slightly parted, her face relaxed. She was different now, a little harder, less innocent, changed by time and circumstances. But Nick believed that deep down, her soul was still the same. The girl he had loved was a little older, a little rougher around the edges, but still the same.

And he still loved her.

Nick took a deep breath and let it out slowly, then curled even more tightly around Kayla and closed his eyes, savoring the thought. He still loved her.

Now all he had to do was convince Kayla of it.

***

Mike stirred, not wanting to free herself from the soft grasp sleep still had on her but being pulled from it anyway because of the unusual stiffness in her back. She stretched then came awake more fully as her feet bumped against something warm and heavy. Her eyes slowly opened, blinking against the sleep, and she realized that she was on the sofa.

And Nick was asleep beside her, his arm wrapped protectively around her waist. She sighed, a soft sound in the quietness around them, then settled deeper into the cushions, curiously content with just lying there for a little while longer.

A crack in the curtains at the living room window showed the sky outside was turning gray, the odd shifting of light between night and day that signaled the approach of dawn. Mike closed her eyes, resenting the pull of wakefulness tugging at her. She wanted to steal a few more minutes, just a few more, before the reality of her world returned with the new day.

Long minutes went by, minutes where she waited for the regret to fill her. Regret for what she had done last night, regret for everything she had said. Her heart beat heavy in her chest and still she waited.

But regret didn't come. Instead, there was a feeling of acceptance. Not an earth-shattering moment or realization of rightness. Just acceptance. And with that brief flare of realization came another feeling: peace.

Mike released her breath in a soft sigh and reached out to run her fingers lightly along Nick's arm, careful not to wake him, enjoying the texture of coarse hair and smooth skin under her touch. Her fingers splayed over his where his hand rested high on her stomach and she opened her eyes, studying their differences. Nick's fingers were long and strong, tapered, his nails neat and blunt, the strength in his hand evident. Next to his, her own hands seemed almost small and feminine. Protected.

Mike sighed again and closed her eyes,

wondering why that particular word had come to mind. Protected? She didn't want protection of any kind, she didn't *need* protecting. She was quite capable of taking care of herself, and had been doing just that for more years than she could remember. She didn't have to rely on anyone, she didn't *need* to rely on anyone. And while there may have been some bumps on her private road, she did just fine. The sudden thought that she needed someone to protect her was laughable. Disconcerting, even.

But on top of that thought came another one, sudden and unwelcome. No, she didn't need anyone. But wouldn't it have been nice to have some company while she traveled that bumpy road? Mike mentally shook her head, wondering why she was suddenly feeling so introspective. The mood wasn't welcome. Since when did she need company? She was used to being by herself, not having to worry about anyone but herself, not having to answer to anybody.

So why was she suddenly wondering what it would be like to *not* be by herself?

Mike shifted, just enough so she could tilt her head to the side and peer at Nick through lowered lids. She blinked quickly, briefly seeing the younger man—the boy, really—from all those years ago beneath the sculpted lines of his face and strong jaw. But it wasn't the boy she had been spending time with lately.

And it wasn't the boy she was afraid she was becoming attached to.

Something had changed last night, shifted somewhere deep inside her and changed the perspective of how she viewed herself—and how she suddenly viewed Nick and the pull he had on her. At first she thought it had just been the music—the slow dance and that song from so long ago. *Their* song. She had blamed the music and the melancholy of memory. Later, she wanted to blame it on alcohol, and would have if not for the fact that she hadn't been drinking. But as she had lain in bed, tossing and turning, unable to get comfortable knowing that Nick slept not far from her downstairs, she had been forced to admit it was more than all of that.

She was attracted to Nick, plain and simple. More than attracted. It went beyond melancholy and nostalgia, and last night she was forced to finally admit it, at least to herself.

Coming downstairs had taken more courage than she thought it would. And opening to Nick, admitting just the little bit that she had to him—that had taken more out of her than she had expected. Bits of what she told him came back to her and she had to resist the urge to shudder at the memory. But she didn't regret saying what she had, or doing what she did.

That didn't mean she wanted to discuss it. And she wasn't going to fool herself into thinking that Nick would let her go without talking about it. Knowing him, he'd want to sit down and go over each word at length, until they discussed everything in so much detail he'd be able to write a dissertation about it.

Which was going to be a problem, because she didn't want to talk about it. She didn't even want to think about it. If she did either, she'd have to confront her own feelings, have to question and reevaluate everything she thought she knew about herself, and she was nowhere near ready to do that. Not even in the privacy of her own mind. She wasn't ready, mentally or emotionally—wasn't sure if she would ever be ready.

What she had told Nick last night was true, it had been a long time since she had felt anything. After the accident, she hadn't been able to allow herself feel. Feeling would have brought memories and pain, and she hadn't been ready to deal with it.

Then, as time moved on, it had become easy to fall into that pattern of not feeling, of not letting things affect her, of just separating herself from emotion. That was how she dealt with things, how she protected herself. Don't feel, don't let anyone too close. And that method had worked just fine until Nick came back into her life. His reappearance, whether by coincidence or fate, was a disruption that was slowly chipping away at her outer defenses, making her feel things she wasn't sure she wanted to feel.

And for the life of her, she didn't know what she wanted to do about it.

Mike sighed, looking at Nick one last time, then closed her eyes and willed herself to drift back to sleep. She wanted to enjoy these last quiet minutes in Nick's arms, not waste them trying to figure out what was going on in her own heart.

Chapter Twenty-Nine

"Yo, earth to Mikey. You there?"

Mike snapped out of her daze and looked up at Jay, who was leaning down in front of her, waving his hand in front of her face. She shook her head and sat back, pushing him away with one hand.

"Yeah, I'm here. Just thinking."

"I'll say." Jay straddled the chair next to her, resting his folded arms across the back then staring at her long enough to make her shift uncomfortably. "Want to share them?"

"Share what?"

"Those deep thoughts you're having."

Mike turned to stare at Jay for a second then shook her head and stood, making her way to the coffee pot on the counter. No, she didn't want to share them. She didn't even want to be having them. If she told Jay what was on her mind, he'd sit and listen to her, probably nod once or twice, then laugh and ask her what she was so worried about. So no, she didn't want to share her thoughts.

She filled her cup, added cream and sugar, then took a long swallow, not bothering to wince at the strong brew. "Don't worry, they're not worth wondering about."

"You sure? Because you look serious. Too serious." Jay's voice had turned quiet and concerned, and Mike closed her eyes against the wave of emotion that swept through her. She didn't need quiet and concern, she needed a distraction. A big distraction, something to get her mind off Nick and all the crazy thoughts she had been having lately. And not just since the other night when she had slept in Nick's arms. No, the crazy thoughts had been happening ever since he had literally walked through the door and back into her life.

"Yeah, I'm sure. Nothing I can't handle."

Jay watched her, one eyebrow raised in question. Or maybe it was disbelief, Mike wasn't sure. She shook her head and finished the coffee, then put the empty cup in the sink, her back carefully turned to Jay so he couldn't see her face. As well as he knew her, he was bound to see the truth in her eyes, a truth she was afraid to admit.

Because she wasn't sure if she *could* handle it. Not anymore. Too many emotions had been whirling through her heart and mind recently, and it had only gotten worse after the other night with Nick. She had been such a fool to say anything to Nick, to open her mouth at all. Worse, to open her heart, even just that little bit. What on earth had she been thinking?

Mike took a deep breath and mentally shook her head. Just let it go, she told herself. Let it go and move on. To do anything else would be disastrous. She took another deep breath and let it out then turned to face Jay, ready to make some light remark, to blow off whatever he had seen on her face earlier, when the alarm sounded. Jay bounded out of the kitchen, Mike right behind him as they ran to the gear rack and got dressed then jumped on the engine, Mike thankful at least for the distraction.

***

Three hours later, Mike was mentally kicking herself for wishing for a distraction. Being called into their captain's office was a bit more than she had wanted. She tried to focus on his words as he sat there at his desk, his monotone voice droning on and on, but her mind kept shutting him out. There was a nudge from behind her and Mike straightened to find the captain looking at her expectantly. She cleared her throat and slid a sideways glance at Jay, hoping for some hint to what she missed.

Captain Nelson blew out a deep breath and shifted in the chair as he fingered the buttons on his clean white shirt. Another long minute went by in silence before he finally stood and fixed the two of them with a hooded expression that didn't quite hide his displeasure.

"Your cowboy tactics are going to stop, both of you. Especially you, Donaldson. I won't stand for anymore freelancing from my crew. The next time either one of you charge ahead like that, I'll see to it personally that days are lost." He leaned over the desk and hastily scribbled on the forms spread out in front of him. Mike turned to Jay and rolled her eyes at him, her patience strained. Jay shot her a warning look that hinted at his anger but said nothing.

The captain finished his scribbling then pushed two identical forms across the desk toward them, placing a pen on each one. He straightened and fixed them both with what Mike guessed was supposed to be a stern glare. Its meaning was lost on her. "I want you both to sign these. Consider this your first and only warning. The next time it happens, I will take stronger action."

Mike glanced down at the paper, not surprised to see that it was a disciplinary action form. Her eyes skimmed the narrative section, her emotions carefully neutral as she read how she and Jay were guilty of insubordination and failing to follow orders. She almost asked if there was a form for cowardice but was stopped by Jay's nudge. She slid him another glance then grabbed the pen and hastily scrawled her signature across the bottom line, then shoved the form back as Jay signed his own. She turned to leave but was stopped by the officer's next words.

"You especially, Donaldson," he repeated. "Your attitude needs a lot of work. Is that clear?"

Mike bit down hard on her tongue then slowly nodded, just a curt motion with her head. "Yes, sir."

She turned her back on him and walked out of the office, careful not to stomp or slam the door, or mutter anything within hearing distance. She made it to the locker room before her temper exploded. "What a fucking asshole!"

"Not so loud, Mike. Do you want him to follow through with his threat? Because he will. You know that." Jay cautioned in a quiet voice as he slumped down on the bench.

"Screw him. Who does he think he is? A fucking coward. I wish to hell they would just promote him and be done with it. This is ridiculous." Mike opened her locker and rummaged through the shelves, grabbing a washcloth and towel before changing her mind and putting them back. She slammed the door closed, the metal echo ringing loudly around them, then took a seat on the bench next to Jay. She leaned back against the locker, welcoming the coolness of the metal against her still-damp skin.

The smell of smoke and sweat was thick around her, and she knew she should just get up and go take a shower. The longer she waited, the worse the smell would be, and the stiffer she would feel later. That's what she told herself, but she still didn't move.

Not when Jay was sitting next to her, anger and frustration rolling off him in suffocating waves. It was one thing for her to be written up. From Captain Nelson's point of view, she probably deserved it. But not Jay. And it was her fault he had been pulled into the situation at all.

"Jay, I'm sorry. He shouldn't have written you up. None of that was your fault."

And it wasn't. Mike was the one who had decided to charge ahead by herself, grabbing the line and running inside before Jay even had time to make it to the front door. And she was the one who ignored Captain Nelson's order to move back.

Yeah, she had heard him. But she hadn't listened and went charging in anyway. It was a simple case of being stubborn, coupled with uncharacteristic tunnel vision.

And what she had thought was a simple room and contents was, in fact, a fully involved dwelling. But she hadn't cared and went charging in anyway, not realizing that Jay had caught up to her. No, she hadn't realized, but she had known he would anyway, because the two of them had worked so closely together for so many years.

And now their captain was pissed because she had disobeyed his direct order while he stayed outside and overheard comments from another crew about his lack of leadership because of it.

The silence stretched around them and Mike shifted on the bench, her discomfort growing with each passing minute. She knew Jay was upset with her, even if he hadn't said anything about it yet. Her eyes shifted to the left and took in the rigid set to his shoulders, the strain in his eyes as he stared at the faded tile floor.

She let out a breath, wondering how long it would be before he said anything.

But the minutes stretched by, filled with tension, and Jay still didn't move. Mike finally stood and opened her locker again, taking out her shower gear and tucking it under her arm.

"I don't know what else to say, Jay. I'm sorry, okay? I just wish, I mean, if you want to yell, then yell. Or something."

"What do you want me to say, Mikey?" Jay pushed himself from the bench and walked over to his own locker, yanking the door open so hard that it crashed into the locker next to his. "It sucks we got written up, but there's not a damn thing we can do about it. And as much as I'd love for you to take the blame, I can't because I was just as guilty. You're right, he's an ass."

Mike watched Jay, not sure what she should say, or if she should say anything at all. He grabbed his own shower kit then slammed the door and stared at her.

"I just wish the hell I knew what was going on with you."

"What?" Mike stared at him, not hiding her surprise. "What's that supposed to mean?"

"It means that you've been so distracted lately, it's like you're somewhere else. But you won't tell me what's going on, so I have no idea how to help."

"I don't need help, okay? I've just got a lot on my mind, and it doesn't concern you."

"Yeah? Think again. It sure as hell concerns me once it starts affecting what you do here."

"What the hell are you talking about?" She was raising her voice but she didn't care. Jay's accusation was coming out of nowhere and she had no idea how to respond.

"Just what I said. You have been so out of it the last week, it's like you're moving on autopilot only in a different world. You're so distracted that you're not even paying attention to anything else going on around you."

"Jay, what the hell? I have not been distracted!"

"Yeah, you have. I have no idea what the hell is going on with you and Nick, but you need to figure it out now, before something else happens."

Mike opened her mouth to say something then quickly snapped it shut. She had no idea what she was going to say, only what she *wanted* to say, and it wouldn't have come out the right way, no matter how she said it.

So, for once, she bit her tongue and said nothing and just stared at Jay. She finally shook her head, pulled her shower gear closer to her, and walked past him. They both needed a few minutes to calm down,

to separate and put distance between them.
 Part of her wondered if she was thinking of Jay.
 Or of Nick.

Chapter Thirty

The presentation was another failure.

Nick studied the students at their desks, noting the bored expressions, the barely restrained sighs, and the closed eyelids. Jay's voice from the front of the room droned on and Nick knew without a doubt that the man was finding it painful to continue.

Nick couldn't blame him. He had been teaching most of these kids for the last three and four years, and even he would have found their decided lack of interest intimidating.

He glanced down at his watch and saw they only had ten minutes left. His eyes searched out Kayla, immediately finding her in the last row, back in the corner. She sat still in her seat, her head tilted down as if the scarred desk held something infinitely more interesting than whatever Jay was saying. She must have felt his eyes on her because she suddenly looked up and met his gaze with a questioning look, as if asking why he was watching her.

Nick looked away, turning back to watch the

students, not surprised that even more of them were now fidgeting in their seats. He finally pushed away from the wall where he had been standing for the last twenty minutes and interrupted Jay with one hand in his direction.

He noticed the brief flicker of relief that crossed the man's face and felt himself smile just a bit in acknowledgment before turning to the class.

The sudden silence caught the attention of most of them. Nick strolled down the second aisle and stopped at one desk, waiting for the boy to look up at him. When he didn't, Nick finally reached over and took the smart phone from the boy's hand, noticing the screen opened to a cover model site.

"Mr. L, c'mon!"

"Not bad, Sam, but let's save this for later, okay?" Nick cleared the phone and powered it down before handing it back with a small smile. "Sam, what do you think the point of this class is?"

"Don't drink and drive." The boy's answer was immediate and monotone in typical teenage fashion. Some of the girls around them giggled and Nick smiled. He had picked Sam for a reason, knowing that he was popular with many of the students, especially the girls.

"Well there you have it, ladies and gentlemen. Don't drink and drive. I guess we should have just let Sam stand up and give the class so we could have all been done by now." More laughter erupted around the room, including Sam's.

Nick continued walking between the desks, making sure to meet as many of the students' eyes as possible. Yes, this is boring and unnecessary but we have to do it, his grin told them. He stopped at another desk and reached over, closing the fashion magazine that laid open in front of another student. "Renee, why don't we drink and drive?"

The girl shifted to look up at him, knowing she had been busted but playing his game willingly. "Because it's illegal."

"Not bad, Renee, not bad at all. I knew there was a reason you guys were all honors kids." More laughter. Nick realized he should have done this earlier, should have taken the lead and gotten the class to relax before anything had even started. Next time, he told himself.

He looked around once more, noticing that all eyes were now on him, including Kayla's. She watched him, her gaze curious, her face relaxed and at ease. For some reason, that made him uncomfortable. He looked away, finally moving back to the front of the class.

"Why else? Anyone?" He motioned around the room, letting the class know that it was now an open discussion.

"Because it's dangerous."

"Because you can get hurt."

"You can die."

They kept calling out the answers, talking over one another, repeating themselves. But it was that one answer, *you can die*, that kept ringing in Nick's ear. He knew the room hadn't grown silent, knew that the students were still shouting out answers and talking, that the simple phrase hadn't had the same impact on them as it had on him.

Everything froze around him. Or maybe he was the one frozen, because he could still hear the students' voices, saw them moving around in their seats, saw their smiles and heard their laughter.

He finally looked toward the back of the room, searching out Kayla, wondering how the sudden eruption around them affected her. But her reaction wasn't what he had expected or feared. He had thought that maybe hearing those words would upset her, that he would see some kind of horror or even blame on her face.

Instead, she was watching him, her head tilted to the side, the green of her eyes so vivid even from this distance. And he didn't see horror or fear or even blame. Instead, he saw concern.

The instant he recognized the concern and realized that it was concern for *him*, everything around him returned to normal. He no longer felt frozen, as if he had been set apart from everything around him for that brief confusing minute.

A bell rang somewhere in the background and he recognized it as the dismissal bell. All around him, the class came to life as students pushed away from their desks and hurried past him, talking and laughing amongst themselves, some even telling him goodbye. He responded, he was sure he did, but the air around him still made him feel as if he was suspended. There but not there, waiting.

"You know, if you had done that to begin with, this whole thing would have gone so much smoother."

Nick shook off the weirdness holding him and turned to face Jay, his mind finally catching up with everything else around him. Jay was bent over the desk, piling his paperwork together with a slight grin on his face.

"Um, yeah. I guess I should have. Sorry, I'll be

sure to do that next time."

"At least they took more of the pamphlets this time." Kayla stopped next to him and held the pamphlets out for Jay then turned to face Nick. "Not bad. It kills me to say this, but Jay was right. You're actually pretty good with them. They listen to you."

Kayla's brief words of praise made him speechless and he had no idea how to respond. But the moment passed as Kayla moved past him to help Jay finish packing. And still Nick didn't seem able to move or to speak. What had happened to make him feel like he was so far removed from everything around him? Here, but not here.

"Hey, Nick." He opened his eyes at the sound of Kayla's voice so close to him and was surprised to find her standing inches away. Her hand rested on his forearm and squeezed. "Are you okay? You look, I don't know, like you're out of it or something."

"What? Oh, no." Nick gave himself a mental shake a forced a smile, surprised at Kayla's concern. "No, I'm fine. Just deep in thought, I guess."

She watched him for another few seconds then shrugged and turned back to Jay. Nick didn't pay them much attention, his mind already back to the last few minutes of the class.

They *had* been more receptive than the previous class. And yes, they had even take a few more of the pamphlets. But Nick didn't fool himself into believing they'd taken anything to heart. What was it Kayla had said that first time?

They thought they were immortal. Invincible.

Nick knew she was right—because he had been the same way.

And had nearly killed Kayla because of it.

He turned back to his desk and absently shuffled through the paperwork and files that never seemed to go away. But he wasn't really seeing them because his gaze was focused on Kayla. She was talking to Jay, laughing softly at something he said, the corner of her mouth turned up in a small smile. Her dark hair was pulled back into a plain pony tail, the end of it swinging against the back of her dark blue polo shirt. She shouldn't have commanded his attention, not dressed as she was in her shapeless uniform, but she did.

And she always had.

Looking at her now, he realized again that she was right, had always been right. No matter what they said or did with these presentations, none of it would get through to the kids because they were invincible.

They had to make it more personal.

Nick thought again about the pictures Kayla had suggested they use, but he still didn't think that would make a difference. The pictures were graphic, yes. Could it bring the point home? To some, maybe.

But the pictures, despite how real and graphic they were, still didn't make it personal.

Nick's breath caught in his throat and his heart stuttered in his chest at the thought that suddenly slammed into him. But no, that was too personal. And he knew that Kayla wouldn't appreciate it.

He didn't think he would, either.

He shook his head, pushing the wayward thought from his mind, and looked up. Both Kayla and Jay were watching him expectantly. He offered them a half-hearted smile and a small shrug, silently admitting that he hadn't been paying any attention.

"Next one's in two weeks, right?" Jay asked,

looking down at the small calendar in his hand.

"Yeah. But it's going to be a little different than these last two. With holiday break coming up, senior faculty decided to have the next one in the auditorium so everyone could participate."

Jay looked up, the surprise clear on his face. "Everyone? As in how many?"

"The entire senior class."

"Nothing like a little heads-up! Shit. When did they decide this?"

Nick grabbed a stack of files from the desk and jammed them into his briefcase. "This morning. I didn't have a chance to tell you when you got here."

"Great. Wonderful." Jay shook his head as Kayla laughed and jokingly elbowed him in the side.

"Don't worry, Jay, you'll be fine."

"Easy for you to say. I'm still not used to talking in front of groups."

"You're fine, stop worrying."

"Well, if it's any consolation, this will be the last presentation, then you're off the hook." Nick grabbed his briefcase and started walking to the door, motioning for Jay and Kayla to follow him.

"Last one? Why?"

"The program was geared to reach the senior class only. And since they'll all be there, you won't have to worry about coming back." Nick pulled the door closed behind them then led the way up the hall, noticing the relief that crossed Jay's face.

"Well, at least there's an upside, I guess."

"Jay, you'll be fine. Just think, you can go out with a bang." Kayla jokingly nudged him again, but Nick didn't miss the expression that quickly passed across her face.

Or was he just doing some wishful thinking? Because he could've sworn something like disappointment had flashed in her eyes and the subtle downward tilt to her mouth.

Yes, some kind of expression had crossed her face. But was he reading into it? He tried to tell himself he was, that he was seeing disappointment where none existed, that he was being foolish for thinking that Kayla might actually miss their forced time together.

But that didn't stop him from hoping.

Chapter Thirty-One

Mike rolled over and glanced at the clock on the nightstand, its green digital numbers staring back at her, bright and bold in accusation.

11:12

She rolled back over with a sigh and kicked at the covers tangling her feet. It was Saturday night, she didn't have to work the next day and what was she doing?

Lying in bed. Trying to sleep.

And not having any luck.

With another heavy sigh, she kicked at the covers once more then pushed herself out of bed, reaching over to turn on the small lamp as she did. Soft light filled the room, just enough to banish the shadows to the corners.

She ignored the chill of the floor against her feet and shuffled over to the bookcase, picking a title at random, not caring what book she chose, as long as it was something to grab her attention. And since every title on this shelf was considered a 'keeper', she was pretty sure it would. At least, she hoped it would.

She sat down in the reading chair, curling her legs under her and shifting until finding the perfect position. She opened the cover of the book and flipped to the first page, hoping to get drawn into the story, hoping to stop the wayward thoughts that threatened to overwhelm her.

A full thirty minutes passed before Mike realized she was still on page one, her eyes drifting over the words without seeing them. She sighed and tossed the book aside then pulled her legs to her chest and rested her chin on her knees.

Sleep was out of the question. Reading was out of the question.

Because she was thinking too much to focus on either one.

With another sigh, she pushed herself from the chair and made her way downstairs, not bothering with any lights until she reached the kitchen. She opened the refrigerator, thinking that maybe a beer might help her sleep.

Except she didn't have any beer, because she had thrown it all out. Just like she didn't have any whiskey or brandy in the house. Not even wine.

Because of Nick and that damned condition of his.

Muttering under her breath, she reached into the refrigerator and pulled out a bottle of water then angrily twisted off the cap. Damn Nick anyway. Who did he think he was, with his stupid conditions?

But that had been more than two weeks ago, and she had stuck by them. She was afraid to admit that it had been harder than she thought it would be, something she hadn't expected.

And she certainly hadn't expected that she would have lived up to those conditions, at least not in the privacy of her own home. She still wasn't sure why she had.

Take that back. No, she was.

Because she had said she would.

Because she wanted to prove, at least to herself, that she could.

She took a long swallow of water, recapped the bottle, then walked into the living room and sat on the sofa. She leaned back and stretched her legs out, staring up at the ceiling.

It was a Saturday night, and she had opted to stay home. Again.

Everyone from work had been surprised when she said she wasn't joining them at Duffy's last night. To be honest, she had kind of surprised herself. But she didn't want to go, afraid she'd give into the temptation and have a drink.

Or worse, give into the temptation of Nick.

Nick's announcement that the next presentation would be the last had surprised her. Not because there wouldn't be more—it actually made sense to do one big presentation instead of a bunch of small ones. No, what surprised her was the brief flare of disappointment that cut through her at his words, and she had to wonder why.

She gave a small laugh, the sound almost sad in the empty room around her. She didn't have to wonder why, she already knew, and part of her was loathe to admit it.

She was going to miss the informal meetings, the routine sparring and even clashing of heads and ideas that had accompanied each meeting.

She was going to miss Nick.

And that's what confused her the most. How could she miss him, when they had resolved absolutely nothing? Yeah, they had talked—but mostly in circles, skating near the edge of things that had to be said without really ever discussing them. The closest they had come had been the other night, when she had come downstairs and confessed just a small part of her confusion.

But they still hadn't discussed anything, not really.

And Mike still wasn't sure if she had forgiven him, if she even could forgive him. But would she have really slept with him if she hadn't?

That wasn't something she wanted to examine too closely, at least not tonight.

She pushed herself off the sofa with a sigh and walked back to the kitchen to turn off the light, figuring it would be best to go back to bed. She wasn't foolish enough to think sleep would come any easier now than it had an hour ago, but at least she would be more comfortable upstairs than down here.

Her foot was on the bottom step when a soft knock sounded at the front door. Mike paused, wondering if she was hearing things, then wondering who would be knocking on her door at this time of night when she heard it again.

She walked over to the door and unlocked it, then stepped back in surprise. Nick was standing in front of her, his face covered in the shadows of night. He moved just an inch, as if he had been ready to step inside, then stopped.

She stared at him, not saying anything, wondering if maybe she was imagining things, that her earlier thoughts had somehow conjured him in her mind.

"Hey." His voice was quiet, pitched low in the night surrounding him, and Mike realized that she wasn't imagining anything. Nick really was standing in front of her. He was dressed in faded denim jeans and his leather jacket, looking every inch the rebel she remembered from her youth.

Only he wasn't, not anymore.

Mike blinked her eyes and stepped back, silently inviting him inside before thinking better of it. "Nick, what are you doing here?"

He gave her a half smile, one corner of his mouth lifting oh so briefly as he walked past her. She closed the door against the cold night air and turned, only to have Nick pull her roughly against him, his mouth descending on hers before she could react.

Surprise froze her in place, but for only a second before her body reacted to his. Her hands came up to his chest, but instead of pushing him away, her fingers curled against the thermal weave of his shirt, her knuckles grazing the bare skin at the opening of the collar. A soft sigh escaped her, immediately lost in the warmth of his breath as his tongue swept into her mouth and pushed all thought from her mind.

Time lost all meaning as the heat of his body warmed her. He turned and pinned her to the door, his body flush against hers so she could feel his erection against her stomach. She sighed again, her hips thrusting against him, searching, as he pulled his mouth from hers and dragged it down her neck, then back up before stopping to nibble at the sensitive lobe of her ear.

"Do you want me to leave?"

She heard the words through the heated fog of passion but had trouble understanding them. Leave? No, not when he made her feel like this. She shook her head, unable to speak as his tongue teased the soft spot behind her ear.

"Tell me, Kayla. Tell me you want me to leave."

"What? No. No, I..." Her words drifted off, her mind trying desperately to understand what Nick was saying, what he was asking from her. She shook her head again and pushed against him, just enough so he would leave her ear and neck alone long enough for sanity to return.

"Nick, what are you doing here?" Her voice was a ragged whisper in the semi-darkness. She looked up at him, trying to gauge his reaction, but the shadows danced across his face, hiding his expression.

But they couldn't hide the burning she saw so clearly in the depths of his eyes. Nick blinked then lowered his face until his forehead rested against hers. His arms tightened around her, holding her more firmly against him.

"Nick, is something wrong?"

He pulled back just enough to look at her, his dark eyes intense. He slowly shook his head. "No. I just needed to see you. Do you want me to leave?"

His words, along with the intensity in his gaze, had an odd effect on Mike, stealing her voice and creating a whirlwind in her mind. She must have been quiet for too long though, because Nick eased his hold on her and started to pull away. The small movement sent a panic through her, a panic she didn't understand and didn't stop to question. She lifted her arms around his neck and pulled him closer, closer until her mouth met his.

Nick held himself still for a brief second but before she could question his hesitation, heat exploded between them. He quickly became the aggressor, taking control of the kiss and demanding her mouth open for him. His tongue swept in, invading, conquering even though she eagerly—willingly—surrendered to each thrust.

She ran her hands around his neck and down, pushing the jacket off his arms before reaching for the button on his jeans. Minutes dissolved as quickly as the barrier of clothing between them.

Nick's touch became more frantic, mirroring her own desperation. He grabbed her around the waist and lifted her, pinning her against the door, holding her in place with one arm while his free hand skimmed her body.

His fingers teased her nipple, pinching and squeezing before moving lower. He stroked the sensitive flesh between her legs, over and over, hard, demanding. Her insides tightened and she thrust her hips forward, needing more, so much more.

"Nick, please."

His mouth closed over hers and she could feel him smiling, felt her own smile in response as he shifted and drove into her with one long thrust.

Her head fell back on a low moan, all sensation, all thought, centered on him. He pulled out, slowly, then drove home again. And again, harder.

And yet again.

Mike cried out his name and shattered, her body exploding into a million fragments. But Nick didn't stop.

He thrust into her, harder, faster.

His breathing harsh, his hold unforgiving.

His body demanding.

Another climax rocked her, long and savage as she clung to him, saying his name over and over, whether in demand or in surrender she didn't know. Didn't care.

His hips thrust once more, grinding into her, holding her in place as his body stiffened. Nick threw his head back, her name a low groan falling from his lips as he found his own release inside her, filling her.

Minutes went by, maybe more, before Mike slowly became aware of her surroundings.

The darkness of the living room, broken only by the light escaping from upstairs.

The quiet hum of the refrigerator, broken by the sudden drop of a cube from the ice maker.

The slight chill against her back from the door closed against the night behind them.

The intensity in Nick's dark eyes as he studied her, reading into her very soul.

"I love you, Kayla."

Chapter Thirty-Two

Nick sat at his desk, holding his head in his hands as he stared at absolutely nothing. Not the reports scattered in front of him, not the ring of condensation forming under his water bottle, not the scratched surface marred from years of use.

He only wished his mind was as unseeing as his eyes as he questioned, for about the millionth time, the wisdom of the last time he had seen Kayla.

He let out a deep sigh and ran his hands down his face. Even that wasn't enough to erase the memory of the look on Kayla's face when he had stupidly told her he loved her. Surprise. Disbelief.

Horror.

What the hell had he been thinking?

Well, he hadn't been. That was the problem.

He still didn't know what had possessed him to go over to her house that night. And not just go over. No, he had sat outside for over an hour, feeling like a stalker as he debated the wisdom of knocking on her door, arguing with himself over the pros and cons.

When the kitchen light had come on, he had taken it as a sign. She was awake, maybe she wouldn't mind some company. At least, that was what he tried telling himself.

He still didn't know why he had gone over there, but it sure as hell hadn't been to take her right there, right up against her front door, minutes after she let him. That hadn't been his intention. He hadn't even remotely considered the possibility of making love to her when he had gone over there.

But he had.

She hadn't stopped him, hadn't asked him to leave. Hadn't pushed him away. And then she exploded around him and screamed his name, her voice as flush and heated as her body.

He shook his head at the image, trying to banish it from his mind, but it was too late. His body was already reacting to the memory. Nick shifted in the hard chair and reached for the water bottle, not knowing if it would be better to take a long swallow or spill it in his lap.

No, he hadn't planned on taking her against the door like that, but he didn't regret it. He would never regret a single second, no matter how fleeting, he shared with Kayla.

His regret was not keeping his mouth shut afterwards.

He closed his eyes and sighed at the memory of Kayla's face. Her eyes widened, a look of horror banishing the warm flush on her skin, leaving it pale. Her mouth snapped closed and he saw the panic overtake her, knew it was happening probably before she even did. Her body stiffened against his as she dropped her legs from their hold around his waist and pushed against him. For a second he had thought he could just hold onto her, apologize and pretend she misunderstood.

But he couldn't. She didn't misunderstand, and he wouldn't take it back. He wouldn't lie to her, and he was through lying to himself.

He loved her. Looking back, he doubted if he had ever stopped.

So no, he wasn't going to lie, not to either one of them. But Kayla didn't want to hear it, that much was obvious. She pushed against him again and stepped away, quickly grabbing her oversize night shirt and pulling it over head. She had remained silent, just watching as he quickly pulled on his own clothes, her mouth a grim line, her arms crossed tightly in front of her.

He didn't need to be fluent in body language to understand what she was trying to say. And yet he still tried talking to her, thought that maybe they could sit down and try to talk things through.

That was when she had asked him to leave, that look of panic-stricken horror still clear in her eyes.

He hadn't seen or spoken to her since.

And now it was time for the big presentation and once again he questioned the wisdom of what he was about to do. He didn't need a shrink to analyze his intentions—he was more than qualified to self-analyze on this one.

And yet he still doubted himself, knowing that a million and one things could go wrong—and only one thing could go right. He had weighed the pros and cons, approached the idea with intelligence and yes, even hope. He wasn't stupid—far from it.

It all came down to whether or not he thought

the payout was worth the risk. Just over three months had gone by, more than enough time for him to realize what he wanted. And more than enough time for him to realize that he was, quite possibly, playing a losing game.

It didn't matter. The payout was worth the risk. He didn't even have to stop to think about that part.

He rubbed his hands over his face once more then looked down at the stack of pictures in front of him. Graphic, brutal. He had once told Kayla he didn't want to use them because they were *too* graphic, *too* brutal. Stark in their realism. His excuse had been that they were too inappropriate for the students.

But he could be honest enough with himself now to recognize that for the lie it was. They were too graphic for *him*. The memories they brought back were still too raw, even after all this time.

He was through lying to himself.

Nick pushed himself out of the chair and grabbed the photos before walking out of the room. He was ready for the truth.

He only hoped Kayla was there so he could share it with her.

***

"You're all set. Is there anything else you need?"

Jay stopped playing with the projector and turned to look at her, his nervousness etched on his face. He cleared his throat and shook his head, trying to offer her a small smile. Mike looked at him, one brow raised in question. She didn't understand why he was so nervous.

"You'll be fine, don't worry."

"Yeah, I know." He wiped his hand down his pants leg and glanced around the stage again. Mike followed his gaze and had to admit that she was impressed with what he had accomplished.

The twisted wreckage of what had once been a compact car sat off to one side, the harsh stage lights reflecting off the torn metal. The windshield, shattered and twisted, rested haphazardly on what used to be the hood of the car. Clumps of bloodied hair stuck in one crack of the windshield, framed by a splattering of even more blood. A body hung halfway out of the car, its face unrecognizable, a pool of blood congealed on the floor under it.

It was all staged, of course. The car was nothing more than a prop, easily carried in pieces and quickly reassembled to resemble the realistic remains of a bad accident. The blood was nothing more than a hardened gel, easily removed by peeling it off the floor like a strip of plastic. The body was merely the top half of an old mannequin, one who had definitely seen better days. Kayla walked over and adjusted the dummy's position just a bit, then stood back and studied the wreck.

"Poor Annie has definitely seen better days," she mumbled before turning back to Jay. He was looking at the wreck, a frown creasing his forehead. He raised one hand and motioned behind him. Stage lights winked off, plunging the corner in darkness and effectively limiting view of the wreck.

Mike walked to the side of the stage and quickly descended the steps to stand next to Jay. He still looked worried, so she reached out and gave his shoulder a reassuring squeeze.

"Relax, this'll be fine."

"Yeah." He let out a deep breath and looked around him. "Yeah, I guess."

"Stop worrying, okay? You got the principal's permission, so it's not like you're going to be sent to the office." Mike walked over and grabbed her jacket from the front row seat then shrugged into it. She had expected at least a small smile at her joke. Instead, Jay fixed her with a look of panic in his eyes.

"Where are you going?"

"I'm leaving."

"What do you mean, you're leaving? You can't leave!"

Mike grabbed the hair at the back of her neck and twisted it, pulling it from under the jacket collar. "Jay, I can't stay. I can't see Nick right now, alright?"

"But you have to stay. You're supposed to review this whole thing and sign off, remember?"

Mike blew out her breath and gave Jay a quick look of impatience before facing the rear of the auditorium. They were the only two people there, but she still stepped closer to Jay and lowered her voice to a whisper. "Jay, you don't need to worry about me signing off, everything is already taken care of. I told you that. And I told you the other day I can't stay, and you know why."

"What? Because he told you he loved you? So what. Big deal."

"It is a big deal. And keep your voice down."

"You're being ridiculous, Mikey. I mean, the guy loves you. Why is that such a bad thing?"

"Because it is."

"Why?"

"Because it just is, okay? Can you just drop it?" Mike looked around them again, afraid that somebody may have come in and heard them.

"No, I'm not going to drop it. All you've done for the last two weeks is walk around in a daze, or walk around looking all panicky. Either admit you love him, or just tell him to get lost."

"You're insane. I don't love him." Sour bile congealed in the pit of her stomach at the words, but she swallowed and met Jay's gaze straight on. She wasn't ready to admit to anything, to even think about any of it. And she certainly didn't want to discuss her feelings about Nick with anyone. Not even Jay.

"The only one you're fooling is yourself, Mikey, so get over it. And you are not leaving. You can't."

"And why is that?"

"Because we're buddies and I need you so you can't leave."

"For crying out loud. Dammit Jay, you have got to be kidding me. You're really going to play that card?"

"Absolutely." Jay fixed her with a steady gaze, his gray eyes boring into hers for a long minute until she finally looked away.

"Dammit," she muttered again. But it was merely for show. She couldn't abandon Jay, not after telling her he needed her. No, she didn't believe him, not really. But she couldn't tell him that. "Dammit, you so owe me for this one, Moore."

He gave her a quick smile and patted her on the shoulder, like he was congratulating her for passing a test or something. She clenched her jaw and shot him a look that said she knew she had been played, then shrugged out of her jacket.

"Fine, I'll stay. That doesn't mean I'm sitting up here. If you need me, I'll be in the back row."

Chapter Thirty-Three

Nick stood off to the side of the stage, watching as the senior class drifted into the aging auditorium. Their laughter echoed around him, the sound tinged with excitement. And why wouldn't they be excited? As far as they were concerned, they were being excused for whatever class they had scheduled for this period. Knowing they were about to be subjected to a lecture on a subject they cared little about did nothing to diminish that excitement.

And why would it? They were teenagers, carefree, worry-free.

Invincible.

Nick wished he could share that excitement. Instead, he took a deep breath and reached up for his tie, nothing more than a nervous habit. His hand came up empty before he remembered he wasn't wearing a tie. Today was faculty casual day, so he was wearing faded jeans and a long sleeve Henley shirt.

He had dressed this morning with an eye to comfort, thinking that being dressed more comfortably would ease any nervousness he might feel.

He had been wrong.

Nick took another deep breath then stepped closer to Jay.

"Where did you say Kayla was sitting?"

Jay looked up from his notes and narrowed his eyes as he searched the growing crowd. He finally motioned with a nod of his head. "About three quarters of the way up. Aisle seat on your right heading out."

Nick stepped forward and moved his head in the direction Jay had indicated, his eyes searching for Kayla. Sure enough, there she was, slouched down in the aisle seat, looking like this was the last place she wanted to be.

He felt the same way.

"So let's go over it one more time, make sure I don't mess this up for you." Jay put his notes down and fixed Nick with a steady look.

"We'll let everyone get settled then I go do my thing, warm them up. Then I do my talk and see what happens."

"You sure you know what you're doing?" The expression on Jay's face was worried, unconvinced—an exact echo of what Nick was feeling. The thought went through his mind once more that a million things could go wrong with this, and probably would.

"Not really, no."

"And you're sure you're okay with the stage set?"

Nick nodded, even though he wasn't sure, not really. He hadn't even looked at the set-up, had no desire to look at it. For that, he was completely trusting Jay. He just hoped to hell he was doing the right thing.

"Okay. If something happens and you change your mind, just give me some kind of signal or something and I'll go straight into the presentation."

"I won't change my mind."

"If you're sure."

"I'm sure." Of that, Nick was absolutely certain. This probably wasn't one of his best ideas, and he was more certain than ever that something—a lot of things—would go wrong. But his mind was made up and there was no turning back.

He took another deep breath and nodded at Jay, then casually walked out in front of the stage. His head turned from side to side, watching the students as they took their seats and settled in. A few of them called out greetings, or made remarks about getting out of class. The mood was still light, the underlying excitement still humming in the air around them.

Nick walked back and forth, trying to calm his nerves as he said a word here and there to a few students. He knew he was smiling, felt it on his face, but it was nothing more than show, a mask to hide his nervousness.

He took another deep breath as the last few stragglers took their seats, his eyes searching out Kayla. She was still slouched down in her seat, her arms crossed in front of her, watching him with an unreadable expression. He smiled at her and felt an instant's gratification when she shifted, sitting straighter and not looking quite so bored.

One last deep breath, and it was show time. He could do this with no problem, he thought. It shouldn't be any different than each weekend when he was up on stage.

Except he didn't have quite so much to lose then as he did now.

Nick pushed that thought from his mind then stepped toward the audience, holding his arms up to get their attention. "Alright everyone, settle down."

A minute went by before the conversations and laughter drifted off to a manageable silence. Nick knew he didn't have everyone's attention, not yet.

That would change.

"Okay, so who can tell me why we're here?" Nick didn't wait to call on anyone, just motioned for people to call out. He let the crowd have their way for a minute, then motioned for silence again.

"Exactly. For the next hour, we're going to learn about drinking and driving." Nick looked down at the rolled papers in his hand, noticed he was absently playing with them. With a mental shake, he flattened the roll and stuffed it into his back pocket. He didn't need notes for this.

"Show of hands. Who plans on going out and having fun this weekend?" Nearly all the hands in the room went up, and Nick included himself, which drew a few laughs. "Hey, teachers need a break, too. So yeah, a lot of us will be having fun. Of course, I'd be surprised if anyone here said no."

His gaze drifted back to Kayla and he was heartened to see a small smile lift the corners of her mouth. "Next question: how many of you here plan on drinking when you go out?"

All hands went down and a few snickers burst from the crowd.

"No fair, Mr. L. You know we're not old enough to drink."

"Touché, Sam, touché." Nick grinned at the athlete and received a smile in return. "So yeah, in a perfect world, none of you drink."

From somewhere in the back came a forced sneeze that suspiciously sounded like "bullshit". Nick glanced toward the back and shook his head. "It's nice to see some things haven't changed since I was in high school. But yeah, let's all just agree that this isn't a perfect world, and that nobody is going to buy the bull that nobody here drinks. Will that work?"

More laughter. Nick smiled, gratified that the students felt comfortable enough with him to relax. "So yeah, we know people drink. And if you're underage, well. That's between you, your parents, and quite possibly the police. But that's not what we're here for."

Nick turned and walked the few steps back to the stage, motioning for Jay to join him. "Some of you have already had this presentation and met Jay Moore, along with his partner Kayla Donaldson. And like anyone who's sat in that class will tell you, they're not here to talk about drinking. What they *are* here for, is to talk about drinking and driving."

Nick nodded at Jay, who took a step closer to the stage. He turned back to face the crowd, noticing the slight discomfort settling over the room. He shook his head and gave a small laugh. "And already I'm losing you. Don't worry guys, we're not here to lecture you. Honest."

Nick offered a reassuring smile to the crowd, going out of his way to make eye contact with as many students as he could. "So, why don't we drink and drive? Anyone?"

As Nick expected, long seconds went by before

one small voice hesitantly offered an answer, followed by another and another until more students were shouting, not worrying if they were repeating answers or not. Nick let the shouting continue for a few minutes then held up his hand to quiet everyone.

"All good answers. But I'm not surprised. I mean, everyone knows you shouldn't drink and drive, right?" He looked around, slowly letting the smile die on his face. He glanced up the aisle to see Kayla sitting there, watching him. "Yeah, we know. But the reality is a little different."

Nick turned his head and nodded at Jay. The man looked at him for a long minute, as if asking if he was sure. Nick nodded again, and Jay raised his toward the back, signaling.

The lights in the auditorium dimmed, throwing the room into near darkness. From the back came the sound of music playing, a generic rock song overlaid with people talking and laughing. Nick closed his eyes, watching a scene play itself out in his memory in time with the soundtrack that surrounded them.

Laughter. Talking.

Music.

The heart-stopping squeal of brakes and rubber squealing.

A split-second pause.

The jarring impact of metal against metal, screeching, tearing. A scream, fading into the backdrop of noise.

Silence. Dead silence.

This isn't real. This isn't real. It's staged. It's only a memory. This isn't real.

Nick took a deep breath and forced his jaw to relax, forced his fists to unclench. He opened his eyes and jammed his shaking hands into his pockets then turned to face the stage. Theatrical lighting was now focused on the tableau off to the side, bathing it an eerie light that only lent more reality to the morbid scene in front of them.

This isn't real. Get it together.

Nick took another deep breath and faced the crowd, unsurprised by the silence and looks of horror etched on most of the faces. But he couldn't look at Kayla. Not yet.

My God, Kayla, I am so sorry. Can you ever forgive me?

The silence stretched around them, almost unbearable. Off to the side, he heard someone sniffle, a small sound in the stillness. Behind him, he heard Jay shuffle, heard him call his name in a voice just under a whisper. Nick nodded and waved with one shaking hand, letting him know he was alright.

He took another deep breath and let it out slowly, his gaze taking in the shocked faces around him.

"A friend of mine told me that teenagers think they're invincible, that they're immortal. They think something like this can never happen to them." Nick didn't turn around to look, didn't need to. He knew Jay was projecting pictures on the screen, awful graphic pictures of real accidents.

Real consequences.

"I'm here to tell you that you're not immortal. That you're not invincible. And if you think it can't happen to you, you're wrong." His voice was louder now, increasing in volume, thick with emotion he could no longer hide. He cleared his throat and looked around, knowing without really seeing that he had everyone's attention now.

Everyone's, including Kayla. He took a deep breath and moved up the aisle, not stopping until he was ten feet away from her. His eyes held hers with sheer force of determination, not letting her look away.

"If you think it can't happen to you, you're wrong," he repeated, his voice carrying through the entire auditorium. "Because it can, and it will. I know, because it happened to me."

The silence continued, charged with awareness and expectation. The tension rolled over him in waves and Nick couldn't tell if it was his own—or if it was coming from the crowd. He didn't care. His focus now was for Kayla, only Kayla.

"Ten years ago, I was out partying. I was invincible, and knew that nothing bad would ever happen. I had someone with me that night, someone very special. Someone I loved. I walked away. She didn't." Kayla was looking up at him, her eyes wide and filled with tears as she shook her head, mouthing *no* in his direction.

He didn't look away, just kept his focus on Kayla for long minutes as his revelation hit home to the crowd in the auditorium. Nick didn't know how much time had passed before Kayla gave her head a final shake and closed her eyes, breaking the trance that had wrapped around just the two of them.

He clenched his fists and turned around, walking back toward the stage, speaking as he went.

"Ten years ago, two lives were changed forever because of something *I* did, because I thought I was invincible. And to this day, I haven't forgiven myself. I don't know if I ever can."

Nick nodded at Jay, his cue to take over, then

turned back to the crowd.
　　Kayla was gone.

Chapter Thirty-Four

Tremors wracked her body, overtaking her like an uncontrollable palsy. And the chill. A deep, bone-penetrating chill that wouldn't be dispelled no matter how much she huddled into herself.

Kayla shifted on the sofa, pushing herself deeper into the corner and hugging her legs tighter to her chest. She pulled the fleece blanket more tightly around her shoulders and clenched her jaw against the latest tremor that shook her.

The sound of her phone ringing drifted down the stairs and she wished again she had thought to turn it off before tossing it on her nightstand. That had been two hours ago, and it kept ringing. Every ten minutes, like clockwork.

She didn't have the energy to climb the stairs and turn it off.

And she was afraid that she didn't have the willpower *not* to answer it. So yeah, it was better to leave it upstairs and let it ring, no matter how annoying the sound was.

Kayla shook her head and reached over for the mug of coffee, bringing it to her lips with a shaking hand. The coffee had long since turned cold but she didn't care, just wanted the hit of caffeine in her system.

No, what she really wanted was something stronger. A shot of whiskey or brandy. But she still didn't have any alcohol in the house, hadn't even thought about buying any until after she came home this afternoon.

After Nick and his bomb shell.

Kayla let out a deep breath and closed her eyes, resting her head on the arm of the sofa. Oh God, she had not seen that coming, had been completely blindsided by it. And she still didn't know what to think of it.

Why would he do that? Why? That was the question that kept repeating itself over and over, from the time she had finally reached the freedom of the parking lot and her Jeep and could actually think.

She couldn't believe he had opened himself like that, had exposed something so deeply personal and horrible and shattering to people who knew him and looked up to him. And she had no doubt that his students respected him, that much had been clear from the very first. So why? Why would he do such a thing?

She didn't want to know why. Was afraid of the answer.

And afraid of what to do about it.

Because she had to do something, that much at least was clear. It was the *what* that scared her. It would be so easy to just forget everything, or pretend to forget. Forget about seeing Nick again, pretend he hadn't come back into her life, pretend that there was nothing there and just go on with her life.

Alone.

Kayla ran a hand over her eyes and sighed, forcing herself to face the harsh reality of her world. Before Nick had come back into it, she had been alone, telling herself that she was happy that way.

Only it had all been a sham. She told herself she was happy because she didn't want to admit otherwise, didn't want to admit she was lonely, that she wanted somebody besides her coworkers in her life. Her friends meant the world to her but they were just that: friends. And she wanted somebody to share her life with.

A few weeks ago, if anyone had told her that someone would be Nick, there was a good chance she would have hit them. But now?

Nick had changed. She had changed. They were no longer the scared kids they had been all those years ago. And while she mourned the loss of what they were, she knew that what they could be was so much better.

All she had to do was let go of the past, to forgive him. And herself.

Silence stretched around her and as the minutes ticked by, a sense of calm filled her. The chills lessened and finally disappeared, and warmth seeped into her. Mike opened her eyes and straightened, letting the blanket fall from her shoulders as she looked around the empty room.

All she had to do was let go of the past, and forgive him. And herself.

And she realized, sitting there in the quiet comfort of her living room, that she already had.

Sometime in the last few months, she had let go of what happened ten years ago, pushing it into a little box labeled "the past" and putting it somewhere on a shelf in her memory. No, she couldn't forget it—she didn't think anyone could expect either of them to forget—but somehow, at some point, it had become just that: a memory, just like any other memory. It may have shaped and defined her in the past, but it wasn't who she was *now*. Who she had been for quite some time.

And with that realization came another: she had forgiven Nick. She had forgiven him years ago and never admitted it to herself. She had loved him then, even after everything that had happened, and she couldn't love someone she hadn't forgiven.

But did she love him now?

She closed her eyes and a picture of Nick came immediately to mind, filling her with warmth. His dark hair, even now just a little on the long side. Dark intense eyes that encouraged her to lose herself in their depths. The feel of his arms around her, strong and protecting, caring, supporting.

She forced the picture of Nick from her mind and thought about what life would be like if she never saw him again. Another chill quickly spread over her, filling her from the inside out. She pushed the feeling of emptiness away and opened her eyes.

Yes, she loved Nick. Not the boy he had been, although that love would never die. She loved the man Nick had become, the emotion for the man stronger than it had ever been for the boy.

A murmur of surprise escaped her at the realization. Had she known already, or was she only now realizing it? Given her reaction when Nick had told her he loved her, she admitted she had probably known for some time, but was too afraid to acknowledge it.

Afraid. Her. And she had acted like a cowardly fool because of it.

Mike tossed the blanket to the floor and pushed herself from the sofa. It took less than a minute for her to shove her feet into a pair of shoes, pull on her jacket, and grab her keys.

The drive to Nick's house went by in a blur, her mind on autopilot until she pulled into his driveway. Close to a minute went by as she sat there, questioning herself and wondering if she was doing the right thing. Then she mentally berated herself, telling herself that of all the things she was, coward was not one of them. So she got out of the Jeep and walked to the front door and knocked on it, hard, not bothering with the doorbell.

And waited.

And waited some more.

The cold evening air drifted around her, chilling the skin beneath her sweatpants and jacket. She bounced from one foot to the other then knocked again, wondering if maybe Nick wasn't home. But no, his car was in the driveway, blocked by her Jeep. He had to be home.

She raised her fist to knock again then stood back in surprise when the door opened. Nick stood in front of her, still wearing the jeans and shirt he had on earlier. Her eyes raked his body, stopping to rest on his bare feet. She felt a smile tilt her mouth as her eyes drifted back up his body to his face.

And her smile left her when she noticed the bleakness of his expression, the shadows in his eyes.

"So. Can I come in?"

Nick stepped to the side, not saying anything, and for the first time Mike seriously began to wonder if she was making a mistake. He closed the door behind her and led the way upstairs, still saying nothing as he lowered himself to the sofa and propped his feet on the table in front of him. She stood a few feet away, uncomfortable as she searched her mind for something to say.

"You, uh, pretty much blindsided me this afternoon, you know? I hadn't expected that."

Nick looked up at her, the expression in his eyes unreadable, and she shifted uncomfortably. "I didn't mean to. My apologies."

"No problem." She didn't like the bleakness in his voice so she stood there, wondering what to do next. "I heard what you said. At the end. About not forgiving yourself."

Nick looked up at her for a long minute then shook his head and closed his eyes. Mike chewed on her lower lip then took a deep breath and closed the distance to the sofa. She sat next to him, leaving only inches between them, then hesitated before reaching out and grabbing his hand. She twined her fingers through his and squeezed.

"So here's the thing. I figure you pretty much have to forgive yourself because," she paused and took a deep breath, squeezing his fingers again, "because I've already forgiven you."

She closed her eyes and waited. Nick shifted on the sofa next to her and she could feel his eyes on her but she was afraid to look.

"Kayla." Her name was a hoarse whisper falling from his lips and she looked up, seeing naked emotion clear in the depths of his eyes. She tried to smile but felt it wobble and fall before she could. She took another deep breath and ran her free hand over her eyes, pushing in on them before running her hand through her hair and finally facing him again.

"I love you Nick. I never really stopped, but it's different now. I love who you are *now*. I've been sitting at home the last few hours, thinking, wondering what it would be like without you in my life and the idea makes me miserable."

"But what about—"

She cut him off with a quick kiss, then reached out and cupped the side of his face with her free hand. "It's in the past. It's been in the past. That's not who we are *now*. That was something else I realized. I love you, Nick. Here and now."

His eyes raked her face, the emotion still clear in their depths, but not as forlorn as before. And slowly, finally, one corner of his mouth tilted in a small smile and he leaned forward to kiss her, a gentle tender kiss that stole her breath and left her whimpering with need and emotion.

"God Kayla, I love you. Now more than ever. You have no idea—"

"I do. So could you maybe, you know, shut up and kiss me?"

Nick laughed, just a small one, and suddenly the heaviness surrounding them lifted, becoming brighter and full of promise. He leaned forward and pressed his mouth to hers, lightly at first, then more demanding, claiming and possessing. Kayla melted against him, surrendering to him just as he surrendered to her.

He finally pulled away and looked down at her,

passion swirling in the depths of his eyes. "Tell me again."

"I love you, Nick."

He smiled and kissed her then stood up, pulling her with him. Before she could react, he leaned down and swung her up in his arms, holding her close as he walked down the hallway.

"Do you work tomorrow?" His question came out of the blue, surprising her. She shook her head and was rewarded with another smile. "Good, because I plan on showing you how much I love you. All. Night. Long."

Kayla wrapped her arms around his neck and held on tighter, laughing as the last sliver of coldness deep inside her melted and disappeared.

And was replaced by something so precious, it filled her with a heat that would warm her forever without fear of ever being burned. She hugged him close and dropped a kiss at the base of his neck, smiling when she felt a tremor shoot through him at the contact.

There would surely be ups and downs as they worked through things, but there was no doubt in Michaela's mind that they would get through everything.

Together.

ABOUT THE AUTHOR

Lisa B. Kamps is the author of the best-selling series The Baltimore Banners, featuring "hard-hitting, heart-melting hockey players", on and off the ice. ONCE BURNED is the launch title of her anticipated new series, *Firehouse Fourteen*, featuring hot and heroic firefighters.

Lisa has always loved writing, even during her assorted careers: first as a firefighter with the Baltimore County Fire Department, then a very brief (and not very successful) stint at bartending in east Baltimore, and finally as the Director of Retail Operations for a busy Civil War non-profit.

Lisa currently lives in Maryland with her husband and two sons, one very spoiled Border Collie, two cats with major attitude, several head of cattle, and entirely too many chickens to count.

Interested in reaching out to Lisa? She'd love to hear from you, and there are several ways to contact her:

Website: www.LisaBKamps.com
Newsletter: www.lisabkamps.com/signup/
Email: LisaBKamps@gmail.com
Facebook: www.facebook.com/authorLisaBKamps
Twitter: twitter.com/LBKamps
Goodreads: www.goodreads.com/LBKamps
Instagram: www.instagram.com/lbkamps/

Amber "AJ" Johnson is a freelance writer who has her heart set on becoming a full-time sports reporter at her paper. She has one chance to prove herself: capture an interview with the very private goalie of Baltimore's hockey team, Alec Kolchak. But he's the one man who tries her patience, even as he brings to life a quiet passion she doesn't want to admit exists.

Alec has no desire to be interviewed--he never has, never will. But he finds himself a reluctant admirer of AJ's determination to get what she wants...and he certainly never counted on his attraction to her. In a fit of frustration, he accepts AJ's bet: if she can score just one goal on him in a practice shoot-out, he would not only agree to the interview, he would let her have full access to him for a month, 24/7.

It was a bet neither one of them wanted to lose...and a bet neither one could afford to win. But when it came time to take the shot, could either one of them cross the line?

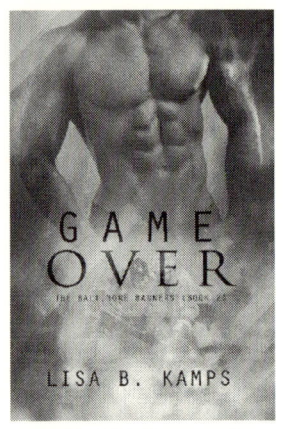

Forensics accountant Bobbi Reeves is pulled back into a world of shadows in order to go undercover as a personal assistant with the Baltimore Banners. Her assignment: get close to defenseman Nikolai Petrovich and uncover the reason he's being extorted. But she doesn't expect the irrational attraction she feels—or the difficulty in helping someone who doesn't want it.

Nikolai Petrovich, a veteran defenseman for the Banners, has no need for a personal assistant—especially not one hired by the team. During the last eight years, he has learned to live simply...and alone. Experience has taught him that letting people close puts them in danger. He doesn't want a personal assistant, and he certainly doesn't need anyone prying into his personal life. But that doesn't stop his physical reaction to the unusual woman assigned to him.

They are drawn together in spite of their differences, and discover a heated passion that neither expected. But when the game is over, will the secrets they keep pull them closer together...or tear them apart?

Kayli Evans lives a simple life, handling the daily operations of her small family farm and acting as the primary care-taker for her fourteen-year-old niece. She knows the importance of enjoying each minute, of living life to its fullest. But she still has worries: about her older brother's safety in the military, about the rift between her two brothers, and about her niece's security and making ends meet. And now there's a new worry she doesn't want: Ian Donovan, her brother's friend.

Ian is a carefree hockey player for the Baltimore Banners who has relatively few worries—until he finds himself suddenly babysitting his seven-year-old nieces for an extended period of time. He has no idea what he's doing, and is thrust even further into the unknown when he's forced to participate in the twins' newest hobby. Meeting Kayli opens a different world for him, a simpler world where family, trust, and love are what matters most.

Baltimore Banners defenseman Randy Michaels has a reputation for hard-hitting, on and off the ice. But he's getting older, and his agent has warned that there are younger, less-expensive players who are eager to take his place on the team. Can his hare-brained idea of becoming a "respectable businessman" turn his reputation around, or has Randy's reputation really cost him the chance of having his contract renewed?

Alyssa Harris has one goal in mind: make the restaurant she's opened with her three friends a success. It's not going to be easy, not when the restaurant is a themed sports bar geared towards women. It's going to be even more difficult because their sole investor is Randy Michaels, her friend's drool-worthy brother who has his own ideas about what makes an interesting menu.

Will the mismatched pair be able to find a compromise as things heat up, both on and off the ice? Or will their differences result in a penalty that costs both of them the game?

Jean-Pierre "JP" Larocque is a speed demon for the Baltimore Banners. He lives for speed off the ice, too, playing fast and loose with cars and women. But is he really a player, or is his carefree exterior nothing more than a show, hiding a lonely man filled with regret as he struggles to forget the only woman who mattered?

Emily Poole thought she knew what she wanted in life, but everything changed five years ago. Now she exists day by day, helping care for her niece after her sister's bitter divorce. It may not be how she envisioned her life, but she's happy. Or so she thinks, until JP re-enters her life. Now she realizes there's a lot more she wants, including a second chance with JP.

Can these two lost souls finally find forgiveness and Break Away to the future? Or will the shared tragedy of their past tear them apart for good this time?

Valerie Michaels knows all about life, responsibility--and hockey. After all, her brother is a defenseman for the Baltimore Banners. The last thing she needs--or wants--is to get tangled up with one of her brother's teammates. She doesn't have time, not when running The Maypole is her top priority. Could that be the reason she's suddenly drawn to the troubled Justin Tome? Or is it because she senses something deeper inside him, something she thinks she can fix?

On the surface, Justin Tome has it all: a successful career with the Banners, money, fame. But he's been on a downward spiral the last few months. He's become more withdrawn, his game has gone downhill, and he's been partying too much. He thinks it's nothing more than what's expected of him, nothing more than once again failing to meet expectations and never quite measuring up. Then he starts dating Val and realizes that maybe he has more to offer than he thinks.

Or does he? Sometimes voices from the past, voices you've heard all your life, are too strong to overcome. And when the unexpected happens, Justin is certain he's looking at a permanent Delay of Game--unless one strong woman can make him see that life is all about the future, not the past.

Jake Evans has been in the Marine Corps for seventeen years, juggling his conflicting duties to country and his teenage daughter. But when he suffers a serious injury and is sent home, he knows he'll be forced to make decisions he doesn't want to. Battered in spirit and afraid of what the future may hold, he takes the long way by driving cross-country.

He never expected to meet Alyce Marshall, a free-spirited woman on a self-declared adventure: she's running away from home.

In spite of her outward free spirit, Alyce has problems of her own she must face, including the ever-present shadow of her father and his influence on her growing up. She senses similarities in Jake, and decides that it's up to her to teach the tough Marine that life isn't just about rules and regulations. What she doesn't plan on is falling in love with him...and being forced to share her secret.

Michaela Donaldson had her whole life planned out: college, music, and a happy-ever-after with her first true love. One reckless night changed all that, setting Michaela on a new path. Gone are her dreams of pursuing music in college, replaced by what she thinks is a more rewarding life. She's a firefighter now, getting down and dirty while doing her job. So what if she's a little rough around the edges, a little too careless, a little too detached? She's happy, living life on her own terms--until Nicky Lansing shows back up.

Nick Lansing was the stereotypical leather-clad bad boy, needing nothing but his fast car, his guitar, his never-ending partying, and his long-time girlfriend--until one bad decision changed the course of two lives forever. He's on the straight-and-narrow now, living life as a respected teacher and doing his best to be a positive role model. Yes, he still has his music. But gone are his days of partying. And gone is the one girl who always held his heart. Or is she?

One freak accident brings these two opposites back together. Is ten years long enough to heal the physical and emotional wounds from the past? Can they reconcile who they were with who they've become--or will it be a case of Once Burned is enough?

Angie Warren was voted the Most Likely to Succeed in school. She was also voted the Most Responsible. And responsible she is: she made it through college on a scholarship and she's even working her way through Vet School. She has an overprotective older brother she adores and a part-time job tending bar that adds some enjoyment to her life. In fact, that's the only pleasure she has. She's bored and in desperate need of a change. Too bad the one guy she has her sights set on is the one guy completely off-limits.

Jay Moore knows all about excitement and wouldn't live life any other way. From his job as a firefighter to his many brief relationships, his whole life is nothing but one thrilling experience after the other. Except when Angie Warren enters the picture. He's known her for years and there is no way he's going to agree to give her the excitement she's looking for. Even Jay knows where to draw the line—and dating his friend's baby sister definitely crosses all of them.

Too bad Angie has other plans. But will either one of them remember that when you're Playing With Fire, someone is bound to get burned?

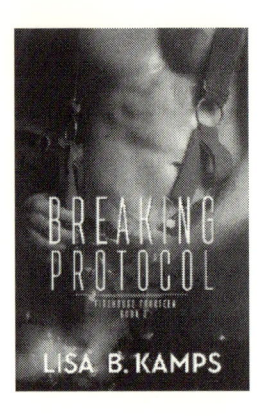

Dave Warren knows all about protocol. As a firefighter/paramedic, he has to. What he doesn't know is when his life became nothing more than routine, following the rules day in and day out. Has it always been that way, or was it a gradual change? Or did it have anything to do with his time spent overseas as a medic with the Army Reserves? He's not sure, but it's something he's learned to accept and live with—until a series of messages upsets his routine. And until one spitfire Flight Medic enters his life.

Carolann "CC" Covey has no patience for protocols. Yes, they're a necessary evil, a part of her job, but they don't rule her life. She can't let them—she knows life is for the living, a lesson learned the hard way overseas. Which is why her attraction to the serious and staid Dave Warren makes no sense. Is it just a case of "opposites attract", or is it something more? Will CC be able to teach him that sometimes rules need to be broken?

And when something sinister appears from Dave's past to threaten everything he's come to love, will he learn that Breaking Protocol may be the only way to save what's really important?

Made in the USA
Middletown, DE
07 September 2019